HANGING FIRE

HANGING FIRE

A JOE NOOSE WESTERN

ERIC RED

PINNACLE BOOKS
Kensington Publishing Corp.
www.kensingtonbooks.com

PINNACLE BOOKS are published by

Kensington Publishing Corp.
119 West 40th Street
New York, NY 10018

All Kensington titles, imprints, and distributed lines are available at special quantity discounts for bulk purchases for sales promotions, premiums, fund-raising, educational, or institutional use. Special book excerpts or customized printings can also be created to fit specific needs. For details, write or phone the office of the Kensington sales manager: Kensington Publishing Corp., 119 West 40th Street, New York, NY 10018, attn: Sales Department; phone 1-800-221-2647.

ISBN-13: 978-0-7860-4298-2
ISBN-10: 0-7860-4298-2

First printing: February 2019

10 9 8 7 6 5 4 3 2 1

Printed in the United States of America

First electronic edition: February 2019

ISBN-13: 978-0-7860-4299-9
ISBN-10: 0-7860-4299-0

To Barbara . . .
for all the wonderful times
with our family in Jackson Hole.

CHAPTER 1

Joe Noose had heard, never trust a man with three names. He wondered if the same held true for women.

Bonny Kate Valance stood there in handcuffs. The wrist restraints were shackled loose with a two-foot chain because she would be riding a horse the next two days. It would be her last ride. Their point of departure was the U.S. Marshal's office in Jackson Hole, Wyoming. At the end of the trail fifteen miles across the Teton Pass over the Idaho border lay the town of Victor. The gallows there would be Bonny Kate's final destination. The notorious female outlaw had been sentenced to execution by hanging and it was Joe Noose's job to get the woman there safe and sound so the state could kill her.

The irony was not lost on Noose.

Noose was a big man. He towered six foot three on a broad, muscular, and rugged frame. His handsome, leathery, unshaven chipped face some said looked like a picture of a Roman gladiator. Noose had never seen a picture of a gladiator, but it had always seemed like a compliment and he took it as such. On his massive block of a head his unkempt brown hair had need of a clipping. His giant hands, big as steer hooves, were encased in leather gloves against the cold. A heavy worn brown duster covered his upper torso over a checkered shirt and red bandanna around his neck. The coat had dark stains that could be mud or blood, likely both. His Stetson was tipped low over his pale blue eyes to shield them from the sharp Wyoming sun breaking over the mountain range near Hoback.

It was there by the fork in the Snake River a month before that Noose had spent a fateful and violent few days. At the end of that misadventure fifteen men lay dead, all but three by his own hand, but the men he had killed were responsible for the murders of the three lawmen and it was justice because the murderers had it coming.

Joe Noose had come out of it with one bullet in him—the other bullet went clear through—a bunch of busted ribs, and a few broken bones but his resilience was high; the massive cowboy was healthy and strong and healed quick. Now save for a few lingering bruises and scars on his person that made him look even tougher, folks would never know the hell he'd been through.

The best thing Noose had gotten out of the nasty Hoback business with the Butler Gang was he had made two friends. The first was standing on four legs right in front of him, sixteen hands high, saddled up, and ready to ride: his horse, Copper. The mighty and fearless stallion was aptly named for his bronze coat; when the light was right as the morning sun was now, its hide gleamed with the metallic magnificence of a suit of armor on a medieval steed. Copper's smart eyes were moist and brown, and powerful muscles rippled beneath its smooth tawny hide. The horse had saved Noose's life, and the love and loyalty it had for its owner, and its owner for it, was palpable.

The other friend Joe Noose had made was walking on her own two legs out of the Jackson Hole U.S. Marshal's office right now. Sort of walking, anyhow. Marshal Bess Sugarland was a young hardy woman, strong and attractive with vigorous outdoor looks and flashing intelligent blue eyes. Her gaze was straight and forthright and her manner the same, although her gait was presently crooked from the wooden leg brace she hobbled on and the Winchester repeater she was using as a crutch. A bullet had nearly taken off her leg in Hoback and the wound was healing slower than Noose's wounds had, but Marshal Bess didn't let it slow her down. She was the law in the town of Jackson now, whether she liked it or not.

The seven-star badge on her small chest glinted in the morning sun. Her chin was firmly set and her composure determined as she limped across the stable behind the U.S. Marshal's office up to Noose and the outlaw standing alongside their horses, getting ready to embark on their fateful journey.

Bess nodded to Noose then turned her gaze to Bonny Kate, choosing her words and tersely delivering them. "It ain't for me to judge you, Miss Valance. It's for the Lord to do that. But let me tell you one thing and you listen so you hear it good. Nothing better happen to my friend, or else."

Bonny Kate smiled darkly. "Don't threaten me with a good time." There was haughtiness in the condemned outlaw's posture, with her large bosom stuck brazenly outward in her denim shirt and her shapely blue-jeaned hips cocked in a defiant pose above her black rattlesnake-skin cowboy boots. Her demeanor displayed neither respect nor regard. Everything about the doomed Bonny Kate Valance seemed to whistle past the graveyard.

Bess leaned in nose to nose with Bonny Kate and spoke in the kind of low, quiet way that got people's attention. "I don't make threats, I make promises, Miss Valance. And I promise if Joe Noose don't come back from your hanging in one piece, I'll dig you up and kill you again. That's a promise I'll keep."

The female outlaw stared at the marshal in disbelief, shook her head in resignation, and chuckled. "The ideas folks have about me. None of 'em true. I swear." The outlaw sighed ruefully and shrugged her soft and delicate shoulders. "But folks best believe what they best believe, and bein' as they all think me to be the Antichrist in petticoats there's no telling any of 'em otherwise, so off I go to be—"

Bonny Kate made a pulling gesture by her neck with her closed fist, cocked her head sideways, crossed her eyes, and stuck her tongue in her cheek, making a popping sound with her lips in a grotesque imitation of hanging. Then she rearranged her face back to normal again and wore a perplexed, confounded expression that was almost comical. "Now, here's the part I don't get. My mama always told me to wear clean drawers, and my whole life that has been just what this girl has done only to end up hanged as an adult and soil myself like an infant. You know that's—"

"Shut up, Bonny Kate. Get your posterior on that horse. You got a date with the hangman and we don't want to keep him waiting." Marshal Bess turned her tight, worried gaze to Joe Noose, who stood calm and patient beside Copper, brushing the horse's golden withers with his big, rough hand. The two friends made eye contact and in their shared gaze was an unspoken shorthand born of friendship. The conversation was had in simple glances.

A nod from Noose telling Bess he was going to be all right. A returned nod and then a second one from Bess told him to be careful. A grin and friendly touch of his finger to the tip of his Stetson from Noose told Bess to stop being foolish and quit her worrying. Joe Noose never had to say a word, and with one easy, powerful sweep of his leg he swung into the saddle of his bronze horse and was mounted up.

This time Bess smiled back. She rounded on Bonny Kate Valance and swept up the barrel of her Winchester, now a loaded weapon, not a crutch, aimed right at the convicted woman's narrow gut below her ample bosom. Again, Bess didn't need to speak. A quick levering of the repeater and couple of up-and-down motions of the rifle barrel communicated the message perfectly well, and Bonny Kate took the meaning clearly. With her relative freedom of mobility in her handcuffs, the woman outlaw grabbed the saddle pommel of her tough old loaned chestnut quarter horse and slung a boot into a stirrup. After a few unladylike grunts and ungraceful clambering of her shapely legs, she struggled into the saddle and sat the horse.

"Let's ride," said Noose. A nudge of his lantern jaw indicated the towering gorge of the Teton Pass to the west, just a few miles south from the spectacular snow-capped peaks of the Grand Teton mountain range rearing majestically against the brightening morning sky to their right.

"Farewell, Bonny Kate Valance," Bess said.

Bonny Kate ignored Bess and with a toss of her fiery red mane of hair skillfully spurred her horse and headed off at a trot west across the field.

"See you soon, Bess," Noose said to the fretting female lawman below him, cradling her rifle and watching up at him with worried eyes.

"You do that," she said. Noose reined Copper around and patted its muscular flanks, and the big majestic bronze horse took off at a steady trot falling in right behind the Appaloosa carrying the condemned woman. Together, the two rode toward the mountains, beginning their long and hopefully uneventful journey to the steep rise of the towering pass a few miles distant. The sunlight still hadn't touched the mountain range and the staggering sloped gradients carpeted with pine trees and yawning rock ravines lay in wait, cloaked with foreboding shadow.

The morning air at the Wyoming high elevations was cold, crisp, and clear, rich with the scents of soil and birch. Joe Noose looked back only twice. The first time he saw Bess now stood at the window inside the U.S. Marshal's office, capably cradling her Winchester as she watched him go. The woman looked confident and calm, for she could still get a clean shot off at Bonny Kate from there.

The second time Noose looked back was half a mile farther on and Bess still stood in the window, a tiny speck, but her gun was down because they were out of range of the rifle. Perhaps it was just how small Marshal Bess's little figure appeared in that window but Noose felt the pain in his friend's forlorn bearing so he didn't look back again. Dutifully, Noose returned his gaze to the fetching, wild redheaded woman prisoner on the horse ahead. Bonny Kate Valance struck him as pretty damn unconcerned about being hanged by the neck until dead, like she was cocksure that was never going to happen.

Did she know something he didn't?

Reckon I'll soon find out, Noose figured. In his favor, he had a Henry rifle in one saddle holster, a Winchester repeater in the other, two Colt Peacemakers freshly manufactured, cleaned, and oiled in his belt side holsters, plus enough ammo for each firearm in his bandoliers and saddlebags to hold off a small army. And he had just one unarmed woman to contend with. What could possibly go wrong?

Probably plenty, like it usually did.

Already, Joe Noose wanted this over with.

CHAPTER 2

The six lawmen were definitely out of their element and a very long way from home. They were dirty and saddle weary and had ridden for three months from the state of Arizona and the town of Phoenix, cradle of their jurisdiction. It had been a hard ride with more hard miles ahead a certainty, but they had reached their destination and there was relief in that. The officers had a job to do and were close to completing it. Still, all six of the posse had to admit the scenery of the Jackson Hole valley at the base of the gargantuan cyclopean snowy peaks of the Grand Teton mountain range was spectacular and took a man's breath away with the sheer scope and scale of the sight. None had seen anything like it. It was impressive country beyond question, even if a man did get winded at the eight-thousand-foot elevation, but this was no vacation.

Sheriff Waylon Bojack knew he had no actual authority as a peace officer in Wyoming but believed the piece of paper in his coat gave him plenty: it was a legal judge's court order—even though the damn government had said the only worth this document had was paper to wipe his butt with.

We'll see about that, the sheriff thought.

Sitting his horse stoically at the head of the posse of five other Arizona deputies, Sheriff Bojack cut a distinguished figure who inspired respect with his silvery beard and clean-cut hair on a leathery, lined, heroic face deeply tanned from the desert sun. Waylon Bojack looked every inch the honest, tough, and incorruptible veteran professional lawman who had seen many gunfights in his forty-year tenure. He didn't need a badge to convey that, but wore one on his coat anyway. His sky blue eyes were piercing and direct beneath the perpetual squint he had developed from a life spent under the blazing Arizona sun—while he didn't need to squint here, it had become his habit. He was a legend in Arizona law enforcement with a formidable reputation and spotless record but nobody in Wyoming knew him from Adam. His suntan made him clearly not from around these parts and he and his men got many inquiring and curious looks from the good people of Jackson they rode past on the streets.

Walking past on the street, a local grocer carrying a crate of potatoes passed Sheriff Bojack's horse and smiled a friendly greeting to the stranger. The lawman tipped his hat and leaned in his saddle with an affable smile. "Sir, may I ask you question?"

"Sure you can." The grocer stopped to talk.

"I'm Sheriff Waylon Bojack from Phoenix, Arizona, and these here are my men." The lawman gestured his hand to the five hearty younger riders as clean-cut and tanned as he was. All of them touched their hat brims respectfully. Bojack fixed the grocer in his manly blue-eyed gaze. "We've been told that the U.S.

Marshal's office presently has a prisoner who goes by the name of Bonny Kate Valance."

"Oh yes, we sure do." The local gave a smile and Bojack immediately lost his. "Can you direct me to the U.S. Marshal's office, please?" he said.

"Straight down Broadway on the right. Can't miss it. Our marshal is Bess Sugarland."

"A woman?" Sheriff Bojack was taken aback. He had never met a female in that position of law enforcement authority and if anybody asked him, he would have said he hoped he never would. The Arizona lawman wondered if this would change the equation.

"Yes, sir," the grocer replied agreeably. "Marshal Bess. She's the law around here."

"Then I look forward to making her acquaintance. Thank you for your help and your time, sir." With another tip of his Stetson, Sheriff Bojack spurred his horse forward and with a fresh sense of urgency rode toward the local U.S. Marshal's office followed by his men on horseback.

Waylon Bojack knew it was almost finished—he just didn't know how it was going to play out.

These lawmen did not look happy when they saw the empty cell, was her first thought.

A few hours had passed since Marshal Bess Sugarland stepped away from the window, feeling weighed down with sadness and dread as Joe Noose and Bonny Kate Valance shrank from view as they headed toward the Teton Pass. The Winchester felt heavy but useless in Bess's hands because it would do her no good at the present. She didn't even want to use it for a crutch even though the length of the gun and bend of the wooden stock fit her height and armpit perfectly. With a weary sigh, the female lawman set the repeater on the gun rack and hobbled back to her desk, sat herself, and spent the morning going over paperwork—reports to file, warrants to issue, and such. It had been an otherwise uneventful morning. A few locals came in with various problems she had to give them advice on, but she could do that from her chair.

One thing Bess was happy about was the jail cell was empty, door left open, and that evil slut lady outlaw was out of her purview. It felt like a great weight lifted and the marshal felt relieved every time she cast a glance across the room and saw the unoccupied cell.

It was around eleven in the morning when the Arizona posse showed up. The sound of their horses outside caught Bess's attention and she looked up at the sound of spurs on the porch, laying eyes for the first time on the six respectable, capable-looking peace officers who doffed their hats in respect as they entered her office.

"Howdy. What can I do for you gentlemen?" Bess said brightly, rising to her feet with some difficulty onto her wood-braced, injured leg.

That's when she noticed the dark, malignant looks the entire posse, especially the leader, gave to that empty cell: six sets of cold eyes fixed on it. For an instant, the lawmen's veneer of polite courtesy vanished, replaced by a bitter, mean-spirited disappointment she could feel as much as see. But the moment passed, and just as quickly, the men assumed the deferential,

gentlemanly attitudes they had led with in making
their first impression walking through the door.

The tall and lean rugged older man with the silver-
back hair and sheriff's badge stepped forward with a
confident, aggressive stride and extended his long
arm to offer his big, weathered hand. He met her
gaze squarely with direct twinkling blue eyes the
female marshal thought were disarmingly beautiful.
Bess shook the man's hand in a firm, solid grip that
matched his own even though his huge fingers en-
veloped her own big hand. His gravelly voice was
mellifluous as he formally introduced himself. "I
am Sheriff Waylon Bojack and these here are my
deputies."

Bess saw Bojack notice her glance at his badge with
SHERIFF. PHOENIX, ARIZONA etched on the metal. "We're
from Arizona."

She met his eyes again with a clear, unwavering
gaze. "Long way from home, aren't you, Sheriff? Did
you get lost?" Bess joked amiably.

Bojack looked at her, not blinking. His grin was
frozen.

"Make a wrong turn in Nevada?" Bess quipped
again.

The sheriff just held her gaze and kept his plastered
grin, but there was no mirth in it.

"I was just making a joke, Sheriff. Wyoming humor,"
she said. "No offense intended."

"None taken," he replied, and the warmth returned
to his grin. "I understand you are Marshal Sugarland
and you are in charge around here."

"On my good days." Bess smiled but he didn't smile
back so she decided to can the humor with these

Arizona boys. "Yes, you understand correctly. How can the Jackson U.S. Marshal's office help you boys? State your business."

Holding her gaze and reaching into his coat pocket, Sheriff Bojack pulled out a folded piece of paper that showed much handling, unfolded it, then presented it to Bess. She took the official document from the Arizona State Judiciary and looked it over. He summarized the contents as she perused it: "This is an extradition warrant for Bonny Kate Valance signed by Judge Warren B. Toller in Arizona ordering the fugitive to be immediately remanded into my personal custody to be returned forthwith to the state of Arizona and there be tried for the crime of homicide." Marshal Bess read over the official courthouse typeset and while it was more long-winded in its verbose legalese, that was clearly what it said. Sheriff Bojack continued with a steely tone of righteousness. "It is my information that a month ago Bonny Kate Valance was captured by bounty hunters and handed over to the U.S. Marshal's office in Jackson Hole for the reward and has been in custody here ever since. We have come to collect her."

Bess looked up and met his eyes with a conflicted gaze.

He shot a hard glance at the empty cell then looked back at her just as hard. "Where is she?" Bojack demanded.

Tapping the extradition order with her hand, Marshal Bess heaved a sigh. "This presents a problem." Her leg was beginning to smart fiercely, so she turned and took her seat behind her desk, trying not to show the discomfort she was in. There, she leaned forward

with her elbows on the desktop, clasping her fists
together below her jaw, and stared away from the
men at the opposite wall. She had a lot of things on
her mind.

"And that problem is?" Sheriff Bojack loomed over
her desk, an edge in his voice now.

Sitting below him standing over her but in no way
intimidated by the disadvantage of her position because she wore the badge and these lawmen had no
authority in her jurisdiction, Bess Sugarland did not
respond immediately. It was clear to her she was on
the spot and had to make smart decisions about what
came next. The clock on the wall ticked. She did not
look at the men or acknowledge their presence, and
to them it looked like she was staring at the wall. But
Bess was in fact staring at their reflections in the small
mirror on the opposite wall, sizing up the six Arizona
peace officers—or so they said—invading her space.

They could be impersonating these officers, was the first
thing she considered. *They could be accomplices of Bonny
Kate posing as lawmen trying to break her out of jail.* Bess
had seen phony badges before and knew how easy it
was to make them but she rejected that idea because
if they were pretending to be lawmen, they would not
say they came from a place giving them no jurisdiction in Wyoming unless they were complete fools.
Their being the outlaw's accomplices was possible
but unlikely.

No, these lawmen were the genuine article. Her
father was a marshal and she had been his deputy;
Bess had been around lawmen all her life before becoming one herself—she knew a real sheriff when she
saw one by the way they carried themselves, and this

man, Waylon Bojack, was who he appeared to be, she felt certain. His men likely were legitimate peace officers, too, although her hackles were raised by the reflection of the truculent postures they currently held, which betrayed open hostility since they didn't think she was watching them.

The clock ticked. Bess's brain did, too. The Arizona lawmen waited.

Her gut told her something about these lawmen was wrong, though, and they were not being forthcoming about whatever agenda they were trying to advance coming here for Bonny Kate Valance. Bess was going to have to speak to these men soon so she guessed their true intentions were they were here to kill the outlaw, not take her back to Arizona for trial. Why, Bess hadn't a clue. The world had a lot of people who had plenty of reasons to kill Bonny Kate Valance. The point was, Sheriff Bojack was not playing straight with her so right there Bess made the decision not to tell him anything—nothing about the impending hanging execution in Idaho, nothing about Joe Noose taking Bonny Kate over the pass. The best thing to do, she decided, was to hold back any information, stall for time, and telegraph the U.S. Marshals headquarters in Cody directly about this supposed extradition order and get the official word.

It made Bess uncomfortable to be one wounded woman among six armed men she didn't trust, even if they were lawmen. She wished Noose were here.

He wasn't. She was. And she wore the badge.

At last, Bess turned, leaned back in her wooden chair, and with a trenchant gaze looked up at Bojack. "The problem is, Sheriff, that I don't know anything

about the extradition order and have no way of
knowing. I am not authorized to disclose any information regarding a federal prisoner. What I will do is
the following: telegraph the U.S. Marshals Service
headquarters in Cody, tell them about this extradition order, request instructions, and get my marching
orders from them. I'll do it now. In the meantime, you
boys should go get yourself a cup of coffee and come
back in an hour."

Standing on the other side of the desk, the formidable figure of Sheriff Waylon Bojack seemed to tense
like a tightening rope. His eyes darkened and clouded
with summer storms of fury, turning the blue of his
gaze behind his squint dull and inchoate. Then the
storms faded and his eyes calmed but the shine of affable blue did not return. "We'll wait," he stated flatly.

"Suit yourself," Bess said, taking the extradition
order, looking it over again, rolling her chair over to
the telegraph, and starting to bang out a long transmission to Cody with a steady tapping.

She didn't need to look behind her to know Bojack
was hovering. And she could hear his deputies cleaning their pistols and checking the loads impatiently.
With her face still pointed at the telegraph, Bess spoke
to Bojack a few feet behind her. "You're staring at me,"
she said. "Why is that?"

She heard a manly chuckle. "I've never met a woman
marshal before. Never knew they existed. I want to
watch you work."

"Knock yourself out. But sit your ass down in a
chair and stop breathing down my neck, Sheriff," Bess
growled. "I'm the marshal, this is my office, and that's
a damn order."

Bess Sugarland smiled as she heard the angry creak of a posterior setting itself in a chair behind her.

Sheriff Waylon Bojack had been grinding his teeth with irritability for thirty minutes sitting in that damn uncomfortable chair waiting for that transmission to come back from Cody, trying to figure out what to do. He knew what the message from the state U.S. Marshal's office would say: his extradition order had been overturned by the federal court in Idaho and had no legal validity.

That damn female marshal wasn't even looking at him, just bent over her desk reading through her paperwork and occasionally signing something or filing some letters in her drawer. She hadn't paid him or his men the slightest bit of attention since she sent the wire, and if that female rudeness wasn't proof positive women didn't have the temperament to wear the badge of a peace officer he didn't know what was. Bojack did wonder what she'd done to get her leg all bound up in that wooden brace, though. Maybe a horse kicked her.

Finally, after another ten minutes had passed and he had no bright ideas how to get the information of Bonny Kate Valance's whereabouts out of this tight-mouthed Wyoming marshal, the sheriff needed to stand and stretch his stiff legs and wasn't about to ask permission.

Avoiding the displeased gaze of his deputies sitting around the office, the old lawman wandered around the room, gazing idly here and there.

A big map of Wyoming was on the wall, impressive indeed in its detailed topography of the mountain ranges and the helpful pin showing where Jackson Hole was. He studied that for a few moments because he loved maps, then his legs ached him so he walked away.

Stopping at the cork bulletin board, Bojack saw it almost by accident. *How could I have missed it?* he thought.

The official U.S. Marshals Service order from the Cody, Wyoming, headquarters addressed to the Jackson Hole office giving written directives for the escort and delivery of the condemned fugitive, one Bonny Kate Valance, to the town of Victor, Idaho, two days from today's date.

His breath caught. He knew where she was. Almost. Switching a sly glance to the woman marshal, he saw her head was still in her paperwork and was purposefully not looking at him like she hadn't been.

Good.

Victor, Idaho. That's where the hanging would be. That's where the other Jackson marshals would be taking Valance right now. He had wondered why the office seemed understaffed, and now Bojack understood.

He just didn't know where Victor was but figured he could find it on the map.

Acting like he was just idly killing time, Sheriff Bojack walked back to the map, and his pale blue eyes tracked a line from the pin in Jackson Hole to the border denotation line of Idaho and quickly found Victor. It was right across the Teton Pass, a big mountain range on the map.

When he shifted his gaze from the map to the window, Bojack saw through the glass about two miles off, the towering forested canyon gorge rearing against an endless, unrelieved sky.

The pass. That's where Bonny Kate Valance was. He couldn't see her but that's where she would be.

The sheriff shot his men a steely glance, loaded with purpose.

He tipped his hat to the lady marshal. "Thank you, Marshal, for your help and your time. Meanwhile, reckon we'll go get that coffee and be back in a few minutes."

Looking up from her desk, the woman saw the six Arizona lawmen were already out the door in a clanging of spur and pistol.

"I know where she is," Sheriff Bojack said when the posse were by their horses out of earshot, as he swung up into his saddle while his deputies did, too. He spurred his horse savagely and took off at a full gallop across the plain in the direction of the Teton Pass with his posse right behind him.

Inside the office, Marshal Bess Sugarland was distracted by the telegraph coming in from Cody, her gaze growing more concerned as she read each word, and when her head shot up to ask some hard questions of the Arizona men they were long gone.

CHAPTER 3

"Are we there yet?"

"Not even close," Joe Noose replied to the insistent female voice behind him. He was riding in the lead now, taking point on the trek the two horses and riders were making up ever-steeper mountainous upgrade. He threw a glance over one shoulder or the other every minute or so to keep an eye on Bonny Kate Valance, but so far his prisoner had not tried to bolt or otherwise cause him any trouble.

Their horses were at the foot of the Teton Pass and towering mountains of granite and pine trees reared above them. The view was dizzying. It looked impassable. From his vantage, a journey up to and over the top appeared impossible for a human being to undertake on horse or foot—a half mile on, the terrain rose almost straight up.

But Joe Noose knew a trail had been carved across the Teton Pass a few years before that could be safely traveled, and some folks even did it in the winter. And if they could, he could, Noose reasoned the first time he successfully rode across the Teton Pass two months ago as a bounty hunter on the trail of escaped Victor bank robber Jim Henry Barrow. It had been late spring and the ground had been dry and snowless but he remembered the two-day ride as a nerve-racking steep traverse of narrow trails dropping off sheer sudden cliffs into hundred-foot chasms. He had simply followed the tracks of the bank robber, who knew his way across the pass, and had gotten to the other side in one piece. The horse he had ridden was dead now, shot in a gun battle with the Butler Gang, and he rode its replacement, Copper, now, a stronger, bolder stallion who he felt more confident on in the dangerous ride to come. Still somehow, gazing up now at the monumental gorge scraping the sky before him, crossing the pass seemed a daunting if not hopeless task.

"We're going over that?" Bonny Kate gasped. She was looking at it, too, with an equal measure of awe and terror. Her horse had kind of the same expression she did, Noose noted with amusement.

"Yes, ma'am. That's the plan." Noose was busy scanning the base of the mountain for signs of the bottom of the trail where they would ingress. He had forgotten exactly where that was, but it had to be around here somewhere. "There's a trail. We're gonna stay on it. It'll get us across."

"How we gonna get up that?"

"On our horses."

"How our horses gonna get up that?"

"With difficulty, at times."

Noose started Copper forward with a flick of his reins and the horses continued on their trek. He looked over his shoulder and the female prisoner kicked her Appaloosa into motion and followed at a steady trot up the rocks and stones and occasional trees. Noose noticed the lady outlaw had lost all the ruddy complexion in her face she possessed earlier, her high color drained to a chalky pale by fear. The woman's large electric blue eyes seemed to sizzle with anxiety below her flowing mane of frothy red hair, her alarmed gaze alternating between the unsteady ground where her steed was placing its hooves and the gigantic mountain looming above her. The sun was now all the way up and its harsh light lit up the pass, piteously revealing all the cliffs horse and rider could fall off and jagged rocks below they could crash onto. "I hope you know what you're doing," she said nervously.

"I do. I've ridden the pass before."

"Good to know. How many times?"

"Once." Bonny Kate didn't look reassured, so Noose tried a joke. "What's the worst thing that can happen to you? You get killed?"

"Very funny." Anger twanged in her melodic voice. "Maybe we should just stop talking."

"Suits me." Noose shrugged. "You're the one doing the talking."

That shut Bonny Kate up for maybe three minutes.

"So who are you?" she asked three minutes later.

"I'm the guy taking you to get hanged."

"They paying you a lot?" Ahead of the female outlaw in tow, Noose simply shook his head and she saw the brim of his hat swing back and forth.

"Why are you doing it, then?" He shrugged. "You didn't tell me who you are," she persisted.

"Friend of the marshal," he replied.

"She's a bitch."

"She's a hero."

"Says you."

"Knows me."

Bonny Kate spat in the dirt.

Noose heard it and rotated his head like a gun turret to target her defiant face. "This is going to be a long ride," he snarled.

Ahead, the smaller conifers parted as they approached the trees to reveal a rock-strewn grassy hill that led up to the base of the trail dug into the mountain. Noose recognized the location from his trip the other way. The sight of it relieved him somewhat because at least he knew where he was going. "There's the trail," he said.

When she didn't respond, Noose looked back and saw Bonny Kate studying him intensely in a circumspect way, scrutinizing and sizing him up. "You don't look like a lawman. I've known lawmen, that's a fact, and you don't look like one."

He pointed at his badge on his shirt. "I'm a deputy marshal, says this."

"How long you been a deputy marshal?"

"An hour."

"What did you do before that?" she asked.

"Bounty hunting, mostly."

"Figures. You look like you killed men before."

"Well, you don't."

"That's what I've been tryin' to tell people."

"That you're innocent and such," he said.

"Not hardly. But innocent of what they are hanging me for, yeah, I am."

"Tryin' to convince me of that ain't gonna change a thing."

"I know that. Think I don't know?"

"Reckon you do."

The trail steepened and both Noose and Bonny Kate had to lean a bit forward for balance on the saddles. Leather creaked. Bridles jingled. The horses had

been watered and fed and were doing just fine so far.
The air was rich with the peaty smells of soil and pine.
A vast blue roof of sky stretched overhead, a scud of
cloud here and there in an otherwise slate expanse.

It was an hour and a half maybe two past full sunup
and both riders had traveled about six miles from
Jackson Hole, riding into the mountains proper now,
and the change in topography had come almost without their notice. Noose understood part of the reason
was how dry everything was: the usual green blanket
of the mountain pines were a sallow carpet of dead
browns, from the leaves on the branches to the grass
on the ground underfoot. A drought had struck Wyoming for the last few months and the dehydrated
vegetation had become parched as kindling from lack
of water. *Fire conditions.*

The day was getting hot, Noose could feel. It would
get hotter, fast, this time of year. For the last half an
hour it had been at their backs, east, and it was a skillet
of flat, hard heat on the back of their necks as they rode
west. Now they were into trees. Sun sparkles needled
through the tops of the fifty-to-hundred-foot-high
conifers, making him squint, creating dense shadows
of the heavy branches that took the edge off the heat,
the weather a trade-off, like much of life, it seemed
to Noose.

Bonny Kate had been quiet for a time, so he swung
a glance over his shoulder and there she was, smack
in the saddle, head thrown back, red tresses off her
face, eyes closed, feeling the sun on her face with a
raw smile of enjoyment. Pleasurably breathing in the
nature smells through her nose, the lady outlaw didn't
say a word for a while until: "It's a good day to die."

"You're dying tomorrow," Noose corrected her.

She opened her electric blue eyes then blinked once or twice. "Well, then, today's a good day to be alive."

Noose shrugged, nudging Copper in a left direction on the narrow, snaking trail up the pass. "Every day above ground is a good day, some would say," he said.

"I beg to differ. Some days in this life I have lived, Joe Noose, I'd've preferred I'd been dead and they had buried me deep."

He was looking over her shoulder back at her and the way her face looked with passing shadows in her hooded eyes lent her words the ring of truth.

"I'm sorry to hear that, ma'am," he replied. "All your suffering will be over soon."

The bullet blew the branch off fifteen feet above Noose's head as a loud shot came without warning from below—*intentional miss,* Noose was thinking, already leaping out of his saddle onto his prisoner and dragging the woman from the horse as the second shot caromed off a rock fifty feet away—*another deliberate miss*—and when Noose and Bonny Kate hit the dirt and he rolled protectively on top of her, quick-drawing his Colt .45, which he thumbed into cocked position, Noose already knew these were warning shots, not kill shots . . . either that, or he was in the presence of the worst shots in the West.

"Stay down!" Noose snarled to his prisoner.

Beneath him, tucked under the broad body shield of Noose's massive muscular bulk, Bonny Kate stared up at him in a naked expression of terror or excitement, he wasn't sure, but it might have been both since she was smacking her lips.

"Don't move," he whispered sharply. "Don't say a word."

She nodded quickly, now very cooperative.

Noose and the female outlaw were hunkered behind some large piled rocks in a gap at the beginning of the trail. The two shots had come from below on the wooded approach to the pass, somewhere down there in the trees, out of sight. Noose threw a glance to Copper and the Appaloosa, both horses ten feet away—the shots had been so far afield neither stallion had bolted.

Bonny Kate gasped, breathless. "Tell me, please, why is somebody shooting at *us?*"

Shaking his head slowly, Noose kept his drawn pistol up, peering over the rocks and listening for any movement. "They weren't trying to hit us, just get our attention. I believe those were warning shots."

"But wh—?"

"Shhh." Noose suddenly put a finger of his free hand to her lips.

Because a forceful male voice a hundred yards below was now calling up to them: *"You two ain't hit because I wasn't trying to hit you! Not yet! Me and my boys don't want to shoot you, Marshal! We respect the law because we are lawmen! We just want the woman!"*

Noose screwed a squinty glance down at Bonny Kate, eyebrow cocked, not making any sense of this.

Again the rough and authoritative male voice below boomed through the trees: *"I am Sheriff Waylon Bojack from Arizona. Maybe you heard of me, maybe not, but I have in my hand a legal extradition order for Bonny Kate Valance authorizing me and my deputies to bring this outlaw you have in your custody back to Arizona to hang for crimes she committed in my jurisdiction! The states of Wyoming and Idaho have chosen to disregard this extradition order and in doing so are breaking the law, but I mean to enforce it and take her back by any means necessary if I have to! Lawman to lawman, Marshal, I hope you appreciate my position! But if you don't, that's too damn bad! Just hand her over and we'll be on our way! What do you say?"*

To his surprise, Noose saw the face of the flaming redheaded woman a foot from him was wild with terror suddenly—he hadn't seen her scared before but she sure was now. Bonny Kate hadn't shown any particular fear of being hanged in Idaho so Noose didn't see why the prospect of being hanged in Arizona was causing her to shake her head *no* at him so desperately right now.

Noose yelled harshly over the heavy rocks: "I say, you boys better back off now if you know what's good for you, because the next bullet comes our way I will kill the man that fired it and kill the man standing next to him directly! I don't know if you are who you say you are and don't give a damn! My sworn duty is to deliver my prisoner to the hangman across the pass and I will do so!"

Bonny Kate gave a coarse laugh, impressed by Noose's sheer nerve.

Noose didn't notice. His gaze busily scanning their woody surroundings, Noose's eyes locked on a fork in the trail just ahead that led up to a granite cliff that would provide effective cover if they made it with the horses the fifty yards it would take to reach it. Getting there, the terrain would be open to view from below and expose them to the line of fire of their adversaries, but Noose figured if he laid down enough covering fire beating the retreat, the other men would be ducking, waiting for him to finish shooting and that would give him time to get Bonny Kate and the horses safely to the rocks.

If nothing went wrong.

Which it often did.

"There's six of us and one of you, Marshal!" yelled Bojack. *"Think about it!"*

"You need more men, if that's all you got!" shouted back Noose.

"Is that your final word?" bellowed Bojack fiercely.

"My final word will be a bullet between your eyes if I don't see the hind ends of your horses with your hind ends on 'em ridin' back down the trail by the count of ten!" roared Noose. While he was doing all that hollering he was busy making quick hand signals with his free hand to Bonny Kate, pointing and gesturing with his fingers, explaining the plan to her, and the woman nodded she understood. Noose put up his finger: *On my go.*

"I respect you, Marshal, for doing your duty as you see it. And I will say a prayer over your grave right after I spit on the grave of Bonny Kate Valance!"

"Go!"

Leaping up from behind the rocks, Joe Noose swiftly drew his second Colt .45 from his side holster and was firing one Peacemaker in each hand into the trees below in the direction of the voice, his boots already backing up, Bonny Kate bolting like a jackrabbit over to the horses and grabbing both reins, running up the hill toward the fork in the trail, Noose giving them cover, firing and firing from the hip, one round after another, fire and smoke exploding from his guns, blowing chunks from the trees below and geysers of dirt and grass in a relentless fusillade of lead.

Tallied up, it took them thirty-two seconds to reach the protection of the cliff: fifteen seconds for Noose to use up all his bullets; twenty seconds for the woman to get the horses behind the crag; seventeen seconds for the man to scramble as fast as his boots would carry him across the open ground for cover . . . but by the seventeenth of those seconds Sheriff Bojack and his deputies had gauged Noose's guns were dry and broke cover, firing everything they had, and Joe Noose spent the next ten seconds running uphill directly in the line of fire with scores of rounds whistling past his head but he was a little faster than they were and got to safety unscathed.

The bullets kept coming until Joe Noose grabbed a Winchester repeater from Copper's saddle holster, levered it, and began blasting around the corner of the cliff.

When he heard the single high-pitched scream and the thud of the body fall Noose knew two things . . .

The bullets had stopped and the number of men shooting at them were one less.

CHAPTER 4

Sheriff Bojack knew the boy. Stood witness at his birth. Now twenty-two years later, stood here, witness at his death.

A bad way to die, a long way from home.

The gut-shot deputy lay sprawled on the grass on his back in his final death twitches, bleeding out copiously from a fist-sized hole in his stomach that spilled his insides. Bojack had just gestured to his men to cease firing and he now knelt by the young man he knew as Ned Hodge, gripping his bloody hand so his deputy didn't die alone, until that hand went limp. The man was dead. The sheriff grimly took off his hat in respect. Crossed himself with two fingers. Reached those same two scarred fingers out to shut the boy's eyelids over his lifeless, staring eyes. The sheriff was regretful his young deputy had to pass over knowing how much dying can hurt.

Waylon Bojack was remembering kneeling over another deputy, barely older than this one, shot in the back.

His boy. Jim Bojack. Twenty-six years old.

Shot by *her*.

It was the true reason Sheriff Bojack was here and why he meant to bring the murderess back to face Arizona justice and be hanged in his jurisdiction . . . or, failing that, kill her here in Wyoming or Idaho by his own hand. Waylon Bojack had a son to avenge and promises to keep.

It all began a year ago when an Atchison, Topeka and Santa Fe railroad was held up at gunpoint by Bonny Kate Valance and the notorious gang of dangerous outlaws she ran with. The one woman and five men used trinitrotoluene to blow the tracks and halt the train then to blast the door off the heavy safe in the bank wagon that contained over a hundred thousand dollars in government payroll. The heist was well planned, brutal, and efficient. Within ten minutes the Valance gang had made off with the loot and left two bank guards shot in the back. One guard survived, one didn't, and Sheriff Waylon Bojack didn't care which one of the gang shot him, just that the robbery happened in his jurisdiction. Word of the train robbery traveled to his office within the hour and he had his lawmen saddled up, armed to the teeth, and galloping hard due southeast past the tracks, where the seasoned tracker quickly picked up the trail of the fleeing outlaws.

Bonny Kate Valance and her crew had made two mistakes he would school them dearly for: the first was robbing a train in the first place and the second was robbing it in Sheriff Waylon Bojack's county—a jurisdiction with a 100 percent apprehension rate for outlaws who committed crimes therein and therefore one of the safest territories in the thirty-eight United States. Bojack was a legend. The lawman always got his man and he was relentless. As were his highly trained attack dog deputies, their fierce, powerful horses, and especially the sheriff's son and head deputy, Jim Bojack, who would succeed him as sheriff when the old man retired.

For five days and nights the Arizona lawmen pursued the Valance gang and drove them to ground on the fifth night in an abandoned Indian pueblo, ambushing the exhausted, beaten-down outlaws while they foolishly slept. Sheriff Bojack and his eight deputies left their horses a mile away and approached the pueblo huts on foot from four sides and went in shooting. Bojack wanted the outlaws captured alive if possible and his deputies aimed for the legs and knees when they shot the first Valance gang thugs.

The train robbers had put up a hell of a fight, taking cover around the pueblos and for fifteen minutes it was a terrific firefight, until the better trained and armed Arizona deputies hammered them back with relentless fusillades of lead, boxing the gang in and capturing them.

Bojack didn't lose a single man that night. Except one. The one that counted most.

It was Jim Bojack who first saw the woman break cover, running away like her ass was on fire and ducking into the sheltering darkness between the huts— Bonny Kate Valance looked so scared as she cowardly deserted her gang, Waylon didn't think anything of it when his son, Jim, gave his father a nod and took off after her. The last Sheriff Bojack ever saw of his firstborn was the back of the strong young man with pistol drawn swallowed into the gloom of the alleyway between those pueblos like a man sinking into tar, and right away the elder Bojack had a bad feeling.

By then, the deputies had rounded up all the rest of the gang and were in the process of disarming and shackling them—this distracted the sheriff for a few fateful moments before that awful loud gunshot rang out . . . in the jagged muzzle flash that lit up the alley he saw Jim crumple, trying to clutch his back.

They found him dead a few moments later.

Never found her. She had shot his son in the back and fled into the desert like a gutless coyote.

They looked. Did they ever. But Bonny Kate Valance was not to be found—not that night nor the following day nor weeks nor months later. She was in the wind that blew hot and dry and dusty across the harsh and arid Arizona desert.

The grief-stricken sheriff Waylon Bojack hunted the fugitive outlaw Bonny Kate Valance clear across his territory from one end to the other, every fruitless day compounding his corrosive hatred of the woman until it destroyed everything he had, chasing her shadow long past when it had become apparent to everyone but him that the female outlaw had safely fled his jurisdiction to points south or north or east or west; it didn't matter, because she was out of his grasp and long gone. Perhaps Bojack knew it, too, just didn't want to, or just couldn't, admit it.

His badge was tarnished in letting Bonny Kate escape. After that, his apprehension rate was officially dropped to 99 percent and his legendary lawman's record was no longer perfect . . . a sullied reputation just the beginning of his long decline as a peace offi-cer traveling into that uncharted and gray country where the law ended and justice began.

Now, finally, one full year and a thousand miles away, Sheriff Bojack was a bullet's trajectory from the

CHAPTER 5

"Are those men who they say they are?"

Bonny Kate was tight-lipped as she met Joe Noose's blunt gaze. He wanted answers. She nodded and said, "Yeah, Sheriff Bojack. I know him."

"So it's true, then."

"The them being lawmen part, yeah."

"Why the hell are they trying to kill you?" he asked.

"For something I ain't done."

"Lady, for a woman who ain't done nothing you got a lot of people want you dead for it."

The two people were walking single file up the narrow gap in the granite crevice between the cliffs, leading their horses carefully, moving single file with Noose in the lead, Bonny Kate tailing him. There was barely room in the tight space for the width of the horses to squeeze through. Noose was walking backward to keep a flinty eye on the opening several hundred yards behind, where they had slipped through, escaping the posse. Noose held his loaded Winchester and Henry rifles, one in each hand, ready to fire, his reins loosely slung over his right wrist because Copper needed little supervision. The bronze horse agilely placed its hooves on the steep, rocky ground, ascending the treacherous draw toward the opening up ahead that spilled out onto some kind of higher ground. The female outlaw brooded, giving Noose a narrow glance.

"I don't give a squat if you believe me or not," she said. "I'm between the hawk and the buzzard anyway and either way I'll be dead in a day or two."

"Can't believe or disbelieve what I don't know nothing about. Why do those lawmen want to kill you?"

"It's a long story."

"It's a long ride. Mind if I ask you a question, Miss Valance?"

"Ain't like I'm stopping you."

"Why is it that you ain't shown a lick of fear about swinging at the end of that noose they got waiting for you in Idaho but that sheriff back there scared you so bad you were quaking in your boots?"

"Was not."

"What difference does it make to you whether you die by a rope or a bullet?"

"Because a noose is quick. Waylon Bojack, he ain't just gonna kill me, he's gonna kill me slow, after he removes my lady parts."

Noose passed the Winchester in his left hand to his right one with the Henry to reach out and take Bonny Kate's hand, helping her lead her ragged quarter horse up a tricky section of path. "Firstly, that ain't gonna happen," he said. "Nobody's gonna kill you before I get you to the gallows to die legal. Them lawmen are interfering with due process and I'll kill all of 'em if I have to. That's on them for breaking the law they was sworn to uphold, but I'm getting you to the noose just like I'm sworn to do."

"Lordy." She looked at him oddly with a penetrating gaze. "You're gonna risk your life, probably get yourself killed or shot up real bad, going up outnumbered against all those men trying to kill me just so the folks in Idaho can kill me. What's the sense in that? Either way I'm dead."

"I have a job to do, you're that job, and I'm gonna put paid on it."

"Well, good for you." She snorted. "You may be big and tough and all and have all them big guns but you ain't got a lick of sense. Not hardly a lick." She shook her head and laughed harshly. "Get yourself killed just so some folks can kill me instead of other folks. That makes no sense."

"Does to me."

"Because?"

"Because I swore an oath to Marshal Bess, because it's the law, and because in this situation it's the right thing to do. I gave my word."

More and more, Bonny Kate seemed to grow fascinated with Noose. Like she had encountered some new animal species not previously known to exist. "You're big on the right thing to do," she observed frankly. "You always done the right thing?"

Noose became distant for a reflective few moments, then said, "Not always. Now I try to. When I can figure out what the right thing is. That ain't always easy."

"You said a mouthful, Joe Noose." The female outlaw unexpectedly smiled warmly then spoke softly and sincerely when she said, "And if it means anything, I do appreciate it. I feel safe with you. Not for long, maybe, but safe for right now."

"Good."

"It is good."

Noose let Bonny Kate's hand go now the footing was more steady in the crevice and returned the Winchester to his left hand, returning his gaze to the receding opening to their rear over his prisoner's shoulder. So far there was no sign of the posse. "Maybe you best tell me the long story of why that sheriff wants your hide. Pardon the language, Miss Valance, but that man has one hell of a hard-on for you. Why is that?"

She sighed, lock-jawed.

Noose shrugged. "I got all day. The night, too. Then the first part of tomorrow. That's about it." He grinned.

She didn't. "Sheriff Bojack believes I shot his son, his own deputy, in the back and killed him outside of Phoenix about nine months ago. The deputy was part of Bojack's posse that was chasing me and my gang for a train robbery we pulled in Arizona, where we stole a bunch of money. A hundred and twenty-six thousand dollars was the take. That part of what they accuse me of is true. We robbed the train. And the law came after us. It happened in Bojack's jurisdiction and he and his boys chased us hard for a week, damn near drove our horses into the ground. Them Arizona lawdogs is some tough honchos, that's a plain fact. After a week we thought we had lost 'em in the desert but we was wrong.

"My gang and me, we had hid out in some pueblos and the sheriff and his boy and probably those men back there shooting at us ambushed us while we were sleeping. The bullets were flying and it was hellfire. I ran. Didn't even have time to strap on my gun belt, and that young deputy, good-looking boy that he was, gave chase and he had me boxed in with his gun on me, but he was an honest lawman, he didn't shoot me though he could have 'cause he was just a kid. I knew when I heard the shot it wasn't his shot, and when the deputy fell with a big hole in his back I saw Johnny Cisco standing behind him with a smoking weapon. Cisco was my man and was always sweet on me but as the good Lord God is my witness it was Johnny Cisco shot the Bojack boy in the back, not me. I was unarmed, didn't even have a gun on me, Joe!"

Noose listened, backing his way up the draw, didn't look at her, keeping his eyes alert for trouble behind them, didn't speak.

"You probably don't believe me, either." Bonny Kate shrugged in resignation.

"Don't matter if I do or don't. Point is, Sheriff Bojack believes it enough to travel three states to come gunning for you. I don't know what happened. I wasn't there."

"It happened just like I told it."

"Why you think he thinks that?"

"Because Cisco told him I shot the deputy. And all those buzzards in that old gang of mine backed up his story. Sheriff Bojack and his deputies captured or killed all of my gang that night. I'm the only one who got away."

"What happened to the money?" Noose asked.

"That hundred grand from the train, you mean?" she retorted.

Noose nodded. "What else?"

Bonny Kate shrugged. "Your guess is as good as mine. My gang had it and the law got them. I got away with two dollars and one buffalo nickel in my britches, and not a damn thing else. 'Cept my life. What I have left of it."

"That was a lot of money."

With a wistful smile, the lady outlaw nodded, whistling nostalgically. "Sure was. Most cash I ever seen or touched. While I was on the run I don't know which I missed more: that money or my beau Johnny Cisco's handsome face, them mooning looks he'd always give me 'cause that man loved me something fierce. Truth be told, I got powerful lonesome in the days since then, knowing I'd never have a man worship the ground I walked on like that again, and I still miss Cisco. He's probably dead now, but maybe he got away with that money and is living in luxury. I rightly don't know. Soon all my worries are over anyhow."

"Reckon."

They had reached the top of the gap and Copper stepped ahead of Noose out onto the top of the cliff face. Noose put his hand out for Bonny Kate to stop so he could check the area was safe. He peered carefully over the edge of the gap that opened up onto a stark plateau, both his rifles at ready as he swung them in a quick 360, his nose going where the muzzles went.

Nobody was up there, nothing moving except the odd birds flying overhead. Insects buzzed. The air smelled hot, dry, and dusty. From Noose's vantage, the rock face ended at a sheer cliff on one side of the draw and on the other side stretched for fifty yards to a scattered tree line of browned and thirsty pine trees that rose high into the colorless sky before the mountains continued straight up beyond in a series of dizzying, jutting crags. A rugged, untamed wilderness. The drought conditions had been severe the last month. The landscape was one big fire hazard,

Noose observed grimly; a single spark could set the entire mountain ablaze. Endless patchwork quilt carpets of once-lush conifers now dun and withered from thirst, green leached from their dried branches, blanketed the steep rising slopes of the Teton Pass in clumps of dead and dying forestation.

Noose could not see the excavated trail everyone traveled across the pass from up here—it lay below out of sight to the south—and there was nothing remotely resembling any kind of trailhead in this remote area; he was going to have to improvise a way on up through the mountains, pushing south, left, with his prisoner and hoping to reconnect with the regular trail without incident.

Time was wasting.

The sheriff and his deputies were after them, and men like these meant to see things through. It was a long way to Idaho across hard country and they had to get moving.

Stepping up out of the crevice onto solid ground, Joe Noose took another look around and then gestured with his rifle to Bonny Kate it was safe to come out. With a few swift, sure steps, she egressed the gap with her Appaloosa in tow and stood beside him on the plateau, looking around in dismay, unsure of where they were to go. A brief, refreshing breeze scented with dry pinecones cooled their faces and dried the sweat. Noose pointed toward what seemed like some kind of natural path in the woods heading west in the general Idaho direction.

He swung into his saddle. She climbed into hers. They rode on. So far, nobody was on their trail.

For now.

CHAPTER 6

Lucky bastard.

Keeping his drawn and cocked SA Army pistol up by his fist, Sheriff Bojack advanced step by cautious step up the narrow gap between the hundred-foot cliff face, leading his horse. His four deputies, on foot like he was, led their horses in single file behind him. The fifth was slung facedown over his bloody saddle, bringing up the rear. The leathery tough old lawman had his eyes fixed to the top of the cliff above them, keenly observant, ready to shoot at the first sign of any movement.

"Eyes sharp, men," he said just loud enough for his deputies to hear. "If he starts shooting at us, it'll be from up there. Soon as we make it up this cliff, remount."

Bojack moved the muzzle of his revolver back and forth with the movement of his head, the barrel going where his nose went, advancing one foot at a time. His gut instinct was the big Wyoming marshal wasn't lying in wait. Instead, he was riding fast away up the trail with his female prisoner, knowing full well Bojack and his lawmen would be delayed having to proceed cautiously through the same narrow gulch they just went through, because the posse didn't know if the marshal would be drawing a bead on them from the high ramparts of the rock formation. The marshal wouldn't be, though, because Bojack, who could read people, figured this one for some by-the-book straight-arrow badge just doing his job, getting the woman to the gallows and not trying to kill Arizona marshals unless he was defending himself and absolutely had to.

Tough, smart son of a bitch.

This Wyoming stud was good. Bojack knew right away not to underestimate the stubborn local marshal he was up against. The U.S. Marshals Service must be paying him a lot of money to be risking his neck to save the life of a prisoner who was a dead woman walking anyway. But it wasn't about the money. Bojack knew what marshals earned in salary and what the states paid to escort prisoners and it wasn't about the money for this man; it was about doing his job. The sheriff understood and admired that.

Bojack instantly respected his adversary. Lawmen like this were hard to come by. He respected any peace officer who did his duty and didn't bend because Waylon Bojack had been that very man himself before he became someone who would kill any man, woman, or child that got in between his gun and the woman who murdered his son. The sheriff felt a stab of deep regret and remorse. He shook it off. Bojack had been proud of who he used to be, proud of all those years of honorable, fearless service and irrationally he envied, if just a little, the marshal he was up against now. In the past, he'd have bought him a drink but now the best the sheriff could hope for was not having to shoot him.

Of course, things could go the other way. This marshal was a dangerous man with brass balls who knew how to shoot—that much was clear. It would be prudent for Bojack to shoot first and ask questions later with this individual.

Hopefully it wouldn't come to that.

Hope for the best, prepare for the worst.

The Arizona constabulary was halfway up the crevice, rifles and pistols drawn, hammers cocked, heads and eyes swiveling, watchful of the ridge above as they led their horses at a snail's pace through the shadows of the rock face. Up ahead in the lead, Sheriff Bojack gestured with his hat for the men to pick up the pace. Nobody was going to take any shots at them—the man and woman they pursued were riding hard and making time. The posse needed to get to the top of this gulch and get after them directly before they fell too far behind.

The lawmen doubled their speed, rigorously trudging up the steep incline leading their horses in single file, their dusty boots dislodging rocks and gravel. The men behind dodged or ducked the stones that came tumbling loose from the feet and hooves of the men and horses above them. One deputy, Jed Ransom, slipped and with a sputtered curse skinned his knee badly through his trousers. The steeds snorted and yanked against their reins, skittish and recalcitrant in the narrow space sometimes so tight the stallions and mares could barely squeeze through. Just a little farther. Another seventy-five yards, Bojack saw, they would reach the top and get back on their horses.

Something gold fell out of his coat and hit the ground with a tiny metallic *clink*. With a sharp intake of breath, the lawman quickly bent down and grabbed it up like it was a fragile, precious treasure.

In his rugged, leathery hand was a small gold locket. Blowing off the dirt, his shaking fingers opened the locket to be sure the contents were intact. Bojack sighed when he saw they were unharmed.

Two photos, one on each side of the oval locket. One a black-and-white photograph of a clean-cut young man in his Arizona constabulary service uniform: his boy, Jim.

The other a photo of a small, lovely woman when she was ten years younger in age, still in full health with light still in her eyes. Margaret Bojack. His wife. His loved ones.

The locket held pictures of a mother and her only child, his son, whom he had let get killed on his watch.

Every good thing Waylon Bojack had done in his life—and there had been too many valorous deeds to count—meant nothing after that. Not to him. And not to Margaret.

She hated him and would hate him until the day he avenged her only boy and took the life of the woman who took Jim from her. His wife told him this every day in her words and her black looks and the grieving and anger that consumed her once-vibrant spirit. Bitterness destroyed her health as she refused to eat and couldn't keep anything down when she did. The great weight of her sadness and misery ground the sheriff down in the early days after Jim's death and he didn't come home to face it, staying out on the trail for weeks on end in the hopeless pursuit of the murderess he knew was long gone.

Half the reason he didn't go home, Bojack knew in his heart, was seeing the accusation in his beloved wife's pained face every time she looked at him. Because every glance reminded him of the lost son the sheriff had loved so much, the boy who was going to take his place and carry on the Bojack lawman family legacy; the son he had gotten killed from one careless mistake he would carry with him to his grave.

The pain was too much for one man to bear, but it would get worse when he came home the last time three months ago and found Margaret Bojack close to death in her bed, wasted away almost to a skeleton, her beauty ravaged by inconsolable mourning. She was attended to by the doctor, who told the sheriff there was nothing he could do for Margaret, who he guessed had a month to live.

Over the entire night, Sheriff Waylon Bojack sat beside Margaret Bojack's bed somberly keeping vigil, holding her hand, which she was too weak to pull away. He made her a vow then, one he swore on the graves of his own father and mother and their lost son, that he would kill the woman Bonny Kate Valance who shot their son in the back and he would do it while Margaret still drew breath, so before she shed this mortal coil she would know her husband had avenged them.

His wife had nodded. Smiled the first time since Jim's death. He saw love in her eyes for him flicker like a candle in the wind.

And she had squeezed his hand, holding on to his instead of pulling away.

Dawn brought a sign from God. His deputy Ransom rode up to the house and burst in, yanking off his hat as he breathlessly delivered the news: Bonny Kate

Valance had been captured by bounty hunters in Wyoming and was presently being held in custody in the Jackson Hole jail.

Waylon had woken the judge and had him draw up and sign the extradition order. By noon, Sheriff Waylon Bojack and his five-man posse were saddled up, fully armed and loaded, and riding hard northeast toward Wyoming.

CHAPTER 7

Noose had the high ground—that was in his favor even if his being one against five of those Arizona boys weren't odds on his side.

Hell, it was nothing but high ground ahead, Noose thought, gazing up at the towering Teton Pass trailhead rearing before him. But difficult as the going was for him, it was more difficult for the men chasing him because Noose was above them and in any kind of armed engagement a man did not want to occupy the low ground. Everybody knew that, and Noose figured the sheriff did, too.

Noose gave Copper a tap with his boots in the stirrups and the good horse picked up the pace up the ridge, its hooves clopping against the loose rocks but finding stable footing with each step. In his right hand, Noose clenched his big revolver, in his left he held the reins to Bonny Kate's mustang.

She was right behind him, throwing a nervous look over her shoulder every few seconds, it seemed like, with a big toss of her red hair. "They're coming after us," she said not for the first time in the last five minutes.

"Thank you for informing me of that," Noose retorted with a roll of his eyes.

"There's six of them, by my count, and just one of you."

"Five now. One's dead."

Bonny Kate took that in. "Okay, five, then. But there's still one of you."

"Your point?"

"I think you should give me a gun."

"Why would I do a dumb thing like that?"

"*Because* then it would be five of them against *two* of us instead of one."

He laughed and shook his head *no.*

"I know how to use a gun!" she insisted, her cheeks getting high color.

"That's what they all say."

"Damn straight." Her eyes flared. "And I ain't gonna shoot you in the back if that's what you're thinking because what would be the sense in that? Them men back there want to kill me. You know it. They said so. If I shoot you then it's one against five again and that would be stupid. I may be many things, Joe Noose, but I sure ain't stupid."

"Never said you was, Miss Valance. Never thought it, neither. I thought anything, it was you may be smarter than me."

"And there it is. I am. You said so yourself. So give me a gun, Joe Noose."

"I don't think so."

The female outlaw stewed. "So what happens if you get shot and kilt and they're coming and I'm unarmed?"

Without looking back, Noose swept his hand in a

gesture to the rifles and pistols on his belt and in his saddle holsters. "If I get killed then you are five feet away from all my weapons, and upon my unfortunate but unlikely demise you have my express permission to avail yourself of any and all firearms you deem fit in the defense of your person."

"Well, that's very big of you."

"Least I can do."

"Can I get that in writing?"

"Think of it as my spoken last will and testament with you being the sole beneficiary."

"You giving me a pistol now might save your life. Just give me a little one."

"I don't have any little guns."

"True." Her smile had sauce. "I noticed that. Everything about you is too damn big."

"Big guns make holes and stop what they hit," he stated flatly. "You might want to remember that if you have any ideas of trying to pull anything. That is, if the hours you have left mean anything to you. Meanwhile, rest assured none of those men back there are gonna touch you. I'll kill any of 'em that try. While you are under my watch, you will be safe until I deliver you to the gallows."

She exhaled an exaggerated sigh of relief.

"Glad we got that sorted," he chuckled.

"I need to pee," she complained.

"Hold it in. Another ten minutes, anyways, till I get us atop yonder ridge. I spy some big rocks and boulders at the crest I can dislodge and roll down on the trail. Give that sheriff a bad surprise if that's the way he's coming."

"You gonna drop rocks on him?"

"I best believe I will. Bullets cost money. Rocks is free."

She threw her head back and laughed heartily. "Joe Noose, you is a funny man. I do say you make me laugh with some of the humorous things that come outta your mouth. My, the way you put stuff."

"Pleased I do. You have a nice laugh. It's good to hear you use it."

"Why, thank you."

"Nice smile, too."

"Joe Noose, can I help you push some rocks?"

"Yes, you can."

"I want to drop me a big damn rock on that Waylon Bojack's head to knock some sense into him."

"On one condition."

"What's that?"

"Stop calling me Joe Noose. Makes me sound simple. Call me Joe. Or Noose. Or Deputy Marshal if you have to, even."

"Got yourself a deal, Joe. On one condition."

"With you, of course there is."

"Y'all call me Bonny Kate. Stop that *Miss Valance* stuff. Makes me sound like I got airs."

Noose chuckled. "Bonny Kate, my name's Joe."

"Under different circumstances, Joe, I'd say it was a pleasure to meet you."

They both laughed as they rode on up the trail that angled suddenly sharper below the jagged ridge overhang above.

"Keep down."

Joe Noose whispered to Bonny Kate Valance, huddling beside him just below the crest of the rocks on top of the outcrop above the trail. He said the words with sufficient authority that she didn't move an inch. They were safely out of sight to anyone approaching below. The two horses had their reins tied to a conifer trunk fifty feet from where the man and woman lay in the dirt, even farther out of sight.

It was very quiet. The rising and falling wind whispered through the pines in a rustle of dried branches from one end of the Teton Pass to the other on both sides of the lonely gorge. It was kind of restful. The wind was the only sound. Even the birds were quiet, as if waiting, holding their breath for something to happen.

It was about to.

Noose's head was cocked in an attitude of keen listening, keeping his ears open for the sounds of hooves or boot steps or creaking of leather or metallic *clink* of gun belt and stirrup that would signal the imminent approach of the Arizona posse.

The only way the rogue lawmen could come that wouldn't take them hours out of the way was up the makeshift trail that Noose and the lady outlaw had just scaled.

Joe Noose was ready.

Both his huge hands were placed against two large boulders he had five minutes ago determined to be loosely positioned on the top of the ridge—one good shove would send both rocks crashing down the craggy slope, dislodging many other heavy, loose stones that would tumble onto the trail and anyone who had the misfortune to be on it.

All he had to do was wait.

Looking at the fearful face of the woman beside him, the man puckered his lips together in a silent shushing expression. She nodded, her own hands on a third, smaller boulder. He gave her a *wait for me* nod.

The wind picked up, died down, rose, and perished again in death rattle rustles of dead foliage across the sprawling expanse of mountainside. It was almost restful.

A hummingbird flitted.

Insects buzzed.

Hearing the clop of a hoof behind her, Bonny Kate whirled with a startled expression, fearing they had been bushwhacked, but saw it was only her Appaloosa of a mustang restlessly pawing the ground atop the ridge with its fetlock.

When she looked back with an exhale of relief, Noose caught her gaze and with a shake of his head and a nudge of his lantern jaw communicated wordlessly that the out-of-state lawmen would be coming from the other direction, up the trail down below.

After that, the lady outlaw caught her breath and composed herself somewhat.

They didn't have long to wait.

First one set of hooves, then another set, then another keeping a slow and steady pace sounded coming up the trail. Noose heard the creak of the saddles of the men astride them, so they weren't empty horses sent as a trick to lure him out in the open so the posse could take a shot at him. That's what he would have done in their position, and Noose was now figuring these Arizona boys weren't all that smart.

Getting a good grip on the rocks, ready to push, he kept his head down. Saw she was, too.

The only thing that worried Noose, as it always did, was that one of the horses the lawmen were riding would get hurt in the rockslide—its skull bashed in or

its leg lamed—and have to be put down. He hated
hurting horses, because they weren't bad, just the
men riding them who were. But this did not worry
him much in the situation as Noose knew that horses
were smart and had good reflexes and the minute the
steeds heard those rocks come down they were going
to run the hell out of there like their asses were on
fire. In fact, he was counting on it. In all the confusion
while the sheriff and his deputies were trying to control their mounts, that's when Noose would leap up
and break cover, shooting down on them with his Winchester like shooting fish in a barrel. The repeater rifle
held twenty-five rounds but he figured he was only
going to use five to ten cartridges. The bad lawmen
had been warned and he would shoot them in the legs.

He knew he had the legal right as deputy marshal
to kill these rogue lawmen, but that wouldn't be right
as long as he could wound them sufficiently to stop
them from interfering with his appointed mission and
sworn duty.

The hooves were directly below.

Noose pushed the rocks, heaving his muscular
shoulders into the effort.

The boulders swayed, then gravity kicked in and
over they went, the weight off his hands as he heard
the falling rocks smash and tumble with a thunder of
impact collision against the side of the ridge as
down they rolled. Now there was a *bang crash boom* of
stone on stone in his ears as the boulders began to
bounce, picking up speed upon acceleration, the
sounds of gravel and stones dislodging to plummet
in a rockslide—beneath the deafening clamor, the
cries of men and bellowing horses as hooves sounded
beneath the din of the falling rocks.

Shooting a glance over to Bonny Kate, Noose could see her face was flushed with effort while she shoved with both her small, and he now saw, dainty hands against the rock but couldn't budge it. He slid over on his seat and helped, using both legs in a pile driver kick to knock the boulder loose, and it, too, fell.

Then he grabbed the woman and held her down, waiting, listening—and there was a lot to listen to as the lawmen on their horses audibly rode for their lives this way and that against all the cascading granite coming down on their heads. They were retreating— Noose heard it.

Three bullets exploded along the ridge, but they were many yards away—the sheriff and his men were shooting at flies, just firing off blind retaliatory shots with no clear targets and might as well have saved their bullets.

When he could wait no longer, Noose quickly popped his head over the edge of the ridge, then got an eyeful of the rear ends of four horses riding at full gallop in three directions away from the ridge back to the cover of the tree line. Sheriff Bojack and his deputies had done the wise thing and beat a hasty retreat from the falling rocks. All five of them.

Wait. Something was wrong. There were just four men down there. Where was the fifth?

Oh hell . . .

Joe Noose was already whirling around on his back, cocking his pistol under the palm of his left hand as the bullet slammed through his left bicep, punching a ragged hole of flesh and cloth and ricocheting off the rock behind him as the slug passed clean through. By then, he saw the rangy deputy who had stepped out of the trees behind him already firing his next shot but the kid pulled the trigger just as Noose got off his first round and the stopping power of his .45 impacting the lawman's chest threw his aim as it sent him staggering back, coughing a phlegm of blood from his punctured lung caused by the clean hole in his chest.

Bonny Kate had covered her head and was screaming but Noose barely heard it above all the gunfire coming from him as he staggered to his feet, bleeding like a steer, fanning and firing his Colt Peacemaker again and again in raw fury. His shots stitched a pattern of red buttons with black burn marks in a tight, neat grouping across the deputy's shirt as the bullets hammered him back in a spastic dance toward the edge of the ridge. One bullet left. Joe Noose put it right between the deputy's eyes. The dead man was blown clean off his feet over the edge of the cliff and disappeared from view as the sound of his broken corpse smacking off the rocks on its way down the hundred-foot gorge grew fainter and fainter until a final *splat*.

There was a lot of cursing going on down there below the ridge in Arizona accents. Noose could make out four voices issuing strings of profanity and swearing eternal retribution.

Dumb sons of bitches, Noose thought. *You wear badges. If you hadn't broken the law you wouldn't be two men short. Go home while you still can because I'm getting this woman where she needs to be and the law is on my side.*

Then, he wasn't thinking too straight.

He'd been shot in the arm and it hurt like hell.

Noose's vision was getting wobbly and he felt a little dizzy so he sat down hard on his ass. There would be a few minutes of relative safety, he knew. The sheriff and his deputies were no threat for at least a short while, stuck as they were at the now-impassable trail below the ridge—he and Bonny Kate would be fine for the time being so long as they kept their heads down.

The next thing Noose knew Bonny Kate was at his side, her beautiful witchy face filling his field of vision, panting an intoxication of sweet breath in his nostrils as she rushed over to help him. The lady outlaw knew enough to keep her head down out of the line of fire of anyone below. Her expression was singularly one of raw concern and worry as she came sympathetically to his aid, in alarm touching his arm with hesitant fingers.

Noose's prisoner made no move to either grab his pistol from his holster or bolt to the horses to grab one of the rifles stashed there—Bonny Kate was trying to help him, tenderly touching his shirt and worrying her fragile fingers around his wound. "You been shot!" she groaned in dismay.

"Bullet went clean through. Flesh wound. I'll survive," he grumbled between gritted teeth.

"Not if we don't get that bullet hole cleaned and bandaged and looked after. You stay here."

Then she was on her feet, hurrying across the ridge over to his horse. Noose wondered just then if this was when Bonny Kate Valance would make her play, grab his Henry rifle from Copper's saddle holster, and pump a few rounds into him but even as he thought that, somehow he knew she wouldn't, and was right— the woman went straight for her own horse, yanked her canteen from the saddle, and rushed right back to his side. "I gotta tear a piece off your shirt to get at that wound and make a tourniquet because I know as we didn't bring no medical supplies."

The pain thudded and burned in the bullet hole

in his bicep and Noose winced. "You know what you're doing?"

"Hell yeah, you bet I do. I'm an outlaw. I patched a lot of bullet wounds in my time, including a few of my own. Now hush." With that, she tried to tear a strip of clean shirt from the sleeve then stopped, looking at his undershirt beneath his checkered shirt. "Better use that," she decided. Unbuttoning his shirt, she grabbed a fistful of his sweat-stained undershirt and tore a large piece of it off with a ripping sound.

Bonny Kate gasped and recoiled, staring speechlessly at his naked chest. *"What the hell?"*

She'd seen the old branding-iron scar at the center of his torso, near his heart: ugly, seared, mottled scar tissue in the oval shape of an upside-down *Q*. It was a sight not for the squeamish. "Somebody branded you like a damn ranch animal!" She choked with an alarmed mix of horror and outrage.

He nodded wearily and sighed. "It's a long story."

"I'm damn well gonna hear it!" she spat. "Tell me now!"

"Just take care of that bullet hole, okay?"

"I'm doin' it. So you can tell me the story about this brand at the same time. It'll keep your mind off the discomfort."

Noose nodded as she started to unscrew her canteen and wet a cloth. Then he began: "The short version is when I was a kid I was rustling some cattle and me and my accomplices got caught. The rancher hanged the others but I was too young, just thirteen, but he figured to teach me a lesson. The son of a bitch branded me to teach me his idea of knowing right from wrong."

Squeezing the water out of the rag, Bonny Kate got a murderous look on her face. "Branding a little boy with a cattle iron is wrong for sure. What the hell was that sick old man thinkin'?"

With a shrug, Noose went on. "He told me that human beings know right from wrong but animals don't, and a man who doesn't know right from wrong is no better than a cattle, and cattle get branded. That rancher figured the branding mark would help me remember to make the right choices. And it has."

"That mark looks like a noose, just like the one they mean to put around my neck." Bonny Kate watched Joe with an intense fascination like she was beginning to figure him out just a little.

"That's how I got my name."

"Now I see."

"So how 'bout you fix my arm so we can get the hell out of here? That sheriff and his boys ain't gonna be waylaid for long and they'll be coming after us. We need to make tracks before we get sandbagged."

"Hold still." It took her less than a minute to clean the wound with splashes of water from the canteen. It slowed her down some and made him flinch in pain when she tried to tear open the bloody, thick cloth of his shirt around the bullet hole. The cloth wouldn't rip. She sighed and looked him straight in the eye with her electric blue gaze. "May I borrow your knife?"

He just watched her without blinking.

She sighed again. "The one in your belt. I can't tear this with my hands, Joe. I need a knife. Ain't gonna stick you with it, I promise."

"You kill me, those men kill you worse, remember that."

"I do. Trust me. The knife, please."

Noose pulled his heavy steel bowie knife out of his belt sheath with his other hand and handed it to her.

The blade looked enormous in her small fingers. Bonny Kate immediately set to work cutting the shirt away with the blade and did so with dispatch. Handing the knife right back to him, the woman splashed water from the canteen on the ragged hole on both sides of his arm, her jaw set in concentration, and dabbed the blood and dirt and sweat away from the wound with the torn section of shirt. Last, Bonny Kate ripped the section of torn undershirt in two halves. She gently but securely bandaged the wound with one long torn piece of shirt and made a tourniquet of the other on his upper arm.

Then the woman stood, offering her hand to help the man to his feet. "That should hold you till we get to Victor."

He smiled at her and took her hand with his good one, letting her pull him up. "Let's get moving," he said.

Keeping their heads down to not catch a bullet, Joe Noose and Bonny Kate sprinted to their horses and swung up into the saddles, untying their reins from the tree then riding out of there up the Teton Pass with the big cowboy in the lead.

No further shots came their way from below the ridge.

Chapter 8

The shootist sat down on the rock and took a load off.

He wanted a cigarette and thought to roll one but then thought better of it, considering the deadly fire conditions of the drought-parched dry forest that engulfed him . . . dumb to strike a match in this place.

Having just now dismounted, his tired horse was tied out of sight behind a copse of trees, enjoying the shade and a bowl of water from the canteen.

The rider stood and admired the vista that lay below. Before him, the top of the Teton Pass opened up on a sprawling overlook of the valley of Jackson Hole, a vast basin of grasslands and river vanishing into a mountain range on the other side beneath the big, blue cloud-jagged expanse of endless sky.

Pretty scenery, just like he'd been told it would be. But this was not a vacation, no, indeed.

It had been a long ride from Arizona. A month had passed since he had crossed the Arizona state line and ridden up to Idaho.

That very morning the shootist had ridden up from Swan Valley into the town of Victor and seen the gallows erected in the town square, the dangling rope ready for a neck that it would never touch—he would make sure of that. One big circus the town was, folks coming from near and far to watch the execution. Popcorn and cotton candy and souvenirs being sold.

The gunfighter personally found it damn distasteful that the hanging of such a remarkable example of the fair sex should be the cause of such a carnival atmosphere . . . Had circumstances been different the gunfighter would have schooled the whole town in manners, which would be the last lesson any of those people would ever receive. Perhaps he would later, come back and burn the hick town to the ground after business was taken care of, but business came first. The shootist had spoken to some lawman and asked about the lady outlaw's whereabouts and it didn't take him long to learn she was being brought on horseback by the Jackson marshals over the Teton Pass to her place of execution. The hanging was tomorrow so the lady and her escorts were on their way.

Armed with that information and his Sharps long-distance rifle, the dusty man had ridden hard out of Victor directly, straight for the Wyoming border a few miles east and a trail that took him high up into the piney elevations of the Teton Pass. Now several hours later, the shootist had since crossed the summit and descended the winding trail to where he now stood, both man and horse catching some rest before the action started.

It had been a long, hard trail from Arizona but the shootist had beaten the sheriff here, of that he was certain. It had been no difficult task breaking out of jail with those half-wit inexperienced deputies the old lawman had left behind to mind him and the rest of the gang . . . just a simple matter of reaching through the bars and breaking their necks when those dumb tinhorns came with the morning coffee, then slipping the keys off their belts. It was harder for the shootist to shoot his two old saddle buddies in the back—boy, they sure hadn't been expecting that—but three's a crowd and the gunfighter rode faster alone.

If the sheriff had not been so blind in his own personal bloodthirsty vengeance, a smart lawman such as himself would have realized the folly of leaving his jurisdiction to chase the woman down. And the old lawman should have kept his voice down, talking about how Bonny Kate had been captured in Jackson Hole, Wyoming, his voice within earshot of the cell where the shootist could easily hear and savvy up a plan of his own.

Sheriff Waylon Bojack had his reasons to come after Bonny Kate Valance but the shootist Johnny Cisco had much better ones, in his own mind, at least.

Once a man saw that woman's face, he never forgot it . . . Once a man kissed those lips of hers, he never stopped thinking about the sweet taste . . .

She'd stolen his heart . . .

And robbed something much, much more important . . .

It was time to get it all back.

Cisco had missed Bonny Kate Valance a lot. Couldn't wait to see her now today.

But the shootist was a patient man when he needed to be and didn't need to ride down the pass to intercept her. No need. Cisco knew she would be riding this way soon enough.

She would come right to him.

He would wait for her here and do what he had to do. Plenty of time to roll a cigarette and smoke it, which he proceeded to pass the time with. Only after he had fingered a pinch of tobacco on the rolling paper and licked the paper did he remember not to smoke here. Almost forgot, and Johnny Cisco was not a man who made mistakes most of the time.

The only things that bothered the shootist were the distant shots he had been hearing since he crossed the crest of the Teton Pass: rifle and pistol fire coming from the direction of Jackson. *Who was doing the shooting? Did it have anything to do with Bonny Kate?* That she had a lot of enemies was a certainty. Cisco had to entertain the possibility that Sheriff Bojack had beaten him to the punch and was chasing her right this very moment somewhere down the pass.

Cisco had no doubt in his mind that a lawman with such revenge in his heart wanted his hand to be the one that took her life, not some hangman's noose. The occasional shots still sounded down the trail off and on. That meant if it *was* Bojack, he hadn't nailed her yet, which meant she was still coming his way. The shootist relished the idea of meeting up with that son of a bitch sheriff again because he had a score of his own to settle, but first he had to get Bonny Kate to safety.

They needed to have a little talk, she and him.

Would she be surprised to see him? Johnny Cisco wondered idly. Perhaps. Perhaps not.

He didn't have long to wait.

Cisco saw the distant movement a quarter mile down the Teton Pass and sat up. His eyes were that good.

A few seconds later, the two horses and riders appeared between the trees on the steep, sheer grade of the rock-and-gravel-rough trail traversing the side of the gorge. He would recognize the red color of her hair anywhere.

Bonny Kate was astride the second horse.

Riding out ahead was a big fellow who looked as wide as he was tall, like a tree with legs. Metal glinted. A badge on his chest. Yes, he sure was big, all right, but that suited the shootist's purposes.

The lawman would make an easy target.

Settling in against the big rock he slid into position behind, the man from Arizona raised the Sharps rifle and cocked the stock against his shoulder, peering through the circular sight. He touched the bolt out of habit but there was already a .40-44 cartridge jacked in the breech.

It took but a second or two to get the crosshairs of the sight fixed on the broad chest of the large marshal, who rode forward with his hat tipped over his eyes, shadowing his face. His pistols were in his holsters.

Slowly, carefully, the shootist thumbed back the hammer of the rifle with a quiet *click-cla-click.*

He licked the tip of his trigger finger and felt the slight wind from the west on his moistened fingertip.

Then Johnny Cisco placed that damp finger on his cold trigger. Adjusting his aim an inch up and to the left of the distant marshal's badge for trajectory in the southeasterly wind, he calculated for windage, elevation, and bullet drop as he felt the chill metal of the trigger resistance against his forefinger.

Cisco was patient when he needed to be.

So long, friend. Nothing personal. You were only doing your job. Just in the wrong place at the wrong time . . .

Hi, Bonny Kate. Hi, honey. Sure did miss you. But I'm here now . . .

Cisco had the marshal dead to rights in his crosshairs.

He pulled the trigger and the deafening explosion shattered the silence, obliterating the stillness with a turbulent discharge of fire and smoke.

Exactly sixty seconds before the bullet was fired, Joe Noose had been on his horse, scanning the winding trail gouged into the pass ahead and wondering how the hell they ever got wagons across in the winter, as he had been told they did—the going was treacherous enough during the dry heat of summer, the way the narrow trailhead bent and curved at a forty-to-ninety-degree angle right at the edge of the cliffs plunging hundreds of feet into the gorge on the left. Granite boulders and slanted spokes of fifty-foot pines formed a porcupine quilt over the precipice. If a horse put his hoof wrong once, over horse and rider would go straight down to oblivion. Noose looked up and saw the Teton Pass rising monolithic against the sky above and ahead.

A glint of sunlight on steel.

Noose saw it for a split second yet in that millisecond of time instantly recognized the gleam off the rifle barrel for what it was.

Already Noose was leaping out of his saddle and throwing his entire body in flight across the two horses, wrapping his arms protectively around Bonny Kate Valance as a body shield as his physical mass propelled her out of the stirrups off her horse, rotating his body around in midair during the fall so he hit the ground on his back with a grunt before rolling on top of her as the heavy-caliber slug meant for him obliterated the leather pommel of her saddle instead even before the long, sharp *crack* of the rifle shot sounded. Long before the echo of the gun blast faded, amplified in the acoustics of the towering wooded ravine, Noose had his Colt Peacemaker out, dragging the startled woman off the trail, behind some boulders before the next shot came.

He had a few seconds, he knew.

That shot came from a Sharps—Noose recognized the distinctive report—and its owner would need three seconds to reload.

Whoever he was.

The smoke cleared from the crosshairs.

Johnny Cisco saw right away he had missed. The two horses' saddles were empty and the marshal had hauled Bonny Kate off her horse onto the ground behind the rocks.

Already reloading, the shootist cocked back the bolt and fingered in a fresh cartridge, was in the process of slamming the bolt into the breech when the bullet from below blew a shower of sparks and stone fragments by his head as it slammed home a foot from his face.

That son of a bitch marshal was either a lucky shot or a damn good one, and Cisco didn't believe in luck.

* * *

A half a mile down the pass, Sheriff Bojack also heard the shots and knew two things right away.

That wasn't just the sound of the marshal's gun.

And the man who fired that other shot was not one of his Arizona deputies.

Which meant the equation had just changed.

The sun's reflection off the metal rifle not only warned Joe Noose just in time but pinpointed the shooter's exact position so Noose had been able to return fire with accuracy, though he missed. Now, hunkered behind the cover of the granite rock, the big cowboy peered up the pass at the dense tree line from where the shot had originated. While he couldn't see any movement right at this second, he knew the rifleman was still there, likely lining up his next shot.

Were there more men with guns up there? Noose couldn't tell.

Who was the shooter?

There's no way that sheriff pursuing him below could have gotten men ahead of himself and his lady prisoner—the pass was a narrow trail with a mountainous, perpendicular ridge to the right and a deep, yawning crevice to his left. The distance was too great and difficult to cross to overtake him, plus Noose would have seen them because he'd been keeping his eyes peeled for any sign of the posse.

The only thing he could figure was that the sheriff behind him had one or more deputies in front, reinforcements who had come over the Teton Pass in the Idaho direction—a flanking maneuver planned way in advance. And a smart one. Noose was now boxed in, facing guns both in front and behind and squeezed between overwhelming firepower.

Swinging a glance to Bonny Kate huddling safely a few feet away, he saw the anxious woman looking a question at him: *What were they going to do?* Noose dropped his gaze to his Colt Peacemaker. It would not be a sufficient weapon to engage with a shooter at this distance, not one clearly armed with a long-range rifle.

His own rifles were on his horse he had just dismounted, which was the problem.

Out in the open twenty feet away, Copper stood with steely nerve on the trail, mindless of being in the line of fire and probably figuring correctly whoever was shooting wasn't shooting at horseflesh. The clever stallion had taken a few steps to stand beside Bonny Kate's mustang, keeping it company and calming it down, as that horse was high-strung and visibly unsettled from having a piece of its saddle shot off. The Henry and Winchester rifles sat in Copper's saddle holster.

Noose whistled.

His horse perked its ears and casually trotted over, taking a few short steps on its hooves to appear nonchalant to the unseen gunman, then when Copper was out of the immediate line of fire the horse charged forward in a burst of speed and got right beside Noose behind the cover of the rock. The stallion timed its move perfectly because as soon as it took off, a single rifle crack sounded and the nearby rocks exploded in a geyser of dirt and stone fragments.

Definitely a Sharps rifle. With certitude, a long-range weapon.

Well, Joe Noose had one of those, too, and knew how to use it.

Patting his good horse approvingly on the flank, Noose reached out a long arm, grabbed the stock of the Henry, and slid it quickly out of the saddle holster with a sound of scraping leather. Bonny Kate was watching his every move, he felt without looking. Noose had seen the puff of smoke through the branches of the distant pines jutting like steeples on a slope three hundred yards ahead, close to where the first shot had come, so the shooter was dug in.

The rifleman was well positioned and wasn't moving. Noose and his prisoner were pinned down and couldn't move. This exchange of gunfire was likely going to continue for a spell. They were going to be here awhile.

At least until the sheriff and his boys, who could obviously hear the shots, showed up and then Noose was going to be in serious trouble.

"Bonny Kate!"

The voice of the unseen shooter echoed across the canyon.

"Bonny Kate! It's me!"

Throwing a glance to the female outlaw, Noose was quite surprised to see the blood suddenly drain from her ruddy features, turning her face the pale color of sour milk with purest raw terror and shock. "Oh no," she whispered in a hoarse stammer.

"I'm here to get you out of this, Bonny Kate! I'm gonna rescue you, honey!" shouted the voice in the trees.

She uttered again, "Oh no."

"Heard you the first time," Noose said. "Who is that up there? You know him, don't you?"

Bonny Kate nodded faintly, turning paler yet. When

she spoke his name she could barely get the words out. "C-Cisco. His name is Johnny Cisco."

Noose saw her face flush with color and took her meaning. "You're full of surprises, ma'am."

"You can't let him get me, Joe."

"I don't aim to. But I'd think you'd want him to rescue you."

"You don't understand. Johnny was supposed to be in jail. Back in Arizona. The sheriff caught him. Cisco, he was the one shot Bojack's boy."

"You don't say. Everybody knows each other shooting at one another this fine day. Hell of a reunion, I'd say."

"It ain't no joke, Joe. That man is crazy. He's lovesick obsessed with me and always says if he can't have me, nobody can. I'd rather be hanged than have him get me."

The loud, rangy voice projected from somewhere up the Teton Pass, carrying directionlessly through the trees of the forest. *"Your lover boy's here to save your pretty fanny, Bonny Kate! You don't worry about a thing now. Johnny Cisco's here, come to your rescue!"*

Was he, now?

A quarter mile away down the trail, Sheriff Bojack could hear Johnny Cisco, and cussed beneath his breath. He knew the voice. It was Cisco, all right. That villain was supposed to be his prisoner back in Phoenix, locked up in his jail. *Son of a bitch.* His being here could mean several things, all of them bad.

Cisco had escaped from Bojack's custody—another black mark on the sheriff's ever-more-tarnished record.

Worse, if Cisco had escaped, he had likely killed the
deputies left guarding him or wounded them bad, because no way those tough young kids would have let
their prisoner out of there unless they had been overcome and incapacitated in one way or another.

   The Arizona posse was still reeling from the shocking sight of one of their own, Deputy Billy Joe Shaker,
plunging over the edge of the cliff, his bloody, bullet-
riddled body smashed to pulp on the rocks below like
a shattered rag doll—the second of their group to die
under the deadly guns of the Wyoming marshal. That
had been barely a half hour ago. For five minutes, the
lawmen had just stood witness, crossing themselves,
saying prayers for their dead comrade, biting back
tears. The bodies of Shaker and Hodge had to be
buried, taken back to Arizona, reclaimed when this
was all over, but all Sheriff Bojack and his surviving
deputies, Jed Ransom, Fulton Dodge, and Clay Slayton, could do right now was leave the bodies where
they lay, to rot in the sun, while they gave chase to the
woman who had brought them all this trouble.

   Looking to his side at the three agitated deputies
cradling their weapons right now, Sheriff Bojack saw
the questions and doubts flicker in his men's eyes and
knew they were figuring it like he was: He'd screwed
everything up. Overconfident and distracted, the old
veteran lawman had been. There had been no communication with the Arizona office the whole two
months the sheriff and his men had been on the trail
and the lawmen should have checked in, should have
not taken for granted Cisco wouldn't try an escape.
All Bojack had been thinking about was flaying Bonny
Kate Valance and stripping her hide from her skeleton, and now things had gone from bad to worse . . .

he'd been making a string of brutally bad mistakes that were costing his men's lives.

His fault. No one to blame but himself. Only one way to make things close to right now.

He had to kill Bonny Kate. Then he would do the same for Johnny Cisco.

He hoped that marshal wouldn't get in the way.

CHAPTER 9

The clock on the wall of the Jackson U.S. Marshal's office struck noon and Bess Sugarland hauled her behind out of her chair. Noon was the time five days a week she had made it a habit to take a ride around the town and keep an eye on things, all part of her peacekeeping duties. She was sure there was nothing doing, there rarely was, but it would do her good to get some fresh air. The walls were closing in on her. Sitting around and stewing about Joe Noose with that slut outlaw wasn't doing her a damn bit of good and besides it was making her leg hurt. With a grunt from her aching wound, the woman marshal rose to her feet and with a jingle of spur stepped out from behind the desk.

Grabbing her Winchester repeater, Bess braced the barrel against the floor and slung her right armpit over the stock, using it as a crutch. On her way to the door, she again considered writing a letter on official U.S. Marshals Service stationery to the Winchester Repeating Arms Company in New Haven, Connecticut, telling Whom It May Concern about what an effective

crutch the rifle made in addition to its other virtues as
a damn fine weapon—if you got wounded, not only
could you shoot the other bastard after you did, you
could use the rifle to hobble the hell out of there.
Bess guessed the gun manufacturer might appreciate
her sense of humor even less than those Arizona boys
did—men lost their sense of humor when a woman
told the joke—but she might send that letter anyway.

Marshal Bess took her Stetson hat from the rack
and screwed it on her head, but left her coat because
it was hot outside and her seven-star badge was there
for everyone to see on her shirt. Pistols cleaned and
loaded and slung in her side holsters, Bess Sugarland,
the law in Jackson Hole, stepped through her front
door to greet the fine day.

The air was clean and refreshing and felt like drinking mountain water, so she breathed it in deep. Her
bosom rose and fell with respiration. Taking a look
up and down Broadway, the marshal saw a few folks
she knew on the dirt street. They waved to her and she
waved back with a grin. It was a damn nice town, and
time to take a ride around the six streets that com-
prised the growing settlement at the base of the valley.
She locked the door behind her, not that she was
worried about anybody stealing anything because
most local folks left their doors unlocked, but just so
people knew she was out doing her rounds.

Using the crutch, Bess walked stiff-legged down the
steps and hobbled across the yard to the corral. Her
horse stood blinking in the sunshine, chewing hay, already saddled. Grabbing a good purchase on the oaken
buck-and-rail with her left hand, Bess stuck the Winchester repeater into her saddle holster and used her
good leg to clamber up on the fence and shimmy into

her saddle. Two months after being shot in the leg, Bess was getting pretty good at this, she had to admit. Reaching down to swing open the gate, the woman marshal gave a short whistle to her horse and gave it a little spur, and the cooperative mare trotted out onto the street.

The town was quiet, the streets rolled up. The marshal knew perfectly well the reason why Jackson was peaceful today was that Bonny Kate Valance was gone. The town was finally rid of her and tomorrow the rest of the world would be, too.

Sitting tall in the saddle, Bess looked left and right at the feed store and the grocery store. The road went right up to the doorways. The town council had been talking about appropriating the funds to build a board-walk on either side of the street like they had in Victor. It would look nice, Bess thought. She looked up at the slate blue sky, puffed with clouds, the sun shining down sharp and hot. Her gaze traveled over to the majestic peaks of the Grand Tetons to the north, capped with snow even in summer, the titanic height and scale of the mountains taking her breath away as it always did no matter how many times she saw them; but once Bess looked at the monumental barrier range, she felt her gaze irresistibly pulled yet again south, along the crags jutting against the sky, to the Teton Pass just west of her. Fear drew her gaze. The pass was cloaked in shadow from the clouds, like a bad omen, and she shuddered.

Try as she might, Bess Sugarland could not stop worrying about Joe Noose and the bad company he was keeping—Bonny Kate Valance could not get hanged soon enough for Bess Sugarland. The marshal's stomach would be tied in knots until noon tomorrow when the execution would take place. Bess had already telegraphed the town of Victor, Idaho's sheriff, Albert Shurlock, requesting he telegraph as soon as Noose arrived with the condemned woman, then again right after the execution when the lady outlaw swung at the rope's end. Shurlock had promised he would.

Trying to shake her uncharacteristic disquiet, Marshal Bess flipped her reins and sat upright as her mare trotted up the street in a brisk, purposeful pace that made its proud rider feel every bit the face of law enforcement in Jackson. A few wagons passed, the farmer owners tipping their hats to her. Bess returned the gesture. Turning her horse onto Pearl Street then riding around on Broadway along the town square, the marshal patrolled her town and gave it a once-over, letting the folks know she was on duty, but everything looked quiet.

This was a good thing, because Marshal Bess wasn't planning to go back to her office just yet. With Noose gone, a powerful sense of loneliness and isolation had blindsided her, making the U.S. Marshal badge on her chest feel cumbersome, and Bess needed to talk to the only other man who understood what that was like— her father—and there was only one place to do that.

With a tug of rein and kick of spur, Marshal Bess turned her mare onto Cache Street after rounding the square, heading toward the open county of Gros Ventre a few miles out. And wouldn't you know it, that's when she ran into the whole group of them.

"Ladies," Bess said, touching her hat in greeting.

The entire Jackson City Council, a political body composed entirely of local women, was standing gathered at the edge of the square right in front of her, clucking like a flock of hens. The Jackson Hole

Women's Auxiliary, who blocked her path at the end of the square, were having some kind of ad hoc meeting. The female marshal rolled her eyes, ready to get her ear bent, because these women always had a lot of opinions on just about everything and never ran out of things to talk about. Heads swung in her direction— they had spotted her, and Bess was going to have to converse with them. It wasn't hard to guess what they wanted to bend her ear about: the hanging.

Every woman in Jackson hated Bonny Kate Valance, Bess included, but for most of the local women this visceral unreasoning loathing of the lady outlaw was fueled with intense personal jealousy because of the seductive effect the gunslinging wench had on their men; husbands, fathers, and sons all ensorcelled and under her spell or so it was believed by the women. Bonny Kate was a notorious outlaw who had the kind of beauty that drove men wild. The women of Jackson, even the most Christian, wanted to lynch her. They considered it an abomination that a slut who they saw as the devil was in their town and couldn't wait until she was gone from their streets, and the face of the earth, forever.

It had been a huge headache for Bess in her early days as U.S. Marshal. For the last month, the local women had gathered daily in growing numbers to protest outside the marshal's office. Holding up signs that read HANG BONNY KATE VALANCE or HANGING IS TOO GOOD FOR HER and suchlike, the disruptive mob disturbed the peace with noisy speeches clamoring for the female outlaw's demise. Bess had gotten sick of reminding people that Bonny Kate's demise was guaranteed and her execution already scheduled at the end of the month. This was not soon enough for the protesters, who wanted her dead and out of town directly and not necessarily in that order.

The men in turn had also protested on the streets against the hanging, claiming that executing a woman was uncivilized and ungentlemanly when what they secretly fantasized about was bedding Bonny Kate. In the last few weeks, Jackson had been having a civil war of sorts, with the men on one side of the street and the women on the other, wives and husbands and mothers and sons shouting and waving signs and fists at one another. In recent days as the female outlaw's execution date approached, escalating tensions between the sexes reached a boiling point among the citizenry in Jackson.

Marshal Bess had spent many long hours sitting outside in a chair on the porch of her office with an 8-gauge scattergun in her lap, keeping the peace and hoping she wouldn't have to use the weapon. Fortunately, except for firing the shotgun in the air two separate times to quiet protests down, she hadn't had to shoot anyone. Luckily, Joe Noose had been there by the marshal's side the whole time, standing on the porch next to her and wading in to break up physical altercations and fisticuffs between spouses and neighbors when tempers flared in the crowd. Noose was so big and tough he would lift the combatants apart, one in each hand, as effortlessly as baby lambs without harming anyone until civility had resumed. The intimidating bounty hunter's very presence was a potent deterrent and order was quickly restored.

For her part, Bonny Kate Valance just sat alone in her cell, amused by the fuss she was causing, her coarse womanly laugh ringing out occasionally through her cell window, an unseen but constantly felt presence stirring up the populace, the lady outlaw seemingly without a care in the world despite her date with gallows that grew closer with each passing day.

Today Bonny Kate had left town under Joe Noose's escort; with her presence no longer felt, a peace and sense of relief was palpable throughout the streets of Jackson as everything returned to normalcy.

Riding her horse up to the gathered women of the city council, Marshal Bess tipped her hat. "Pretty quiet today, isn't it?"

"Is she gone?" Florence McCoy tugged her bonnet around her head worriedly, looking up at the peace officer, who nodded. "She hanged yet?

"Tomorrow. My deputy is taking her over the pass right now as we speak."

"Thought I heard shots up there coming from the direction of the pass a couple times this morning."

"I did, too. But it's nothing to worry about. You hear gunshots out there all the time from hunters and trappers and such during the summer."

"What if Bonny Kate escaped?" wondered Eleanor Rittenhouse, a well-liked and outspoken wealthy aristocratic woman from all the way in Philadelphia who had just bought a ranch in neighboring Solitude and served as council treasurer.

"No chance of that." Marshal Bess shook her head decisively. "I deputized Joe Noose to take her to Idaho." All Bess had to do was mention Noose's name and that pretty much silenced any concerns, but not today, it seemed.

"What if that evil harlot outlaw shot Noose?"

"Impossible, Eleanor. Noose took down the entire Butler Gang single-handed, and may I remind you it was the Butler Gang that captured Bonny Kate Valance in the first place and brought her to Jackson. If she couldn't kill any of those men you best believe she can't kill the man that did."

The crackle of very distant gunfire echoed again, seemingly from the direction of the Teton Pass, but it was hard to tell for sure in the tricky acoustics of the valley basin. Bess Sugarland turned her head to stare out at the pass, still cloaked in shadow on the sunny day. Her eyes narrowed, and she chewed her lip. The other women were looking in that direction, too.

Florence spoke up again. "There was a bunch of lawmen asking around this morning about Bonny Kate Valance—you think it could be them up there?"

Above them on her horse, it took a beat too long for Marshal Bess Sugarland to respond and return the upturned gaze of the other ladies. "Nope, it couldn't be. I didn't tell those Arizona lawmen which way Noose was headed with Valance. And besides, they're out of their jurisdiction."

Bess tipped her big Stetson hat. "A fine day to you, ladies."

The group of women stood at the edge of the square, quiet for once, and none of them said a word as they watched their tough no-nonsense lady marshal ride her tall horse down Cache Street toward the empty open country of Gros Venture. None of the women said it but they were all thinking it:

The only thing out there is the cemetery.

CHAPTER 10

*Build her gallows high, the judge had said, and so
they had . . .*

The stark wooden scaffolding loomed against the
sky in the Idaho town of Victor as the workmen put
the finishing touches on the crossbeam dangling the
thick, oiled rope noose, the trapdoor and lever, and
the platform ten feet off the ground, giving ample
room for a body to drop and neck to snap like a rag
doll on a string. The sound of hammering filled the
air. The gallows stood grimly ready for duty in the town
square of the small town . . . it was twenty-one miles,
thirty yards, and two feet from where the convicted
woman and her escort were on the Teton Pass trail at
this exact instant.

Sheriff Albert Shurlock stood below looking up
at the hanging structure, glad his own neck was not
in it and hoping it wouldn't be anytime soon. He was
a lean, leathery lawman with an amiable, weathered
face and twinkling, watchful eyes. Al Shurlock had
been sheriff of the growing town of Victor for as long

as anybody could remember, since the first barn had been raised twenty years before. He was an affable fixture. His squint was friendly but savvy and he smoked a corncob pipe that lent him an avuncular air. The lawman knew everybody within a hundred miles, and few who mostly came in by train and made their way in and out of Victor across the Teton Pass to Jackson Hole didn't make his passing acquaintance. It was hot and sweltering with that hard and dry insistent Idaho country heat at this hour so the lawman was soaked with perspiration, but he was used to it.

His three deputies were a few blocks away at the office or making their patrols on the streets, but so far there hadn't been any trouble except for a few drunks that had to be rousted. As a precaution against unforeseen circumstances relating to the impending hanging, each one of the lawmen had been issued a Winchester repeater in addition to the Smith & Wesson SAA .45s in their belt holsters they routinely carried but rarely had cause to use.

Shurlock swung his gaze to the empty railroad tracks ending in the deserted Victor station, the end of the line. Dust and dirt blew across the trackside railbed and trestles, accentuating the emptiness and sense of anticipation of the arrival at 2:13 A.M. tomorrow morning of the Oregon Pacific steam train departing from clear across the country in Philadelphia, which would be pulling in after its lengthy journey, bringing the last spectators for the hanging of Bonny Kate Valance. The town could hardly handle any more people, and the sheriff would be glad to see the vultures go, despite being grateful for the temporary infusion of revenue they were pouring into the local Victor businesses. The town could use it.

There were too many strangers in Victor the last few days for the sheriff's liking. Too many people he didn't know. He preferred the faces he knew or the transient ones just passing through to Jackson. Al Shurlock was a man who didn't like surprises.

Victor had increased its population from 75 to nearly 320 residents in the last seven years. It had been formally established just the year before, in 1887. The town had been named after the sheriff's friend George Victor Sherwood, a dedicated and cussed-natured mail carrier who always delivered the mail despite of threat of Indian attacks. Shurlock had been proud of seeing the town grow. It used to have just a few buildings and a rooming house. Now it had two hotels and a saloon and a boardwalk on one side of the main street. The railroad had been routed to Victor as the end of the line. The train traveled from as far as Philadelphia and brought rich folks and wealthy gentry eager to visit Jackson Hole and taste the West, as something about Jackson fired upper class easterners' imaginations. There, the wealthy New York and Pennsylvania aristocracy bought ranches and rubbed shoulders with cowboys and outlaws. They took the train to Victor, got off, and rode wagons across the Teton Pass down into Jackson. That was the problem, Shurlock knew. Victor until now had been little more than a train station, a place to pass through on the way to Jackson. All that was about to change.

The platform that had elevated Victor, Idaho, into the public eye was indeed this very gallows platform built for the sole purpose of the hanging by the neck until dead of the notorious outlaw Bonny Kate Valance, the first woman executed in the history of the United States, and a powerful campaign symbol for the state politicians' law-and-order agenda of driving the outlaws out of Idaho and Wyoming and bringing the Far West states into the twentieth century.

In the politicians' view, it was all about civilizing the Old West in the hopes of a prosperous future for the citizenry in a brand-new century.

In Shurlock's view it was a disgusting spectacle, hanging a woman in the center of his town, and with that thought the lawman spat on the street in disgust in the shadow of the hanging platform.

While he watched the workmen finishing the gallows, Sheriff Shurlock looked around at the town at the grotesque Fourth of July tone of the decorations and celebratory banners filling the square. This hanging was a major historical event with people coming around the country to attend it and Victor was smack at the center of it. Mayor Ralph Wiggins would give a speech he had been rehearsing for months in front of thousands of people from all the thirty-eight states and reporters from every major newspaper across the country. There would be brass bands and trick riders on horseback, shooting contests, and barbecues. Soon, two days from now, the air would be filled with the scents of burning hickory and roasting pork and husked corn. Shurlock could already smell it with the cotton candy. Hangings were public events in the Old West, and the sheriff wondered sometimes how civilized it was for folks to have picnics watching others drop on ropes, but who was he to judge?

This hanging meant dollars.

That's what mattered.

Bonny Kate Valance held the key to Victor's future

and she was on the way, being delivered to him on a horse. In a sense, her neck in the noose prevented his town from being in a figurative one if the economy didn't improve while Jackson continued to grow.

The lawman felt confident the lady outlaw would be delivered on schedule for her date with the rope— he knew the bounty hunter Joe Noose, the man who was taking her across the pass, pretty well. Two months before, Sheriff Shurlock had dealings with Noose, who took on hunting the thousand-dollar bounty on a bank robber named Jim Henry Barrow who had shot a guard in the Victor town bank before fleeing across the pass and ending up in Hoback. There, from what Shurlock heard, things got murky, with another gang of bounty killers tangling with Noose on the claim over Barrow's dead body. It was a mess.

One thing Al Shurlock always liked about Joe Noose, doing business with him over the years, was when the bounty hunter chased dead-or-alive claims, he always brought his quarry in alive if he could. Shurlock had no doubt the other bounty hunters had killed Barrow in cold blood and supposedly, from the conflicting stories he had been told, it was a big to-do. Noose had ultimately collected on the reward, but Shurlock heard a lot of men got killed in the process, including his two friends, the U.S. Marshal in Jackson, Jack Mackenzie, and his deputy, Nolan Swallows. The Hoback Marshal Nate Sugarland's daughter, Bess, was now U.S. Marshal in Jackson and she was the person Shurlock had been dealing with via telegraph on the Bonny Kate Valance business.

These events were all very confusing and way too much excitement for a simple lawman like Al Shurlock was. Let the town of Jackson have all that excitement—

he preferred the peace and quiet of remote Victor, where he hoped to end his days. All this disruption would be all over soon after the execution. Joe Noose was a tough, reliable man and he should be halfway across the pass with the woman by now.

Sheriff Shurlock had to smile when he reflected that a man actually named Noose was taking Bonny Kate to the gallows.

Ironic indeed.

CHAPTER 11

Into the tawny rolling rural hills of Gros Ventre
rode the lone woman on the horse. She had ridden
this way having noticed the yellow wildflowers like
bright pools of butter against the brown grasslands on
the banks of the bend of the Snake River. The flowers
grew because of the nearby water. They were perfect.
Marshal Bess Sugarland dismounted her mare and
walked to the banks, taking many patient moments to
select the prettiest flowers with the biggest petals
whose stems she carefully cut with her bowie knife
into a proper bunch she wrapped in her handkerchief. Then, flowers in hand, she got back on her
horse and rode away from the river onto the road to
the cemetery.

It was quiet up here and lonely and peaceful in the
big empty of the valley in the shadow of the Grand
Teton mountain peaks; the area was named Solitude
for a reason. Bess felt it was a good place to spend
eternity, which is why she selected the local graveyard
as her father, Nate Sugarland's final resting place. Her
old man had loved the wide-open spaces and rode out

often to fish the river, and she knew he would be happy to be buried here.

It was a small graveyard surrounded by a small black corrugated fence below an unmarked metal archway; inside the several-hundred-foot-square plot lay thirty-five gravestones and head markers in uneven rows. Some had fresh flowers on them, some dead flowers, some none at all. Bess thought it was a lovely little cemetery and she felt close to her father when she came here, and she always came alone.

Sitting in her saddle, Bess took off her hat and shook her hair loose. She carefully slid out of her stirrups, placing her good leg onto solid dirt, carrying the yellow wildflowers with gentle care with both hands. It hurt to walk but she wasn't about to use a repeater rifle as a crutch while visiting her father's grave, because that was not respectful.

Feeling her eyes begin to water the moment she stepped through the gate, Bess Sugarland was wiping tears by the time she reached the handsome granite headstone ten paces inside.

NATE SUGARLAND
Born 1837 – Died 1888
Loving father and dedicated lawman.

It was here Bess stood, shut her eyes, and breathed her father in the smells of fresh air and mud and grass and sunlight where he rested. As always, she could smell his skin and hair and leathery scent in those natural outdoor aromas. For her, now he was near.

And she could talk to him again.

Somewhere her father was listening, she felt in her heart.

So Bess spoke to him as she did when she needed to, when she came out here alone.

"Hi, Pop. It's me, Bess. I miss you and think of you every day. Think what you would do. Try to do what you would do. Make you proud of me. Gosh, I been U.S. Marshal of Jackson two whole months and they ain't fired me yet. Guess I must be doing something right. It's all the women in the council that keep me in the job, I reckon, 'cause they like having one of their own wearing a badge. Owe 'em for that, I figure. You'd have hated these ladies, Pop. Talk-too-much women always drove you crazy. But I wouldn't be marshal without them. And I wouldn't be anything without you, Pop. You set such a good example and were always there for me and . . . it's hard, sometimes it's so hard you not being here to talk to . . . and it gets so lonely like the weight of the world is all on my shoulders. Pop, you ever feel this job was too much for just one soul to handle? I feel that way sometimes, yes, I do."

Bess began to sniffle as she bent down and placed the pretty yellow wildflowers on Nate Sugarland's plot, near the headstone. All of a sudden, a big cloud passed from the sun above and a wall of golden sunlight fell over the cemetery and Bess felt its warmth as if in answer. She smiled, wiped her tears, and rose.

"I know. You always told me nobody does it alone. You had me. I had you. Then, ever since, I have Joe Noose. Yes, I do. I'm lonely today, that's all, feeling sorry for myself, being foolish. It's just 'cause Joe is gone. Joe will be back. And if he don't come back, I'm gonna go after him, Pop. Because Joe Noose ain't alone, neither. He has me."

Bess kissed her fingers and pressed them against the warm marble of the tombstone. Then she saddled up. Bess rode at a hard gallop away from the cemetery, shrinking in the distance as she sped in the direction of Jackson. There was an empty plot right beside her father's. Hers when the time came.

She wanted to be buried beside him.

CHAPTER 12

"You think you killed him?" It was a breathless question from Bonny Kate.

"I don't know," Noose tersely retorted, lifting his head to peek over the rock around the curving, steep trailhead and the sweeping vista of forest. "Keep your head down."

"You think we lost 'em?" she asked querulously. "Those others behind us, I mean."

"Not likely." Noose reloaded his Henry rifle, then his Colt pistol, with rounds from his belt and pockets in a *clatter* of rifle bolts, *clink* of different-caliber cartridges, and *whirr* of revolving cylinders. "They come this far."

"What are we gonna do?"

"Stay down, I said." Noose pulled Bonny Kate lower behind the rocks they took cover behind, away from the potential line of any fire. "What do you care? Same end for you there as here. Might be quicker for you with a bullet."

"Maybe I want to make the most of the time I got left. I like breathing."

"I do, too."

"So what we gonna do?"

"This ain't what I signed up for," Noose groused. "This whole thing has gotten a hell of a lot more complicated than I figured. All I thought I had to worry about was you."

"Welcome to my world, Joe Noose."

"I'd like to have skipped the visit."

"So now you're gonna insult me? That's your big answer to everything when there's bullets flying everywhere and there's guys trying to kill us—"

"—You. You're the one everybody wants to kill, remember?—"

"—Kill *us* because *you're* with *me*, and all you can do is insult me instead of getting me to Idaho so they can hang me like you swore a duty to do!"

Noose shot Bonny Kate a cocked-eyebrow scowl. "So you get killed there instead." He shook his big head. "You don't make no sense, lady. Nothing that comes outta your pretty mouth does."

Tossing her red hair like a fiery mane, Bonny Kate shot him a defiant and challenging glance. "Well, I say I prefer to be hanged, I do! If I'm gonna die then that's the way I choose to go! A person should be able to choose their way of dyin', I say."

"Don't often work out that way." He smirked. Noose swung his fierce bird-of-prey gaze left and right, looking up and down the pass, squinting into the blankets of trees above and below, scouting for any sign of movement. There was none for the moment. The mountains had gotten very quiet all of a sudden. Too quiet, his expression read.

"Are you even listening to me, Joe?" Bonny Kate rolled her eyeballs in naked exasperation. "Do you hear a word I say?" She glared at him in a blaze of her intense blue eyes.

Continuing to ignore her, Noose rubbed his stubbled jaw on his unshaven granite chin, assessing their surroundings. "Your voice carries," he responded in a preoccupied voice—still thinking, now deciding.

"I ask you again," the lady outlaw said quieter as she caught her breath and regained a semblance of composure even as she switched her glances around herself skittishly. "*What are we going to do?*" she half whispered, half hissed.

"We're going to get off the pass, is what we're going to do."

At that, she just gaped, looking awestruck up at the sheer rock faces and perpendicular slopes rising into cyclopean peaks of rugged, untamed wilderness. The trail they were on was primitive and dangerous enough, but the uncharted woodlands rising on all sides appeared completely impassable. "How?" Bonny Kate choked.

"Didn't say it would be easy." Noose took the woman by the hand and pulled her away from the stack of boulders, both of them crawling on their hands and knees, deeper into the woods away from the trailhead, until they were out of view of anyone who might want to take a shot at them. Then, when they reached safe cover, Noose rose to his feet, clicked his teeth, and Copper trotted over beside him. Bonny Kate's Appaloosa remained standing near the trail, uneasy and shifting from hoof to hoof. Noose, good with horses, spent a few minutes gently whistling to it and making eye contact, and finally, reluctantly, the other horse advanced and stood beside Copper. The lady outlaw carefully got to her feet and brushed the dirt and gravel off her skirts. She was still scared out of her wits.

"Saddle up," Noose barked, picking up Bonny Kate by both shapely hips and depositing her onto her horse. Then he got a boot in his stirrup and swung into the saddle of his own bronze stallion. Keeping the Henry rifle ready for action in one fist, he gripped the reins tightly in the other and rode out in front into the woods.

Noose reined Copper to the edge of the gravel trail where it met the grassy, muddy mountainside. Tilting back his hat, he studied the topography of the incline between the trees, charting a possible trail. "Think I can see a way through this first part at least."

"Our horses can't—they won't make it."

"They don't, we don't."

The woman was speechless. He rode up alongside her and looked her square in the eye, his voice calm and steady. "Look, Bonny Kate. Listen good. We're sitting ducks back there on the trail out there in the open. The sheriff and his posse back there, they're gonna figure we're ahead on the trail because nobody in their right mind would ride up into these hard mountains."

"Nobody in their right mind would."

"So they'll keep following the trail and I don't think they'll follow us. Don't even think they'll know where we went. Keep in mind they're strangers here. Men unfamiliar with this country. I'm not. We get a little lucky, our horses don't break their legs, I best believe we can forge a trail up through this hairy range."

"Okay, okay." She nodded, studying him with growing confidence. "With Bojack that may work. But he ain't the only one gunning for us. There's Johnny Cisco. What about him?"

Noose just shrugged in response. "I don't know. Got no measure of the man except he's a crack shot. You know him better than me. He a good tracker?"

"He's a good *everything*. You're tough. He's tougher."

"Suppose we'll find that out and see what we'll see. Meantime, savvy we need to get our behinds off this trail directly and up into those hills. It ain't gonna be a picnic. I need your cooperation. Do I have it?"

She nodded. "Yes. You do. Lead the way."

"Don't put a bullet in my back."

"I don't have a gun."

"Wouldn't put it past you to keep one somewhere nobody would look."

Bonny Kate laughed coarsely, loud and pleased. "You make me laugh, Joe Noose." She turned her horse to follow him as he flipped the reins and started up a narrow hundred-degree draw off the pass and into the mountains. "Don't think I ain't done it in the past, mind you," she quipped.

"I wouldn't put it past ya."

"Thing was, the whore that taught me that trick, one day she farted and the gun went off and she's doing different work now."

It was Joe Noose's turn to laugh.

Their horses disappeared into the upper elevations of the tree line as their laughter shrank into the distance, carried away by the wind.

The posse was not far behind.

Back less than a quarter of a mile east below their quarry on the winding declination of track carved out of the mountain and tracing the edge of the gorge, the Arizona sheriff and his three deputies cautiously rode their weary horses around a sheer cliff wall, moving at a slow trot, guns drawn and held at the ready, anticipating shots to come in their direction at any moment as they rounded the towering bend in the rough-hewn trail. Bojack rode in the lead, letting his men know he was the first to take a bullet if any had their name on it. His hard, keen eyes were fixed straight ahead, studying the imposing mountain face beyond as more of it was revealed to his field of view around the corner of the granite wall they rounded; the marshal could be anywhere, lying in wait, targeting them now, for all the sheriff knew. He was ready, but a man could be only so ready. Because his attention was fully focused on what lay ahead, Bojack did not see his three perspiring deputies, Jed Ransom, Fulton Dodge, and Clay Slayton, exchanging furtive and doubtful glances on the horses straggling behind his own.

"I ain't so sure about this, Sheriff," Deputy Jed Ransom finally piped up.

"Sure about what?" Bojack shot back.

"All of it, sir . . . This."

"Didn't your mama teach you English, Deputy? You got something to say, spit it the hell out." Sheriff Bojack gave Ransom the side-eye as the posse struggled to get their horses up the narrow draw, one behind the other. The footing was treacherous, and the loose rocks and pebbles toppled under their stallions' tentative steps. Fact was, Bojack knew what was on Deputy Ransom's mind. It was the same thing on all of his men's minds the last few hours, from the doubtful, worried looks and glances Ransom, Dodge, and Slayton

gave one another when they thought Bojack wasn't
looking. From the whispers that had started when they
thought he was wasn't listening or too far ahead. Hell,
Waylon Bojack heard everything. Had been blessed
with sharp ears ever since he was a kid. It was a blessing and a curse: a blessing when he was tracking a
villain and could hear a twig crack at four hundred
yards, a curse when he could easily overhear the dissen-
sion in the ranks of his deputies as he had been clearly
overhearing now—the hushed talk had been getting
worse the last few hours since Ned Hodge had been
gunned down in front of them and death became real.
Then Billy Joe Shaker's bloody demise little more than
an hour later made it even realer.

The surviving deputies were facing the genuine
prospect that some of them might not make it home,
and the fun and games were over. If Sheriff Bojack
had been deaf as a post, he could not have helped but
feel the tightening garrote of tension in air. *Best just
deal with it. Get it all out in the open. Let them air their concerns.* These deputies were good men. *His* men. He
owed them that much.

"Speak your mind, Mr. Ransom," the lawman said,
pulling up his horse.

They all cast furtive glances up and around at the
their towering surroundings, walls of granite and slate
and conifer, but the area seemed secluded enough
that they were safe for the moment . . . safe enough
to talk.

The Arizona posse pulled their horses into a tight
circle formation and kept their voices down by professional training and habit.

Ransom tugged off his hat and wiped dirty sweat
from his brow, his blue-eyed honest and direct gaze

looking Bojack respectfully in the eye. The sheriff liked the young man and knew he was his natural successor, as his late son, Jim, should have been. The deputy spoke respectfully, choosing his words. "Sheriff, speaking for myself, I think we may be making a big mistake here."

Bojack just watched the younger man spit the words out with an unblinking eagle-eyed stare over his gray beard—plainly, the old man was listening and giving the boy his full attention but wasn't going to make it easy for him.

Ransom went on. "Sheriff, sir, we need to rethink this. That girl outlaw is being taken to be hanged and the deputy marshal taking her there is a man who knows his business. Justice is being served. I know you got good reason to be the man that pulls the trigger and ends her life, sir." Deputies Dodge and Slayton nodded their agreement. "We all know that, because of what she done to Jim. But we're breaking the law here. And we're out of our jurisdiction. And we're a long way from home. And mostly, we already lost Ned Hodge and Billy Joe Shaker. Two of us are dead." Ransom broke Bojack's gaze and swiveled his head to regard Slayton and Dodge in the posse, his steady face bearing a grim expression. "And I'm—we're— getting a bad feeling about this."

Screwing his hat back on his head, Deputy Ransom shrugged, his piece said. His body language said he couldn't speak for the others but that was how he felt. Bojack saw the other deputies' eyes were on Ransom, not himself, so he spoke up. "You all know who Bonny Kate Valance is. You all know *what* the woman is. Seen it firsthand. Let's say she doesn't get to that hanging. Let's say she shoots that deputy marshal who is of use to her now, protecting her against us. You know how this witch thinks. The first thing Valance will do when she thinks her ass is safe from us is kill that tough hombre she got protecting her and make her escape."

Looking at his men, Waylon Bojack saw doubt and uncertainty mingled with a return of the purposeful sense of mission they had started out with. He was getting through to them and suppressed a smile. "Let me point out to you men, if I need to remind you, another Goddamn good reason we gotta finish her." The Sheriff pointed up into the mountains to the east, where the last shot had come from. "Johnny Cisco is up there trying to rescue her, come all this way after busting out of our jail, and we all know how dangerous this man is. We all know if Bonny Kate don't kill that deputy marshal then her lover boy most surely will—unless we're here to stop it and kill both of those outlaws first instead."

The posse of lawmen nodded—everyone except the one deputy who spoke up. Ransom just listened with a circumspect expression. Bojack settled his gaze on the young man and addressed him evenly. "Yes, Mr. Ransom, we _are_ breaking the law. But there is what's legal and there is what is just and what needs to be done. Right and wrong is real simple in this here situation. What _is_ wrong is Bonny Kate keeping her life. What _is_ wrong is her getting away and living happily ever after with Cisco. What _is_ wrong is them murdering that marshal up there. _What's right_ is us making sure that doesn't happen. _What's right_ is making her dead and making sure she stays dead. _What's right is Bonny Kate Valance gone from this world._"

"What if we wind up killing that marshal?" Ransom pointed out. "How is that right, sir?"

Sheriff Bojack's eyes clouded for he had no ready answer. Instead, after a pause, he said, "One thing I know is the same as you all do for damn sure . . . Bonny Kate Valance ain't got no intention of getting hanged. That degenerate outlaw means to slip the noose. She'll do what she has to do unless we stop her. It's up to us. Each man here."

Sheriff Bojack looked his deputies in the eye, one by one. One by one they nodded—Slayton, Dodge, even, finally, Jed Ransom.

Away they rode.

CHAPTER 13

She was full of surprises and he wondered what else she had in store for him.

Joe Noose had suspected Bonny Kate Valance would be a mouthy handful the two days he had to get her over the pass but never doubted he could handle one unarmed woman. He'd expected her to try to make a break for it but she hadn't tried to escape yet. This surprised him because it was the first thing he expected her to do. What he hadn't been expecting was a posse of lawmen vigilantes all the way from Arizona to complicate things, let alone this rifleman trying to help her escape. A lot of surprises for one day. His plate was full with this woman.

Noose sat in his saddle atop his bronze sure-footed horse, eyes fixed on the daunting crevice rising above him, steering Copper with a touch of his boot or flick of his reins now and again up whatever semblance of path presented itself. Noose could hear Bonny Kate behind him, the *clop* of her mustang's fetlocks following in his own horse's hoof steps. Now and again,

Noose swung a glance over his right shoulder to check Bonny Kate was still there and she always was. The subdued female outlaw was very quiet.

Something didn't sit right with him about this whole situation and he wasn't sure what it was. Not exactly.

"One thing I don't get, lady," Noose said over his shoulder to his prisoner as they rode carefully up the steep, tricky incline.

"There's a lot of things you don't get, trust me on that one, mister," Bonny Kate snorted petulantly.

"One thing mainly."

She responded with an affected yawn.

"What I don't get is why that sheriff and your old pal Cisco spook the bejesus out of you but getting hanged don't."

The question visibly threw her. She blinked. "Who said I wasn't scared?" She shrugged with a slippery glance. "Course I'm scared."

"Then you sure don't show it. Not like how scared you looked of getting shot by that sheriff back there or by whatever you think Cisco means to do to you. One's as bad as the other, I'd think. Don't make sense."

"You don't know women."

"Know 'em well enough."

"You don't know me."

"True. Not more than a few hours, anyways."

Her flashing eyes drilled into the back of his head. "So don't judge me. Enough people been doing that already. The whole world's been judging me my whole damn life and that's why I'm in this here predicament."

"You put yourself here. Tied the rope around your own neck by your own deeds.

"You weren't there. You don't know. Like you said."

Noose nodded: *Fair enough.* "Still looks to me you're more scared of the men after you than of being hanged and it just makes me wonder why."

Bonny Kate was off her horse!

She was there and then she wasn't.

Moved so fast Noose barely had time to react before the woman had flipped herself head over heels over the back of her horse, landed squarely on both boots, and took off at a dead run down the hill.

"Dammit!" Noose swore, dismounting in one smooth movement and hitting the ground and tearing off after her but Bonny Kate Valance was gone.

Noose figured maybe she wasn't so keen on getting to that gallows after all.

Throwing a quick glance back to Copper and the Appaloosa, Noose saw the horses weren't going anywhere, so he scrambled down the grassy and rock slope in the direction the flash of color from her denim shirt had disappeared. He had to admit the woman could move when she had to. It was like chasing a jackrabbit.

Where the hell did she think she was going?

Fortresses of pine trees rose on either side of the uneven narrows of the draw they had been riding up. The ground was undisturbed. Noose stopped and took a moment to study the area and realized she had not fled the way they had come.

What the hell way did she go?

A lot of dry brush and parched thicket to the right, just off the horse path. There were broken bushes but it didn't look like she had run through that. Chaff. Weeds. Scrub. Unnatural beds of parchment-dry fallen leaves crunching under his boots every step he took.

The lady outlaw couldn't get far without making noise in this dried-out terrain. It was like walking on matchsticks.

Listening carefully, cocking his head to concentrate, Noose couldn't hear much beneath the wind crackling through the dry-as-kindling treetops. Because of the drought conditions, the tree line that would normally be verdant green was brown and arid, dead crackling leaves on the branches. No fleeing footsteps and grunts of exertion came from below. Bonny Kate could be hiding. Keeping her head down. Waiting for him to pass by. Maybe holding a branch she could bushwhack him with when he went by, steal his guns and horse, and make a break for her freedom. Noose thought he might try the same if he was in her position.

He parted the brush and squinted at the descending ridge below. He swung his head and looked up, seeing a flash of blue denim above him farther up the ridge— Bonny Kate was scrambling for the higher ground through a wall of rocks.

She had a good head start to nowhere.

Joe Noose leapt into action and scrambled up the hill after her, charging on his pumping muscular legs in long strides over the rocks and boulders, shoving dehydrated branches and desiccated sticks out of his way. She was a hundred yards directly ahead of him above. That's why he hadn't heard her. The clever woman had taken an escape route over the rocks rather than the beds of dry leaves below that would have made so much noise.

Hand over fist, Bonny Kate scrambled up the rocks, but she kept losing her footing and it was one step up and two steps back.

Noose charged up the rocks and clambered over the boulders on his big hands and feet with the speed and prowess of a cougar, quickly gaining ground on her. Down below a few hundred yards away, the horses looked up and watched their two riders with lazy disinterest, then went back to munching on grass that had become as dry as straw.

Throwing a wild look of fury and fear over her shoulder behind her flowing red tresses, Bonny Kate cursed, "Damn you, Joe Noose!" Her hand met a loose rock and it gave her an idea. She stopped climbing suddenly and used both arms to knock the heavy stone loose, sending it tumbling with sharp rhythmic *crack*s down at Noose. As the rock lifted off the ground and bounced, picking up speed and velocity, Noose dodged it just in time as it smashed past. Had it hit him it would have taken his head off. His face colored with anger as he looked up and saw Bonny Kate rolling more rocks down at him, using both legs to dislodge the small boulders. A second stone tumbled. He rolled to the side to avoid it. Gritting his teeth, he snarled up at her, "Woman, you don't stop right there, I'm gonna pull my gun and put one in your foot!"

"Do it if you're man enough!" she crowed, and shook loose another rock from the ridge but this one missed her pursuer by a mile.

"I don't care about you hitting me, but if one of those rocks hits my horse you'll be in a world of hurt, lady!"

"Like I ain't already!" Bonny Kate was climbing again, scampering up the granite face like a lizard.

"Dammit!" Joe Noose swore, and in a surge of strength he cleared the fifty-yard space between them with a few powerful leaps, and his fist closed around her ankle.

"Lemme go! Lemme go!" Bonny Kate was kicking and punching and thrashing with all the fight she had in her, but she was a small woman and Joe Noose a very big man so it took him less than a minute to get her facedown in the dirt with her shackled arms pinned beneath her, his knees on her legs, holding her down. "You big son of a bitch, let me go!" Noose was frustrated and upset with the lady outlaw but he never hurt women and didn't use any more force on her than it took to subdue her. "Let. Me. Go."

"Are you done?"

"Just let me go." It was a bleak, hopeless moan.

"I got a job to do, lady, and you're it."

She rolled onto her back and looked up at him with wet lips, radiating raw animal carnality. "What do you want? Me? Go on. Take me. Then will you let me go? Go on, take off my drawers. It'll be worth it. I promise." She shimmied her hips against his, licking her lips salaciously, wiggling her thighs, but he stood and put a space between them. She lay back, foiled again, glowering up at him.

"No chance," Noose said.

"Are you kidding me? I ain't never had no man ever say no to me."

"There's a first time for everything, I reckon. Now, get on your feet, get back down there, and get on your horse." He pulled her to her feet and began helping her down the rock-strewn slope.

"I'm sick of you bossing me around," she grumbled.

"This time tomorrow you won't have to worry about it. Or much else, I savvy."

She snorted in retort.

As they reached the trail and he dragged her sulky, recalcitrant figure back to her mare, he said, "Your best bet is with me. The end may be the same but them that are after you want your end to be prolonged and you don't want that."

"So you're protecting me?" she said with dainty sarcasm as he lifted her fitfully back into her saddle.

"As far as it goes," he replied, swinging into his own.

CHAPTER 14

Johnny Cisco was closer than Noose imagined.

Somewhere in his bloody and storied career the dangerous gunfighter Cisco had picked up the nickname *The Ghost* because he moved like one—a tricky killer whose movements were invisible. The sobriquet stuck; you never saw him coming and he usually came up from behind. Cisco's trademark was shooting men in the back, because he always found a way to get behind his target. This wasn't cowardice on Cisco's part so much as pragmatism: it was safer to kill a man putting a bullet in his back where he couldn't face you and draw down on you. The mathematics of the fearsome tradecraft of the shootist were to stay alive and make sure your opponent didn't, as Cisco understood the basic equation. Honor and fair play had never entered the gunfighter's thinking—he considered those niceties he couldn't afford when there wasn't anything nice about killing a man with a gun to begin with; the killer had no intention of playing the game by different rules now. Stick with what works, was his motto.

An hour ago, as soon as he saw the marshal ride off the trailhead of the pass up into the untamed wild elevations with the woman—a smart move by a capable lawman—Cisco's respect was growing, for as he grew to realize he had to watch out for this one. Figuring out their plan was to cut straight up the mountain, the outlaw had abruptly backtracked. He began riding hard west and as straight south back up the mountain across the rugged terrain as his horse could manage, thereby closing the space between him and his quarry the quickest way possible. In a quarter mile Cisco would have to cross the pass into the northern elevations the two people he was after had ridden up into, and the southern side of the mountain merged with the trailhead soon.

Cisco double-checked the loads on his guns with his skinny, skeletal, and callused fingers as he perched in the saddle, watchfully surveying the area and keeping his sharp ears alert for any sound of irregular movement. The going was tough, his big brown stallion having trouble clambering up the steep hill over the roots of the tightly packed pine trees, but the rider and his horse were making steady progress and covering ground. He didn't think the Wyoming lawman would see him coming from his right because he was watching his rear mostly . . . Cisco's guess was that this marshal was more worried about Sheriff Bojack and his deputies than he was of Cisco.

Just one thing gave Johnny Cisco pause. He'd counted only three deputies a short while ago. Yet he had seen five ride off with the sheriff back in Arizona. Somehow Cisco doubted two of the lawmen had turned back or quit; these were dedicated individuals and the sheriff was a hard-ass tyrant. Cisco had clearly heard crackling reports of gunshots in the distance over the previous hours so it was simple math that two of the deputies had been gunned down by this fearsome marshal already. Cisco figured he had better watch his ass and not underestimate this Wyoming stud who had his woman under escort . . . the heavily armed ape was good.

But Cisco knew he was better—had been up against tougher, gone up against the very toughest, and still lived to tell, which told the whole story.

But something else stuck in his craw. Despite the badge, this Wyoming marshal didn't look the usual lawman with his wild, unkempt appearance. Instead, he looked like an outlaw himself. Truth be told, Cisco was smart enough to admit he didn't know anything about Wyoming law enforcement or what breed of individual it employed. About the only thing he knew about the place called Jackson Hole was Butch Cassidy had once hid out here.

Play it careful, play it smart, he told himself repeatedly as he rode across the mountainside, on the lookout with his guns at the ready. With his narrow, saddle-worn face and austere, bony physique, Johnny Cisco looked like a raggedy scarecrow astride his stallion, and his passing scared away a few crows that took flight into the bleached, lowering skies punctured by parched trees that looked like rows of brown arrowheads.

Presently, as he approached the nearing trail of the Teton Pass, the dry forestation thickened and the shootist dismounted with a rusty *clank* of spurs and led his horse on foot. Ducking down a ravine, sidestepping, his weathered boots kicking loose pebbles and dirt, Cisco made for the trailhead. The ground was uneven and tightly packed with trees and bushes.

Prickly, spiky brambles caught and snagged on the loose, stinking clothes on his wiry, lupine frame. Thorns sliced his flesh, drawing drops of blood. Undeterred, still he kept his clench on his big, fully loaded Sharps rifle and forged ahead. Using the weapon's wooden stock, the gunfighter beat back branches that got in his way and gradually covered the distance. Through the branches, he saw the rugged, excavated dirt road of the pass about three hundred yards ahead. Shouldering through the trees, he strode past some large boulders and made out a clearing between the tree line where he could reach the pass itself.

He was almost there.

Then they were. Ducking down quickly, Johnny Cisco took urgent cover below a pile of rocks just as the four horses of the Arizona posse of lawmen rode up around the bend. Their sudden appearance had been concealed behind a large massif of a granite wall on one of the many sharp bends on the trailhead in the eastern direction leading back down to Jackson. From where Cisco hunkered with his gripped rifle locked and loaded, listening hard, he detected no change in the tempo of the horses' hoof steps so the sheriff and his deputies likely hadn't spotted him. Looking up, he brushed a sweaty lank of long black hair from his stinging brown eyes and swept a wolfish gaze over his surroundings. There were titanic conifers on all sides, branches thickly meshed, and he had cover.

The horses stopped. He didn't hear the sound of their stepping fetlocks anymore. Deciding he had suitable cover, Johnny Cisco carefully risked a cautious glance over the edge of the rock to scope out the enemy.

A hundred yards west, the posse had come to a

standstill as the gunfighter had surmised, and weren't looking in his direction. A swift glance at the barricade of branches and leaves he stood behind told Cisco they couldn't see him from their vantage point even if they were looking straight at him.

Instead, the deputies' gazes were focused on their boss, who was getting his fat ass out of the saddle and struggling with his stirrup as he dropped to the ground.

Sheriff Bojack in plain view. In killing range. The shootist could easily drop him with his long rifle. It was too damn good to be true. For a few brief, impulsive seconds, all thoughts of Bonny Kate Valance vanished from the gunfighter's mind, replaced by a red haze of murderous rage that filled his skull.

Johnny Cisco raised his Sharps rifle to his shoulder, leveled his aim using the boulder for leverage, then stuck his finger through the trigger guard to touch sweet, sweet curved steel.

Take the shot.

Boy, was it tempting. He had that fat old bastard right in his crosshairs. For a moment Cisco didn't move a muscle, the weapon socked to his shoulder, its long, heavy barrel unwavering in his sure and steady heft. His only movement was the infinitesimal twitches in the touch of his forefinger on the trigger, applying the tiniest smidgen of pressure, just enough to feel the trigger depress a fraction of an inch, one *click*, a hair away from firing. Down the barrel, between the gunsights, a hundred yards away, Sheriff Waylon Bojack stood beside his horse he had just dismounted, looking up at the rise of sheer, steep mountain topography leading up off the trail. The old lawman was completely unaware of being under the gun whose owner

had already adjusted for trajectory and wind velocity
and had him dead to rights and a bullet with his name
on it aimed right at his head. Cisco wanted to blow
Bojack's brains out—or his head clean off, which was
more likely with this caliber at this distance—he wanted
to so much he could taste it.

But Cisco was a careful man measured in his dead-
liness, who would wait until just the right moment to
strike and when he did, it was without hesitation or
remorse and fatal as a scorpion. Moments passed as
the tarnished Sharps rifle remained trained on the
Arizona lawman, muzzle tipping slightly as the heavy-
set sheriff knelt to check the trailhead of the pass for
sign, tipping up again as he rose and looked up at the
mountainside above, rubbing his jaw in thought.
Cisco's finger never left the trigger and his aim never
wavered off his target.

But there were those three other deputies.

He knew and hated their faces, too, but if he took
the shot he'd have to take them on. Cisco did some
swift mental calculations: there wouldn't be time to
reload the Sharps before their guns came out, but his
own twin Remington 1875 .44 caliber pistols would be
out of their holsters and he figured he'd drop one of
them before the sound of the rifle shot faded and
Bojack hit the ground dead. His position was safe
and secluded behind the rocks amidst the copse of
trees but there would be an extended exchange of fire
as the last two of the Arizona posse took cover and he
engaged them. Let's say he plugged them without incident. Cisco figured he probably would. But there
would be a lot of chaos and that damned marshal protecting his woman would no doubt exploit it to his
advantage. Might even sandbag Cisco, knowing the

shootist was pinned down. No, there were too many
damn variables. Johnny Cisco stayed put. And he
didn't shoot.

He dropped the gunsight to resist temptation.

Cisco kept his attention focused on the posse,
knowing he could see them but they couldn't see him.

*Did you feel me, Sheriff? Did you just then feel the hand
of death touch your shoulder like some kinda cold breeze? Because you don't know how close you just come to meeting
your Maker. You got no idea in hell, and hell is where you're
going . . . 'cause me, Johnny Cisco, is gonna send you there
soon, real soon. Just got some business to take care of first.*

Cisco listened in from his place of concealment.

The lawmen were talking. The tall canyons of the
pass acted like an echo chamber as the acoustics of
the deep gorge amplified their voices even though the
men were speaking quietly and stood a good distance
away. They had all dismounted now.

The gunfighter caught snatches of words, snippets
of sentences. Something about there being no sign
and the marshal having left the trail and riding up
into the mountains. Nods. Agreements. They were
going to follow, it looked like.

Then the sheriff was shaking his head.

No, looked like they weren't, after all.

Bojack pointed up the trailhead carved out of the
pass, a rideable route hugging the mountainside wend-
ing in a rough, dusty path ever higher up into the
pine-crusted crags of granite scraping the clouds.
More words. Curt orders. "*It is faster that way,*" the sheriff was saying, making some hand gestures that were
plain enough: *take the trail, get ahead of them, cut them off.*

Cisco pondered that. *Maybe might make sense except
this tough marshal for sure must have thought of that and*

had some other plan in mind. The posse staying on the pass was okay, though. This would help Cisco. Let them try to get in front of the marshal with the woman he was trying to get away from them. The marshal would be looking ahead, dealing with what was in front of him then, all his attention focused forward. He wouldn't be watching his back, wouldn't see old Johnny Cisco sneak up behind, and when he did it would be too late. The shootist's plan was to pursue his quarry up into the mountains following his exact footsteps, shadowing him, then wait for his moment to shoot. He wouldn't miss this time. Put one .44 Remington centerfire slug in the marshal's back— maybe two more for good measure, because he was a big son of a bitch—then get his woman back.

A hundred yards away through the trees, the four-man sheriff's posse swung back up into their saddles and rode off at a brisk canter up the Teton Pass.

Johnny Cisco was suddenly glad he hadn't killed them, after all.

CHAPTER 15

It looked like the coast was clear, but they still had a long, hard ride ahead.

Noose regarded the intimidating crags of granite massif ahead jutting up hundreds of feet into the sky. The pass was difficult enough to cross staying on the trailhead, but now he and his prisoner had left the road and were recklessly trying to make it up through the actual mountains themselves. Impassable steep, rocky slopes and vertiginous grades that ended without warning in knots of tree trunks that blocked the path. Horses had never been ridden here and the only creatures that passed were bears and cougars and deer. It was a hopeless fool's errand getting off the trail, the worst idea in the history of bad ideas. Forging forward was a step-by-step process, going a few feet at a time and being constantly, tensely vigilant of where the horses carefully put their fetlocks. One misplaced hoof would break a stallion's leg and then it was all over, because one horse could not take two people through this fearsome terrain and they hadn't brought a spare.

Luckily for Joe Noose he was riding Copper, because a regular horse wouldn't have stood for it and just stopped—stubbornly refused to budge or turned straight around. The average stallion wouldn't have dared struggle up this mountainside, but Copper was no average steed—Noose's tough, brave horse would do anything for him, and seemed to enjoy the challenge. The bronze stallion stared straight ahead with a determined, dogged gaze and kept pushing forward, deliberately and stubbornly taking the lead. Copper forging a path through the forest allowed Bonny Kate's nervous mustang to follow its hoof tracks, showing the other, lesser horse that the passage was indeed possible.

The problem was it was slow going—very slow going. The horses and riders were covering about a hundred yards every ten minutes and the people could have walked faster. Noose's worry was that the men after them were going to catch up. He couldn't hear or see them but for all he knew they had dismounted and, unhorsed, were catching up on foot. Truth be told, in their position that is precisely what he would do. Noose didn't think the Arizona blood posse would leave their horses for a two-legged chase, this was his instinct, anyway, but the gunfighter might well be traveling on foot.

Noose had considered abandoning the horses several times over the last hour, but something made him not leave Copper. Like it was bad luck. It felt like leaving a friend. No man, or horse, left behind.

Looking over his shoulder, Noose saw his agitated prisoner looking visibly uneasy as she clung to her saddle. "How you managing, Bonny Kate?"

"You sure about this?"

"Nope. But it beats the alternative. It's slow for us, it'll be slower for them."

"If you say so." She suddenly brightened and shot him a jaunty grin. "I ain't in no hurry." This woman changed moods like hats, it seemed.

He couldn't resist grinning back. "No, reckon you wouldn't be."

"You know what they say, Joe Noose."

"What do they say, Bonny Kate?"

"The best party to go to is the one they can't start without you."

He laughed. "Fact."

"So what did you do before you was a marshal?" She made conversation as they rode to keep their minds off the horses' struggle clambering up a treacherous arroyo below a huge cliff precariously laden with boulders that seemed like they might fall on their heads at any time.

"I'm a bounty hunter by trade. Not really a marshal in the job sense, just a deputized one for this one job."

"So you're an outlaw. Like me." She smiled knowingly.

"I ain't an outlaw. Used to be, not now. Not for a long, long time. I chase legal, legitimate bounties. Only use my gun when I have to."

"Dead-or-alive bounties."

"A lot of the time."

"You bring 'em back dead, it's the same price as you bring 'em in alive?" she asked.

"Yeah."

"How many men you killed?"

"More than I wanted to. Like to think none I didn't have to."

"But you *are* a bounty hunter. You *do* kill men for the reward money."

"No, I bring 'em back alive when I can," Noose answered. "Most times I do bring 'em back alive, in truth. Once I get the drop on a man, they know I got 'em dead to rights, and most usually make the sensible choice, meaning surrender."

"I believe you, Joe. You ain't the killer type. You ain't got it in the eyes." She thought for a second and an idea occurred to her, lighting up her gaze. "So you bein' a bounty hunter and all, you must have heard of me."

"I think everybody's heard of you, Bonny Kate Valance. You're a famous woman."

"*Notorious* is the word most would use."

"Same thing."

"Reckon. I'm surprised our paths didn't cross before with the big reward on my head. You ever hunt me for the bounty?"

Noose shrugged. "No. I been working Wyoming and Idaho the last five years and when I got wind you was in Wyoming, before I could go after you for the reward, heard other bounty hunters already claimed it."

Those words drew an angry response from Bonny Kate Valance. Her eyes blazed in abrupt fury and she spat contemptuously onto the ground from her saddle. "Frank Butler and his dirty sons of bitches gang of vultures. Twelve against one. Me against all them. Yeah, those pigs got me, delivered me to the Jackson marshal like livestock. They don't know how to treat a woman, that's a truthful fact. Those is bad men, Joe Noose. You don't want to meet up with 'em."

Joe Noose sat straight in the saddle and looked forward with a stony hard stare. His voice was low and gravelly, like rocks ground together when he said: "I did. I killed 'em."

A gasp came from behind him.

"You killed Frank Butler?"

He nodded.

"The Frank Butler?"

"And his men. The whole Butler Gang. Last month."

With a vicious whoop of savage joy and a coarse, bitter laugh, Bonny Kate clapped her hands, rattling the steel shackles in a noisy *clank*ing of metal. Noose shot her a narrow glance and pressed his finger to his lips, warning her to stop making so much racket. He pointed around them, indicating that people might be listening. She nodded back soberly and drew her finger across her own lips as if to seal them, whispering now. "*Good for you.* Goddamn good for you. Did you have a bunch of guys with you?"

"Just me."

"Just you? One man against all of them?"

"And Bess Sugarland, the Jackson U.S. Marshal, but she wasn't then. I did most of the shooting but she helped. I'd have been dead if it wasn't for her. That's why I took this deputy job to help her out, 'cause she hurt her leg in those troubles with Butler and, well, 'cause I owe her."

"Yee-haw! Joe Noose, if you'd have ridden with my gang we'd have been unstoppable. We'd have taken over the whole damn West." She whistled in admiration. "One man took down the Butler Gang. Hot damn."

"Wasn't easy. They were a lot of trouble. A real handful. I got shot twice. Barely survived."

"But you did."

"I did. They were stupid. Plus, they were greedy. They were a pack of mad dogs and mad dogs get put down. Did get this horse out of it, though, Copper here. Took him off one of those boys. He likes me better."

"May I inquire what made you mix it up with Butler and his boys? What was in it for you?" she asked.

"It was what was in it for them. Butler framed me for shooting Bess's father, the marshal in Hoback, then tried to hunt me down for the reward."

"So you got the reward, then?"

Noose gave her a screw-eyed, squinty glance. "You got a mind like a cash register, lady."

"I'm a woman. I keep my eye square on the bottom line. So you're rich, right?"

Noose just shook his head. "Change the subject."

"Joe Noose!"

"Let's talk about something else, I said."

"I'm gonna be dead tomorrow. I should damn well be able to talk about what I please my last day breathing living air."

"Not with me."

Suddenly, Bonny Kate hissed. "*Shush!*"

Quickly reining Copper to a standstill with the lead in one hand, Noose quick-drew his Colt Peacemaker from his holster and cocked the hammer, utterly alert, his gaze sweeping the forest around them.

"You hear that?" Bonny Kate whispered.

Brow furrowed, he looked her a question. Hard.

Her eyes were wide and wild, fixed to his own, as she silently pointed to her left. Then she nudged in that direction with her jaw.

He nodded imperceptibly. Noose adopted an attitude of intense listening.

The woods were quiet—too quiet. The branches

and leaves, dry as parchment, were still. There was no wind. The silence that descended was deafening.

A *crack*. Faint but distinct.

Perhaps fifty yards away, in the depths of a dry thicket.

His eyes swiveled to Bonny Kate, who was holding her breath. Her face had a high color. The two of them sat stone still in the saddles, surrounded by thick trees and undergrowth on all sides. The two horses sensed the tension of the owners and remained absolutely stationary. Noose remained braced and alert, gun barrel held up beside his head, thumb on the hammer.

Another *snap*, like a breaking twig beneath a foot. Closer this time, maybe forty yards distant, approaching.

Bonny Kate shot him a glance. Her gaze landed on his pistol.

His thumb was slowly cocking back the hammer, one notch at a time.

A movement in the bushes.

The Colt Peacemaker was fully cocked and Joe Noose levered his gun arm like a lowering boom to fiercely, directly aim his revolver at the source of the sound.

A flurry of movement.

He pulled the trigger.

A rabbit suddenly charged out of the bushes up the hill in a blinding blur of motion.

Noose caught the hammer with his thumb before it made contact with the shell, sparing the bullet and the noise it would have made.

With a loud exhale of relief, Bonny Kate sagged.

The loud gun discharge instantly followed at an earsplitting decibel in the amplified acoustics of the

ravine—it came from the other direction and from
below, Noose already swinging in his saddle and
squeezing off two shots in the direction while roaring,
"*Get down!*"

Heaving herself clean out of her saddle, Bonny
Kate covered her face with her shackled hands as she
flew from the stirrups and hit the ground hard, rolling
over and over with a grunt to end up hugging the
ground on her belly in a settling cloud of dirt.

Lapping tongues of fire came from the cluster of
dead pine trees below, where crouching figures of several men had rifles and pistols drawn, shooting up at
them. The figures were concealed by branches and
hard to make out. Noose swung Copper full around
and loosed off several more wild shots down at them
but he didn't see any horses—Sheriff Bojack and his
posse had abandoned their mounts to pursue on foot
after all; it was why they had caught up so fast, as he
had anticipated. Bullets whistled past Noose's ears
and flashed in his eyes as bright scintillating glints of
metal. Rounds punched holes in trees nearby, showering chunks of bark. It was harder to hit a moving
target so Noose got his horse moving fast, galloping
straight for a tightly packed copse of pine trees
clumped thirty feet away where he could dismount
and keep Copper out of the line of fire for now the
horse was a big and obvious target. Noose needed to
be on foot and quick.

As he rode charging past Bonny Kate—the lady
outlaw was safely hidden flat in the grass and intact for
now—he snatched her horse's reins and hauled the
second steed with him toward the cover of the trees.
Seconds later Noose was unhorsed, his boots hitting
solid ground, and in several swift movements he had

lashed the reins of both animals to a branch while
snatching his Winchester repeater and a bandolier of
.45 ammo from his saddle.

In deafening fusillades of lead, the bullets from the
dug-in Arizona lawmen below exploded everywhere,
relentless strings of fire coming in staccato bursts
with scarcely a pause to reload. Jets and geysers of
dirt kicked up at his feet as Noose hurriedly departed
the safely sheltered horses and ran in a swift, low
crouch back toward Bonny Kate, levering and firing
his Winchester rifle over and over down the hill in the
direction the shots came from. He saw muzzle flashes
in the branches below popping like a string of fire-
crackers. The air was already thick with a hanging haze
of gun smoke. The bullets all seemed to be coming his
way, Noose noticed, quickly realizing that the Arizona
constabulary were trying to kill *him* first—because that
vengeful sheriff would want to be the one to shoot
Bonny Kate, not allowing her to die by a stray bullet.
It was a strategic awareness that gave Joe Noose a slight
advantage as he dove to the ground beside Bonny Kate
and crawled into a good shooting position.

Noose got his left elbow crooked on a ridge of dirt
that gave him leverage for aiming his rifle as he slapped
some fresh cartridges into the breech, cocked the lever,
and began firing more discriminately this time.

Other than feeling the sweet body heat radiating off
her, Noose was paying no particular attention to the
woman beside him so it came as a big surprise when
he felt the fully loaded Colt Peacemaker snatched from
his right holster before he could react . . . Noose
snapped a fearsome glance over to see Bonny Kate gripping the revolver in a two-hand grip on the ground and

taking careful, well-placed shots at the half-glimpsed posse below.

"Gimme my damn gun back!" he snarled.

"Shut up and shoot!" she snapped, blowing one shadowy deputy to his knees. Noose cocked an eyebrow, actually impressed. This was one woman who knew how to handle a gun.

"For the last time, give me that gun!"

She shot him a potent, loaded glare. "We're outnumbered and outgunned, mister! Two guns are better than one! Let's take care of these fools and when it's over I'll give you your damn gun back!"

As a heavy-caliber round exploded an inch from his face, Noose had to admit she had a point: another knowledgeable gun hand in this sticky situation they found themselves in was clearly an asset. Glaring back at her as she returned her gaze to sighting down the barrel of her stolen Colt, Noose took aim with his Winchester and shot a piece off another deputy, who went down and flopped around, hollering a string of profanity.

A hundred yards below the roaring guns of the tough marshal and his fiery prisoner defending their desperate position, the lawmen were advancing, even the wounded ones. Exchanging hand signals back and forth with seasoned professionalism, the determined posse gained ground and fearlessly came on in a deadly phalanx. Noose realized besides being disciplined, these Arizona men were tough sons of bitches because some had bullets in them and were still on their feet and not slowed down. Respecting them for this, it was with some regret Joe Noose realized he was going to have to kill each and every one, because that was the only way to stop them.

At his side, Bonny Kate chose her shots wisely. She didn't waste bullets. Seconds passed between each time she pulled the trigger as she carefully squinted and locked on a target. Four, then five shots sounded.

Then the hollow click of a hammer on an empty chamber.

"I'm out of bullets," she said.

"Good," he replied.

"Gimme more ammo. I need to reload."

Noose just grinned and shook his head. Bonny Kate grabbed his arm and jammed her face in his. "Listen to me, Joe. I have a plan. Load me up and let's split up. Let me head left down that hill and you and me, we can flank them. They're shooting at you, in case you ain't figured that out yet. Bojack ain't gonna let one of his men shoot me, he wants to do that, but he needs you dead first. Flank 'em is the smart play. From their position they won't see me make my move. They'll keep coming to you. Let 'em. You keep me covered and I'll get down there and hit them from the side."

His heart pounded from adrenaline and something else he didn't quite recognize. Noose looked in the mesmerizing whorls of Bonny Kate's blue eyes for what seemed like minutes but was probably less than a second. "That's a good plan," he stated flatly.

She didn't react, just held out her open palm in a *pay the girl* gesture.

He grabbed twelve .40-44 cartridges from his gun belt. Stuffed them into her small fist. Lightning fast, she flipped open the cylinder of the Colt Peacemaker, stuffed in six rounds, closed the gun, and stuck the rest of the shells in her pocket. "Cover me," she ordered, giving him a steely parting glance, then took off in a

low crouch down the side of the hill under the tree
line below the enemy's line of sight.

If the posse saw her, they didn't try to shoot her,
Noose saw, but they sure as hell were shooting at him,
getting ever closer and their shots more accurate by
the foot.

Noose paused to reload, hugging the dirt as lead
screamed around him. He doubted Bonny Kate would
use the opportunity to flee because she wouldn't get
far. It struck him as odd that the person he felt he
could most depend on right this very second was the
prisoner he was taking to be hanged, but the world
was a strange place. This entire situation had a whole
lot of irony; it had from the start. That was more thinking than Noose was used to or comfortable with and
with his Winchester chock-full of rounds he got back
to what he was comfortable with, which was shooting people.

Waylon Bojack whirled and saw her right there in
the flesh staring straight at him.

Bonny Kate Valance stood no more than ten feet away.

It was the last thing the old lawman had been expecting and to say he was at a disadvantage would
have been a considerable understatement.

Once back on his farm in Arizona a whole litter of
his black Labrador dog's pups had been killed and
eaten by a single dangerous coyote and on that night
he had woken to the awful sounds of the puppies'
hideous cries outside as they were torn to pieces.
Within less than a minute's time, Bojack was out of
bed and had grabbed his rifle and rushed outside but

the pups were gone and so was the coyote; no blood, no anything. All night the sheriff had sat up in his chair on the porch with his rifle, hoping to get a shot at the miserable cur that had savagely massacred his beloved dog's litter. Bojack remembered staring out into the darkness and seeing nothing, hearing nothing, just the mother dog's mournful mewling that her children had been taken from her. As dawn broke, the man fell asleep, only to wake up and open his eyes to see the coyote standing ten feet away looking him straight in the eye, well fed and visceral and defiant in its feral stare locked to his own, the look saying, *I killed them, I'd do it again, and I can take anything you love anytime I want.* Bojack had been so shocked and half-asleep he had become flummoxed and forgotten he had set his scattergun down on the porch, and in his groggy disorientation had taken a few seconds too long to pick it up and by then the coyote was long gone. He never forgot that baleful look the predator gave him.

The same exact look Bonny Kate Valance was giving him now.

The old man was so unnerved by the unexpected sight of the woman that he fumbled with his gun. It was that evil smile on her face that undid him. Her triumphal blue eyes locked on his.

So that he noticed the leveled revolver in her hand a fraction of a second too late, and by then it was going off in a bright, hot flash of fire and smoke and all he could do was wait for the hard impact in his chest but instead that's when he saw the blur of his deputy Clay Slayton leaping in front him and the next thing he felt was the hot, salty blood from the bullet wound the man suffered.

Sheriff Bojack let out a frightened little whimper when he looked up.

She was gone. Vanished in thin air. Like Bonny Kate was the devil himself but then he already knew that.

"*Pull out! Pull out!*" Bojack screamed to his men, as he dragged Slayton's body by the arms even though he already knew the man was dead from the fist-sized hole in his chest and all the blood left on the leaves in a gory snail trail from the exit wound crater in his spine. The sheriff was totally unnerved, in an utter panic, and his men didn't know what to do so they followed orders and retreated.

Nearby, up the hill, Noose couldn't believe his eyes. Wasn't sure what he just saw. A moment before, Bonny Kate had snuck behind the posse in the flanking maneuver she worked out and fired only one shot. She had the sheriff dead to rights but a deputy had jumped in front, taken the bullet, and been shot dead. Her sudden armed and unexpected appearance seemed to have rattled the Arizona lawmen so badly that they just pulled out. It was at Bojack's orders and Noose could clearly hear the fear and panic in the man's voice. For now, the posse had fallen back and the gunfight was over.

For now.

Noose figured once they settled down, they'd come back to finish what they came to do . . . he harbored no illusions about that.

Joe Noose rose and stood up, certain no bullets

would be coming his way. The area had gotten very quiet and still and the fog of drifting gun smoke was dissipating.

When the smoke cleared, Bonny Kate Valance was standing five feet away, holding his Colt Peacemaker in her small left fist—somehow, the big gun fit her like a glove. The weapon wasn't pointed at him, but it wasn't pointed away, either.

Noose froze. Did some quick mental calculations: The barrel of his Winchester was pointed down—it still had two .45 rounds in it—if he was fast, he could swing the barrel up and get a shot off but Noose had seen the woman handle a pistol and had no doubt he would be dead the exact same time he pulled the trigger when she shot him—Noose guessed he'd be alive long enough to drop Bonny Kate with his single round—but it would be a wash . . . they'd both be dead.

The female outlaw wore no expression on her face. She flipped the pistol out of her hand, stock spinning, and caught it by the barrel.

And she handed it back to him.

He took the gun and spun it back in his left holster.

Bonny Kate was once again unarmed. The lady outlaw smiled mischievously, knowing what he had been thinking like she was in his skull and could read his mind, but didn't mention it. "I bought us some time," was all she said.

"Thanks." It seemed like the proper reply, so he gave it.

"Don't mention it." She winked.

They stood facing each other.

Finally she shrugged. "Well, what the hell are we waiting for?" she quipped. "We got a hanging to get to."

Noose had to grin, showing his crooked teeth, and was extra gentlemanly as he helped the lady into the saddle of her horse, then swung a leg over his own and off the two rode into the higher elevations.

CHAPTER 16

Marshal Bess Sugarland hated him on sight.

It was just after three in the afternoon. The new Jackson peace officer was in the office cleaning her Winchester repeater, even though she had little need to as the rifle had been getting more use as a crutch than a firearm lately, and having a cup of coffee. Her leg was hurting more than usual today, as the bullet wound continued its slow healing process. Another trip to the doctor was in order so she could have the dressing changed and the wound treated with ointment. Marshal Bess had been offered a bottle of laudanum several times by the local physician but she had demurred, not wanting to be under the influence of narcotics while she held her U.S. Marshal's office post and bore those duties. So she bit the bullet against the chronic pain literally and figuratively, a .45 round clenched in her back teeth this morning. Most of the time she kept it in her cheek but when the waves of pain came on she bit down on it. In that way, the U.S. Marshal's daughter was like her father in her stubborn insistence on keeping a clear head and taking physical pain straight. The cartridge in Marshal Bess's mouth looked to most folks like she had a wad of chewing tobacco in her cheek and nobody seemed to notice she never spit.

The female lawman was antsy and restless today, feeling on pins and needles, her mood edgy and pre-occupied. She kept glancing out the window at the grand vista of the Teton Pass, imagining Joe Noose's progress with Bonny Kate Valance and squinting at the barely visible mountain road amidst the distant pines, trying to pinpoint where they would likely be even though they were far beyond the scope of her vision. Bess couldn't help herself; she would not be able to relax until noon tomorrow when Bonny Kate took the drop and she would know Noose had made it to Victor safe—she had twice telegraphed the local sheriff, Al Shurlock to send her a wire when her depu-tized friend arrived with his prisoner. Bess was also worried about that Arizona posse that had ridden through that morning even though they were long gone and she had not given them any information about Valance or Noose or where they were. In recent hours Marshal Bess fancied she heard the echo of gunshots coming from the direction of the pass a long way off, but they could have been anything. She had to stop her fretting.

But she couldn't. Luckily it had been a slow day in Jackson save for that dodgy sheriff and his deputies that morning, and not one person had walked through the door of the U.S. Marshal's office until he did.

Just ambled right in like he belonged here, even like he owned the place.

The cowboy was tall, rangy, clean-cut, square jawed, and arrogant as hell in his straight posture and upright bearing. His jeans were too tight. His Stetson and denim shirt and jacket were clean and pressed, boots spit and polished. Below close-cropped blond hair, his Johnny Appleseed scrubbed face was covered with red freckles behind a corn silk–colored, groomed beard.

The man looked about thirty and had confident eyes that let folks know he could handle himself as he swaggered inside. A sweep of his unblinking, indolent gaze took in the modest office. Everything about this kid rubbed Marshal Bess the wrong way; mostly, it was the flat expression of aloof disregard of her office that irritated her, like he was checking into a hotel and felt the room looked too cheap. Plus, he kept his hat on his head like it was cold, and didn't remove it, displaying another lack of respect for her office. And, worst, the jerk looked right through her, like he was looking for somebody else. *I'm the damn marshal,* Bess thought to herself, *so who the hell else would you be looking for?*

Therefore Bess Sugarland gave the young, cocky interloper the stink eye while he stood there sucking her air—didn't even bother to greet him like she normally would anybody else.

After a moment, the man strode right up to the desk, barely acknowledging her presence. "I'm looking for the marshal," was all he said.

Biting down on the bullet in the side of her mouth hard enough that she felt molar enamel grind on polished brass, Marshal Bess simply locked eyes with him, leaned back in her chair, then lifted open the side of her coat, displaying the seven-star silver badge on her bosom.

The look of surprise and disadvantage on the man's face almost made her feel better, even though he seemed to be staring equally at her badge and her breasts, so she closed her coat and leaned forward on her desk with her hands clasped together in half fists, staring straight up at him and raising an eyebrow, which told him to state his business.

"You're the marshal?" the youngster said, cracking an annoying grin that broke into a guffaw as he let out a hee-haw laugh that reminded her of the jackass she completely took him to be.

Now Bess was angry. "Yes, and who the hell are you and what are you doing in my office? State your business."

"Yes, sir, I mean, ma'am, I mean, Marshal. I am Nate Sweet, your new deputy."

"*What?*" Her eyes widened. "What the hell are you talking about?"

Nate Sweet took a folded official paper out of his denim jacket and presented it to her with a flourish. Warily, she snatched it from his fingers and opened it and the first thing she saw was the U.S. Marshals Service stamp on the letterhead. "I was dispatched from headquarters in Cody last week and ordered to report to the new marshal in Jackson but they didn't tell me the marshal was a *she.*"

"You got a problem with that?" Tired of sitting with this annoying new deputy looking down at her, Bess rose to her feet and felt a sudden stabbing pain in the bullet wound in her leg, wrapped in the wooden brace that caused her to flinch and buckle over slightly as she stood up behind her desk to be eye to eye with him. Immediately, Sweet saw her leg injury and was dumb enough to point at it.

"They didn't tell me you was a cripple, neither. I can see why they sent a man to give you backup. Must be why they figured you needed some help, ma'am, I mean, Marshal."

"That's it, junior." Marshal Bess's face flushed with a high color and she glared at him..

"Didn't they wire you that they were sending me—?"

"Shut up."

He did. Now his eyes were wide.

"No," she continued. "Cody did not wire me that they were sending a deputy. If they had, I'd've sent you across the pass with that damned lady outlaw instead of my friend, so thanks to you, and them, for nothing."

"I-I'd just heard, I mean, they just told me, that the old marshal and his deputy had got themselves shot last month and that there—"

"Which part of *shut up* don't you understand, junior?"

He closed his mouth and kept it closed. The first smart thing Bess Sugarland had seen Nate Sweet do since he walked in.

"You have any experience?"

Sweet nodded.

"How many years with the U.S. Marshals Service?"

He held up two hands and showed seven fingers.

"Can you shoot?"

Another nod.

"Can you ride?"

Nod.

"Ever shot a man?""

Sweet shook his head.

"Ever been in a gunfight?"

Another head shake.

Walking around the side of her desk in a tight limp, Marshal Bess got nose to nose with Sweet and looked him straight in the eye. "My name is Bess Sugarland. My father was a U.S. Marshal for thirty years and I was his deputy for ten of those so that's my experience. For your damn information I ain't no cripple. I got shot in the leg in the line of duty during a gunfight and I *have* shot men dead. I have not shot a deputy yet but there's a first time for everything, *Deputy*. Cody assigned you here, fine, but this is my jurisdiction and you will do what I say when I say it. If you perform those duties to my satisfaction then we will not have a problem. Understand me? You may speak now."

"Yes, ma'am," Nate Sweet answered respectfully.

"Marshal," she corrected him.

"Marshal."

CHAPTER 17

The lowering sky above the pass had begun to color with late afternoon as Joe Noose and Bonny Kate Valance rode their horses at a relaxed pace along the natural trail. For the last hour they had traveled in safety, their transit unmolested, and Noose sensed no immediate danger in the woods around them. At least for the present. While he kept one eye peeled and one hand near his gun, Noose felt looser and began a casual banter with Bonny Kate. He admitted to himself he enjoyed talking to her. She was funny, bawdy, and ribald in conversation. In another time and place Noose might have taken a genuine shine to Bonny Kate as many men had, to their considerable disadvantage, he reminded himself. But for right now the ride and the company were pleasant enough as the traveling companions talked easily about this and that and even shared some jokes, and the cowboy grew comfortable enough to ask his prisoner something he'd been meaning to since they set out from Jackson.

"Mind if I ask you a question, Bonny Kate? Kind of

personal, I reckon. Don't have to answer if you don't feel like it."

"You can ask me anything you want, Joe. Not like I have any secrets worth taking to the grave."

"Could be it's a question can't be answered."

"Won't know if I don't hear it. Ask away."

Noose's brow knitted as he tried to properly word his question. He fell back on Copper to ride alongside Bonny Kate, and when he finally looked over at her saw she held his gaze honest and true. Noose spoke softly with a rough sort of kindness in his voice. "How did you go wrong, Bonny Kate? How did it all come to this? I know why men go wrong 'cause I know how men think. Reckon that's because I am one. But I don't lay claim to understand women, and what makes one good like Bess or bad like you. How did you go so wrong, what brought you so low?"

"If this is your idea of small talk, Joe, you need some lessons in talking to girls." She grinned, and he laughed, embarrassed.

"Shucks, you don't have to answer."

She looked ahead while they rode and thought it over. "No, it's a good question. You mean when did I make the decision to turn outlaw, to rob banks and shoot people, when did I decide this was the life for me?"

"Something like that."

"I don't think I chose the life, Joe, I think it chose me."

"I can understand that."

"But *when* you want to know? What was my story? What was my family like? Before."

"Yeah, I suppose," he answered.

Then the conversation took a sideways turn when Bonny Kate asked Noose an offhand question.

"What's the story with you and that Marshal Bess back there?"

"It's complicated." He shrugged.

"Always is. I got time."

"I work for her."

"That's all?"

"Bess has big boots to wear in town, being the only law in Jackson—one woman running the U.S. Marshal's office, so I help her out when I can."

"You're a bounty hunter."

"Sometimes. Sometimes I'm a deputy marshal. Whatever she needs."

"Reckon it's handy having you around."

"Depends on what side of the law you're on."

"It's handy her having you on hers, is what I meant. A woman likes a strong man watching her back. Makes her feel protected."

"Bess can handle herself. She's a heck of a lady. And a hell of a marshal."

"I can see that. A woman marshal, now, that's damn impressive. Never met a lady marshal or sheriff once before her, not in my entire career. This may sound strange coming from me, but I say it is high time women wore a badge. If a woman had been enforcing the law, I'd have been brought to justice years ago. It's because of all these stupid men holding lawman positions I've had the run I've had, believe it. Women are smarter than men. We're the superior species. They say I'm historical because I'm making history being the first female outlaw to get hanged, well, that's a lot of hooey because it don't take no brains to get yourself killed. I just got caught, was all. Historical is your marshal friend back there. Bess Sugarland is the one who made history, becoming the first female marshal."

Noose nodded in agreement and Bonny Kate, on a roll of rhetoric, whistled in admiration. "The guts she must have. All the crap she must have had to take from men, especially lawmen, because of her sex, her wearing that badge. Earning the respect of men like those. Hell, earning the respect of a man like you. That's something. I take my hat off to Marshal Bess Sugarland. She's a great lady and you can tell her I said so."

"Don't take this the wrong way, but I don't think the feeling's mutual, Bonny Kate."

The lady outlaw sighed, shrugged. "Sad, but I know. Stands to reason she don't like my kind and truth be told she got good reason not to. I don't hold that against her. But Bess and I, we got more in common than she wants to admit to herself."

Noose chuckled. "You got rocks in your head if you believe that, lady. The marshal ain't nothing like you. She enforces the law and you break it. That's why she's wearing a badge and you're wearing a rope necktie."

"I'm serious, Joe. Bess and me, we got us plenty in common. We're independent women who live on our terms, play by our own rules. Strong women who both distinguished themselves and made a name for ourselves in a man's world by not letting men tell us what to do. It's a lonely road when most of our sex get married and push out babies and end up forgotten by husbands who cheat on them with the other kind of woman that sells sex for money. Those are the two choices that a woman is born into in this life with, Joe Noose. Bonny Kate Valance and Marshal

Bess Sugarland—us, we're two of a kind. Broke the mold, you might say. Mavericks each in our own way. Free women who think for ourselves, living by our own wits God didn't give us because there ain't no damn God, but our mothers did. It's a man's world, Noose, not built for females, so take it from a woman, any way she can skin this world is her business."

"You both have guts, it's true. But you want to know the difference between you and Bess, Bonny Kate?"

"Yes, I do."

"The truth?"

"No, tell me lies like every other man always has. Of course I want you to tell me the truth."

"You make excuses for your misdeeds and try to justify your wrongs when all you care about is yourself, Bonny Kate. You don't feel sorry for anything you've done, all you ever cared about was not getting caught. Bess always tries to do the right thing and makes the tough choices and decisions when it ain't in her interest, just the opposite. She makes sacrifices and takes responsibility because that's her duty. What Bess has, it's called *character*. That ain't a word you know the meaning of, Bonny Kate, and responsibility for other people ain't in your vocabulary because the only thing you feel responsible for is yourself. That's why she's a lawman and you're an outlaw."

After this exchange they rode in silence for many minutes as Bonny Kate Valance fell into deep thought and introspection, reflecting on what Noose could not hazard a guess. Noose was never sure what women were thinking. But he wondered just the same. As the two companions climbed the lonely trail on saddles undulating with the steady rhythm of their horses' steps, the sound of the hooves and exhalations of the

stallions added to the sense of silence and solitude of
the high elevations. It seemed like they were the only
two people in the whole wide world. Noose waited for
the woman to speak but had no idea what she would
say when or if she said it; half the time he was amazed
at what came out of the lady outlaw's mouth—she was
unpredictable, he'd give her that.

When finally Bonny Kate spoke after clearing her
throat, it was in a calm and reasonable manner. "The
difference between an outlaw and a lawman ain't so
large. I think you know that. Look how many outlaws became lawmen. Doc Holliday. Wyatt Earp. Look
at yourself. You ain't no stranger to the wrong side
of a gun."

Noose was surprised but also wasn't to hear Bonny
Kate still justifying herself; his words had not gotten
through to her and he should not have expected anything he said to change her. Some people knew the
difference between right and wrong and some didn't,
and the only reason Noose did was the ugly brand on
his chest that had forged a conscience into him at a
young age.

"That's true." Noose nodded, his expression saying
he wasn't proud of it. "But I ain't half the person Marshal Bess is and you ain't less than half of what she is.
Bess Sugarland's better than me. And she's better
than you, too."

As Bonny Kate perched cocked in the saddle, her
blue eyes sparkled as with a saucy little smile she studied Noose. "You like her."

"We're friends." When he looked over at her, Bonny
Kate held his gaze in her own like a warm fist. Noose
did not expect what she said next:

"She's in love with you, you know."

Noose was at a loss as warmth spread through his insides and flushed his face, which got suddenly hot.

"Ain't," was all he could say when he found the word to speak.

The lady outlaw beamed at him with a teasing affection and amusement. "I seen the way she looks at you."

"It ain't like that."

"I seen the way you look at her."

"Ain't nothing between us."

"Nothing but air, huh?"

"We're just friends." He nodded to himself. "Good friends, is all."

She laughed as if that was absurd. "Are you really so thick skulled you can't see how that lady feels about you?"

Hearing this from another woman, even a bad one like Bonny Kate, made Joe Noose's heart lift in a way he didn't understand but he showed no expression or tried not to. "She's way too good for the likes of me."

"You both are meant to be together, Joe. You do know that. If any two people in this world were made for each other, it's you and Bess."

He shifted awkwardly in the saddle, lips unable to form words.

"Why ain't you made a move on her?"

"It's complicated."

"Joe, that part of what goes on between men and women ain't complicated at all."

"I took something from Bess she can't get back."

"Her heart?"

"Her father."

"You killed her father?"

"Not me personally. But I might just as well have."

Noose looked ahead into the distance while he spoke but Bonny Kate could tell he was looking into the past as she watched him from her saddle. "Few months back, I disputed an illegal bounty claim made by that man Frank Butler and his boys. I had taken the fugitive in alive but the Butler Gang sneaked up and shot him then stole the body from me and took it to the Hoback U.S. Marshal's office to claim the reward. Just should have let it go. That's what I should have done. But the bounty was mine because I'd caught the guy. So I didn't let it go. Mostly, it was because Butler murdered this man in cold blood for no damn reason since I had captured the fugitive alive and unharmed. Butler probably figured it didn't make no difference because it was a dead-or-alive bounty but what he did was illegal and it was murder, pure and simple.

"Like I said, Bonny Kate, I didn't let it go because it didn't seem right. I followed them bounty killers to Hoback, where Bess's father was the marshal and she was his deputy and I brought the dispute to them, told the marshal the truth of what Butler done, just not figuring . . ." Noose trailed off. "Doesn't matter what I did or didn't figure, because on the spot Butler shot that marshal and framed me for his death, getting a fat reward put on my head and he and his gang rode after me to collect. I killed 'em all, but Bess lost her dad and she got shot and it's all my fault."

"You were trying to do the right thing, sounds to me." Bonny Kate was a good listener when she wanted to be.

"I'm responsible for Marshal Nate Sugarland getting murdered and even though I brought the men responsible to account, that won't bring Bess's dad back. That's on me."

"I don't think she blames you, Joe."

"She should."

"That's the past. It's history. You and her now, that's the present."

"I have to do right by Bess, got me an obligation to do what her father would have done now he ain't here."

"You ain't her dad, you're a man, a man who can love Bess and that's what she wants, you damn fool."

"I need to make it up to her, even if I never can."

"You think too much!" Rolling her eyes, Bonny Kate shook her head in exasperation. "Screw all that thinkin' an' hesitatin' nonsense. You gotta take what you want in this life. You love that woman. You know you do. She loves you. Take her. It's what she wants you to do, even if she ain't got the guts to say it."

In the saddle across from her, he just sighed and looked straight ahead, staring into space.

"You hear old Bonny Kate, Joe. You drop me off at the gallows then ride straight back to Jackson and marry that woman."

"I ain't the marrying kind."

"When you find a woman like Bess, you hold on and don't let go, Joe, don't ever let her go." Bonny Kate's eyes were tearing up, filled with emotion. It seemed important to her that Joe and Bess found love.

Noose looked at her, unsure of how to react to the raw, exposed look he saw in her eyes. He didn't know why Bonny Kate was saying all this or what she was getting at. So she spelled it out for him: "If there is any reason for you and me to be sharing this last ride, Joe, any reason fate brought us together, any higher purpose to our paths crossing, if there be anything for someone like me to impart to someone like you, it is this: to tell you to love that woman hard as she loves you until you draw your very last breath. Don't let her get away. Don't let that one go, Joe."

Noose watched her a long moment and didn't blink. "What do you know about love?"

Bonny Kate dropped her eyes, embarrassed of exposing her true feelings. "I know what it's like not to have love. There, I done said my piece, Joe, and if you're too dumb to take the gift of a condemned woman's advice then you're stupid. All men are stupid. I wouldn't have gotten as far as I done if men wasn't so stupid."

They rode on into woods in silence but something had changed between them as the roof of the sky began to dim.

CHAPTER 18

The sun was going down.

Joe Noose looked up at the sparkling red flares exploding through the tree branches, the crimson ball of fire moving behind the western pines flashing in and out of his eyes with each step of his horse. He gauged they had an hour of daylight left. Full dark in this part of Wyoming came fast this close to the Idaho border, he knew. The tree canopy would bring on darkness that much quicker. They were a mile from the top of the pass but wouldn't reach it today. Riding off the trail through the treacherously uneven pine woodlands was difficult enough during day hours and would be suicidal once night fell. The horses wouldn't make it ten yards before one put a hoof wrong and snapped a leg. The sanguine radiance of decreasing sunset deepened and shadowed in luminosity to paint the riders and horses and the trees towering around in one sinister color: a gruesome shade of blood, a hellish gory hue that even now was fading to black.

Scanning the surrounding woods in the failing light

from his saddle, Noose spotted a small clearing nearby
that looked like it might make a suitable campsite.

Swinging a glance over his shoulder, he saw Bonny
Kate Valance's ruddy face bathed in red twilight, the
glow infusing her red hair with witchy incandescence.

"We have to make camp," he said.

"Stop, you mean?" she replied.

"Can't ride in the dark. You know better than that."

"But they're coming. They're all still after us."

"They can't ride in the dark, neither."

The sun sank.

Looking nervously around herself with a shiver,
the woman pulled her coat tighter around her shoulders. "Good, I guess. Camping here, I mean. Lordy,
my ass hurts from all this riding and I'm getting cold.
Ain't you?"

"It ain't cold. Not yet."

"It will be good to get warm by a fire."

Noose shook his head slowly, firmly. "Ain't gonna be
no fire. That will point us out to those that's after us
like a signal flare. We're camping in the dark, because
dark is what it gets up here."

"You're making me look forward to getting hanged
so I can get this all over with."

"You'll get your wish soon enough. Tomorrow, if we
survive tonight."

She had no response to that.

He clicked his teeth and flipped the reins, steering
Copper for the small clearing under the lofty over-
hang of the pine trees and his horse trod toward it.
Bonny Kate followed cooperatively on her Appaloosa.
All around, the dense woods were growing quiet
and very still in the onset of nightfall. The shadows

deepened. The closer they rode, the more Noose saw he had picked a good spot. The area was flat and un-cluttered by roots. The brown pine-needle carpeted ground looked soft enough to make a reasonable ap-proximation of a bed. Best of all, there was a natural obstruction of a log on one side and tight growth of conifer trunks on the other that afforded a natural defense and cover. It would do.

In the branches high above, the chirp of birds and buzz of insects sensing the approaching nightfall created a noise that somehow added to the sense of silence. It was serene, restful even. For the first time since Joe Noose rose that morning and rode out of Jackson with his fateful cargo, Noose began to feel himself unwind and relax—he sat loose in his saddle, eager to get off his horse for a few hours.

The dark descended fast. The two horses and riders approached the clearing. Swinging out of the saddle, Noose swiftly tethered Copper's reins to the nearest suitable tree and patted his four-legged friend's nose. Copper showed its teeth and bucked its head in friendly response. Rounding on Bonny Kate, Noose saw she was still up on her horse, sitting in the saddle and looking around to get her bearings. From the calm ex-pression on her face, the camp seemed to suit her.

The last of the sunset winked out on the horizon, like a glint of red light on the sharp blade of a knife; a sudden gloom descended over the campsite as the red afterglow extinguished in the deep shadows' descent—it was very quick; the only remaining light was the faint crimson glimmer of the twilit sky barely glimpsed through the interlaced black skeletal silhou-ettes of the branches high above. Already, Noose could barely make out the bronze shadow of Copper standing by the tree.

"We're safer now than we've been the whole day. The dark just took care of that. I don't expect no trouble till dawn." Noose helped Bonny Kate off her horse, easing her to the ground, where she stretched her aching limbs.

"We at the top yet?" she asked.

"Hard to tell. Just about, I'd say. The trail is a few miles to our left and not being on that I can't say for sure, but my guess is an hour's ride at dawn and we'll arrive at the declination."

"Declination?"

"Means we'll be riding downward. On the Idaho side."

They made camp. Both sat across from each other as night fell and the world went dark.

"My last good night's sleep where I wake up to a new day." She stared off into space.

Noose looked at her grimly. "Waking up to a new day ain't guaranteed for nobody, Bonny Kate."

She gave him an ironic, melancholic smile. "Well, for me, *no days* after tomorrow is definitely guaranteed." She sat on the ground, knees pulled up to her chest, hugging her arms around them.

For a while, Noose didn't respond. "I'm sorry about that."

She just shrugged.

The quiet moment and relaxed surroundings as well as saddle fatigue had Noose in a reflective mood. "I don't know what to say, I suppose."

"You don't got to say nothing. You don't owe me nothing."

"Reckon all I can say is I hope you had a hell of a

time in this life. Don't know you too well, Bonny Kate, just a day, but you seem like you ain't that bad a sort. Definitely met worse. If what you say is true, or some of it is, then you've been wronged by them hanging you like they mean to. It ain't right. But it's the law, and it ain't for me to say."

Her smile was genuine. "Thank you."

It was his turn to shrug.

"You're okay, Joe Noose. Don't exactly understand you, but as males of the species go, you're okay in my book."

He grinned, then tipped his hat.

"I'm gonna cut you loose, Bonny Kate."

"Say *what*?" Her widened eyes gleamed in the moonlight.

"Gonna take the cuffs off, so you can sleep comfortable. You got a big day tomorrow, need your beauty rest to keep your wits about you."

"You trust me that much?"

Noose didn't answer, just edged forward on his big knees through the pine needles, drawing his key ring from his belt as he reached for her hands. "You ain't afraid I'm gonna run off?" she asked.

"Where to?" He gestured to the woods. All around them was pitch-darkness so stygian black the nearest trees ten feet away were visible only as lighter shadows against the darker impenetrability beyond. The moonlight did nothing to light the area.

"Grab your gun or something while you're asleep?" Bonny Kate asked as Noose inserted the key in her manacles and undid the lock. The shackles opened and the chains dropped with a muffled *clank* on the soft bed of pine needles. She rubbed her wrists.

The moonlight glinted on his cracked grin. "I ain't

gonna sleep. I'll be sitting right by that tree yonder with my eyes and ears open, standing watch."

"All night?"

"All night. So I ain't worried about you going for my gun, and it ain't you I'm staying up to watch out for anyway."

Noose settled back against the tree. He bit the cork out of a bottle of whiskey, took a swig, corked it, and tossed it over to Bonny Kate. She caught the bottle, took a deep swig, and whistled in satisfaction. "That warms a body right up." The lady outlaw tossed the whiskey back to Noose. "It's kind of nice without a fire. Just the moonlight. Cold and all, but nice."

"And safe."

"I feel safe."

Noose grunted in agreement. Soon he felt her eyes gleaming in the dark on him. Presently, Bonny Kate said, "So being as we got this time to spend together . . ."

He raised his gaze to meet hers, watching her evenly.

Bonny Kate took a deep sip then thought a minute before she recorked the bottle to throw it back over to Noose. She regarded him a moment. "You mind if I could sit next to you, Joe? Seems stupid us tossing this bottle back and forth, us keeping getting drunker because soon we'll miss and break the bottle and then there won't be no more whiskey."

"I'm not drunk."

"I'm getting there."

"You're fine where you are."

He held her raw, aching gaze. Finally she said, "Fine, you want me to say it, I will: This is my last night on earth. I want to sleep my last night in a man's arms. What's so wrong with that?"

Noose sighed, shifting uncomfortably. "Ain't a good idea, Bonny Kate."

"You think I'm gonna steal your gun and shoot you with it while you're asleep if you let me get close?"

"I told you I ain't sleeping tonight."

"Then, what you worried about?"

The two people sat across from each other in the camp in the middle of the woods, just outlines to each other in the dappled moonlight falling through the boughs. Noose could see her eyes shining in the dark, glittery with tears. "Ain't worried about nothing," he said defensively.

It was quiet for a while then he heard the woman's soft sobs and in the dim saw the heaving of her shoulders as she wept.

Noose shifted awkwardly. "C'mon, Bonny Kate. Don't do that."

Louder sobs and sniffles. He couldn't see her eyes anymore and it took him a few seconds to realize that was because her face was in her hands.

"Stop crying, will ya? C'mon, I hate to listen to a woman cry."

"I-it ain't you gonna hang tomorrow. I'm scared. I'm scared to die. It's only gonna be a few hours now. That's all the time I got left. I never felt so . . . alone. So terrible awful alone."

Regarding her bleak and dismal form in the shadows, Noose felt a tug on his heart, because the woman looked like a discarded little girl's rag doll, utterly bereft and forlorn. Unable to help himself, he set the bottle down and sat up, getting up on his haunches and approaching her in an unthreatening crouch.

She sat slumped, her hair over her hands pressed against her face, weeping uncontrollably in racking sobs.

Tentatively, Noose reached out and as gently as he knew how, took one of Bonny Kate's hands and pulled it toward him. "Come on. Come over here with me. I'm sorry. You can sit over here with me."

Her hand was limp in his, as if the strength and will to live had left her body. Noose was shaken up by how spent and fragile the woman appeared to be. Tenderly as he could manage, he pulled again and she didn't resist but it was like he was dragging an unconscious person. "Easy, lady," he said. Scooping her up off the ground in both big arms, one under her legs, the other under her shoulders, he rose to his feet, stood up straight, and carried her the fifteen feet across the camp to the big pine tree trunk he had been sitting against. There, Noose set her gently down with her back to the tree, with all the care he could muster. Her head hung limp, her froth of red hair about her shoulders. But as he released her hand she gave his a delicate squeeze, and there were signs of life in her again. Bonny Kate had stopped her crying, drying her wet face with the back of her other hand.

"Thank you," she said sweetly.

Leaning back against the tree, Noose slid to a sitting position beside Bonny Kate. Immediately, she rested her shoulder against his big left arm and laid her head against his chest. She felt warm and alive and her being this close to him was more agreeable than he cared to admit to himself, so he did not move.

With his right hand, he picked the bottle of whiskey up off the ground then bit out the cork. It was half-full, and the amber liquid sloshed around inside. They passed it back and forth as they sat together and watched the idyllic moon fingering through the branches of the forest canopy as minutes seemed to turn into hours, feeling the alcohol warm their insides with each swig. The soporific effect of the booze did not make Joe Noose drunk for his tolerance was high, but he felt himself feeling closer to Bonny Kate Valance than he had all day, as she lay against him.

All of a sudden, her lips were on his. Hot, moist, sweet.

Noose broke the kiss with Bonny Kate.

"Please," she begged.

"It's tempting, ma'am. It sorely is. But it ain't right."

She smeared her lips against his and threw her whole hot body behind it, wrapping her arms around his back but gently he pushed her way. The passion in her smoldering flesh radiated raw heat off her and Noose wanted the woman bad. It took all his will to break away. "I couldn't take advantage of you like that."

She grinned saucily. "Take advantage all you want, cowboy. Ain't like I'm gonna mind this time tomorrow. Girl's got to get her kicks while she can. Hell, it ain't like I'm gonna get with child."

"Sorry." He pulled back and watched her stonily. His face was a wall.

Bonny Kate cooled off, her rapid breathing slowing, at a loss for words. She regarded him incredulously. "Nobody's ever turned me down before."

"Let's just say you're not my type."

CHAPTER 19

The 2:13 train to Victor was scheduled to reach the station in less than an hour. That was the end of the line. The big Pacific Northern steam engine had a full head of steam on as it barreled across rural Idaho, nine cars long, pulling six passenger wagons, one horse truck, and the brake van. Its single headlight lanced through the gloom, steam and smoke belching from the locomotive's high stack. The train hurtled across the lonely landscape through the night, nearing the end of its long journey.

It was just past midnight. Bill Tuggle snapped his pocket watch shut and settled back on the hard seats of the passenger compartment as the coach rocked and shook around him as it clattered down the rails.

He looked down at the bag of Idaho potatoes in his lap. Idaho was known for its potatoes and he'd purchased a bag.

There was not a free seat on the train. The coach was packed, booked to capacity. Folks on this railroad were coming from far and wide for the hanging party. A watchful Tuggle scrutinized the cross section of people on the train, which made for an unlikely if interesting polyglot—farmer families with kids, cowboys with sidearms, reporters with notepads and box cameras and tripods stashed in the overhead compartments, fancy wealthy men in fine coats and top hats with their perfumed, groomed women in lace dresses and silk petticoats rubbing elbows with grubby, saddle-worn wranglers both male and female sitting side by side with them on the wooden seats. Nobody seemed to mind; they were all just waiting to get to the show many had traveled clear across the country to see.

Tuggle himself was a large, stocky man in his late forties, wearing a leather duster and rough gray felt shirt. His old cowboy boots were weathered and dusty, the spurs rusted, and the heat in the coach was making his feet swell painfully. Beneath a thick beard, the man's scarred, leathery face was tanned from the desert sun, where he spent most time. Thinking he had never been this far west before, the rugged man looked out the window at the passing moonlight forest rolling past. The spectacles he wore for distance were perched on his nose; he adjusted them. Big, handsome country, what he could see of it. His side of the train faced south and somewhat east, and Tuggle realized he was probably looking at this side of the Teton Pass. Down below, out of sight from this vantage, was the valley they called Jackson Hole. Occasionally there was a flash of sparks and cinders through the window as the wheels bit some rough section of track. Coal smoke would curtain off the view now and then only to blow clear and reveal the Idaho vista again, bathed in cold moonlight.

The muffled percussive timpani of the steel wheels

of the steam train on the rails and trestles below was a comforting, even soothing, sound—the steady *click-a-clack* of the wheels on the tracks combined with the rattle and sway of the wagon made Tuggle want to go to sleep but he couldn't do that; there was much work to do before dawn, and Bill Tuggle had a job to do.

It was why he was here. Why they were all here.

Swinging his gaze across to the six men in the weathered dusters or heavy coats seated beside him and across in the facing seats, Bill Tuggle saw a few of them getting rest. Hats tipped over eyes. A few snored. It had been a long, tedious train ride from Ohio. He wasn't worried about any of them. Not Jim Gannon, not Zane Flannery, not Horace Comstock, Luke Mesa, nor Mad Cow Hondo—they were professionals and would be ready when the time came.

Jack Varney, a husky ruddy-faced cowboy, was wide-awake. His dun brown eyes swiveled back and forth behind his perpetual squint, taking in the other passengers, watchful for any signs of trouble. He and Tuggle exchanged glances, both keeping an eye on things. Neither man wanted any surprises. Tuggle looked over the other people on the train again, saw the same mixed, incongruous bunch. Some men and women were very well dressed in the latest eastern fashions, wealthy personages who had boarded the train in Philadelphia, having come from as far as New York. Others were obviously journalists from various newspapers, judging by their cheap suits, bow ties, and the pads of paper and pens in their hands. Then there were the bedraggled-looking cowboys and ranch hands, some perhaps outlaws on the run. Nobody Tuggle recognized. Everybody was coming for the hanging.

Just like they were.

There were no lawmen or Pinkerton agents seated in the coaches, nobody who looked to create any trouble for Tuggle and his crew. Not that they couldn't handle any who did. Tuggle himself had done a perspicacious walk-through of all the passenger wagons each station they had stopped at during the two-day train ride, checking faces and clothes, but had spotted nobody who raised any red flags. He and his men had originally boarded in Hocking Valley, Ohio, and the last stop had been six hours ago in Salt Lake, Utah. The railroad compartments were full to capacity, and everybody was riding to the end of the line in Victor, where history was to be made with the snapping of the neck of the first female to be executed in the territory.

It amused Bill Tuggle to know he was going to be part of history . . . and they all said he would never amount to anything. For the next hour the man sat back and watched the view, reviewing the plan over and over in his mind, convinced they had covered every detail. Out the windows, in the darkness, the vast massifs of the mountainous Teton Pass rose against the sky.

Bonny Kate Valance was out there on the pass somewhere—he couldn't see her but he could feel her. It looked cold out there, through the window, and she must be freezing her damn ass off.

The train decelerated, its brakes locking as it slowed to pull into the Victor station. A distant steam whistle far off at the front of the train announced their arrival.

Tuggle looked out the window at the small settlement of the town slowly coming into view out of the wilderness and passing lazily by the slowing coach;

the hammered-together, threadbare buildings looked primitive and makeshift in the shadows under the cloudy moonlight. The place was just as he remembered it from the trip he took here two weeks ago. Tuggle had memorized the layout of Victor and scribbled a map on a thumb-worn notebook but there wasn't much to commit to memory—it was a whistle stop of an outpost, built up around the railroad junction and the road to the Teton Pass that led to Jackson, the biggest town in the area. People came to one on their way to the other. Victor was a place people mostly passed through.

The man eyeballed the familiar buildings as the train decelerated. There was the feed store. There, the corral. The streets were deserted at this time of night. This was good. Once the passengers on the train got off, he and his men would get the horses, put them in the corral, and get to business directly. He and his men had not booked rooms like the other passengers because they would not be sleeping tonight. It would be in and out, and they would be long gone by sunset, if everything went according to plan.

No reason it wouldn't.

The steam train slowed to a crawl and pulled into the station. There it was.

The gallows.

The foreboding structure slowly rolled past the train in the town square, unoccupied at present. The dangling noose swung lazily in the night breeze, a curlicue shape in the darkness.

It looked like some effort had been expended building it. The fools could have spared themselves the trouble.

The streets would be empty again in a half hour, once the passengers had checked in to their accommodations, and the streets would be theirs. They had work to do and a plan to execute.

As the locomotive lurched to a stop there was a hiss of steam and a smoky haze wafted over the windows, obscuring the view of the town outside.

The door to the passenger coach opened and a conductor stepped in. He addressed the people inside. "Victor. Last stop. Everybody off. Please watch your step."

We're here, Tuggle thought. *Time to get 'er done.*

His six associates were all awake now, exchanging alert glances, blending in with the other passengers who rose from their seats and rubbed shoulders, grabbing their luggage. Comstock was helpfully assisting an old woman with her satchel. Tuggle and his crew looked like any other bunch of cowboys come to town to work a local ranch or hire on to wrangle cattle or sheep in Jackson after a ride across the pass. They had no luggage other than the arsenal of Winchester and Henry rifles and belts of ammunition they had concealed under their long coats.

Plus the bag of potatoes.

Tuggle took the spuds with him as he rose from his seat. The seven men filed with the others out of the passenger coach. Stepping onto the forward platform, they breathed in the refreshing cold, crisp Idaho night air before disembarking in single file formation, descending the metal gangway behind the tender and locomotive wreathed in hazy clouds of steam expelled from the brakes. Their large, imposing silhouettes were dark shapes in the billowing steam, mysterious figures rim lit by the lunar brilliance of the moon above in the star-spangled skies of the Far West.

The rest of the passengers waited in a small mob on the platform, milling around, waiting for the porter to bring them their baggage.

The seven men did not wait.

Instead they marched to the back of the train, where the horse truck was, five cars down. The doors to the wagon were opened by a trainman and a wooden ramp was dropped, then one by one, seven big warhorses, fully saddled and tacked, were led down to the platform to their waiting owners, who saddled up.

Without a word exchanged, they rode into town directly.

CHAPTER 20

Noose didn't remember nodding off.

Only that he was having the nightmare again, the one he so often had he would never be rid of . . .

Always Noose feels the heat first, hotter and hotter, not like a dream but like reality, as it had been . . . that sizzling red-hot brand getting closer and closer . . . In the dream Joe Noose is just a boy again, underage, branded because he was too young to hang like his friends had been that terrible night . . . the old man's severe hooked face and hard pitiless eyes without a trace of mercy . . . his eyes glow in the light of the coal fire with little flames and sparks dancing in the retinas . . . the blazing Q brand ever nearer, glowing like melted metal behind the heat waves . . . the old man's shot-apart hand with no thumb or forefinger . . . a disfigured chicken claw of a hand clutching the fiery brand over young Noose's chest, and he can't escape it because he is tied down with rope . . . "You don't know right from wrong, good from bad, do you, boy?" . . . The faces of the two frightened small boys standing behind the old man, their father . . . "My sons have me to teach them right from wrong but you never had nobody to show you good from bad, and that puts you at a powerful disadvantage." Noose

*remembers those two dark towheaded boys now, the intense
fear in their impressionable gaze being forced to watch a boy
their age being branded, but the old man makes them watch
as he leans over Noose, his eyes reflecting the campfire flames,
his evil soul lit by hell from within . . . "You're too young
for me to hang 'cause you ain't a man yet and it's wrong to
kill a boy. You're still a boy but you ain't ever gonna be a man
'less you learn right from wrong, son. A man with no conscience is an animal, no better than cattle, and cattle get
branded." . . . The Q brand smoking and glowing as the old
man presses the hot brand hard against young Noose's chest
and holds it there, pressing harder and burning Noose to
where he can smell his own skin sizzling like charbroil . . . the
searing brand feels like it is roasting its way right through his
whole body, setting his heart on fire . . . he is screaming as
the old man presses down on the handle of the brand and
puts his mark permanent on the boy's chest with it . . . finally
he takes the iron off and throws a bucket of water over the boy
and leaves the brand etched in Noose's chest for all time . . .
In his dream the nights he has it, Noose always sees the
smoking Q on his chest . . . but not tonight . . . tonight he
sees the faces of the old man's two young sons, his own age,
one a bit older than the other, their eyes horror holes forced to
watch him get branded . . . and Noose feels sorry for that old
man's sons even more than he does for himself . . .*

  "Thanks for keeping her warm for me."
  The voice woke Joe Noose suddenly and he
snapped open his surprised eyes to see Johnny Cisco
wearing a big old grin, looking him square in the
eyeballs. The barrel of the Colt Dragoon pistol in
the shootist's hand looked as big as a cannon. Then the
outlaw's finger pulled the trigger, there was a huge,

3:35. Tuggle snapped closed his watch. The whole town was getting some shut-eye so folks could be rested for tomorrow's big event less than eight and a half hours away . . . the hanging by the neck until dead of the notorious female outlaw Bonny Kate Valance.

The seven men were weary from travel but had no plans on resting this night. They had work to do. Everything had been rehearsed. They each knew their jobs.

Sunrise would be in three hours, and they needed to be in place by then.

Tuggle gestured with a brisk hand signal and the men on the big horses moved forward at a slow stealthful trot, Stetson hats pulled down over their eyes. Varney, Gannon, Flannery, Comstock, Mesa, and Hondo rode alertly behind their leader.

The layout of the town was very familiar to them, for it had been scoped out earlier in the week by Tuggle, who blended in with the other people that had come to Victor. Tuggle had drawn them a map when he returned to Ohio a few days later and made them commit it to memory. There wasn't much to the place, just a few streets and a square and a train station. Across town in the distance, the darkened behemoth of the steam train sat at repose, hulking and motionless against the stars, like a slumbering dinosaur, moonlight gleaming off the black-iron-and-steel Pacific Northern locomotive. As they were in most of the other buildings in the rest of Victor, all the lights in the train cars were extinguished.

The street ahead the seven men rode down T-boned into a side street to the left, and a soft burnished glow in the square shape of a window loomed large against the opposite storefront. Tuggle could see from his saddle that would be the light from the sheriff's office next to the jail. No surprise there, since none of the men who just rode into town expected the Victor constabulary to be sleeping on the job. Not this of all nights.

Even ridden quiet, the horses were making noise and the men did not want to attract unwanted attention, so the sooner they were on foot, the better. The town corral would be around the corner to the right, down a block, across from the train tracks. The plan was to go to the stable directly, stash the horses, then do what they came here to do. Tuggle put two fingers together and pointed the way. Careful and quiet, the men rode very slowly around the corner onto the next street, staying to the shadows, which were plentiful.

Nobody had spotted them, as far as they could see.

Three minutes later, the seven men had ridden down the side street that kept them parallel with the stationary steam train, looming huge and dark against the buckshot pattern of bright stars in the clear night sky. No light came on in the windows of the wagons, and the horses were not making too much noise. Ahead, the gated fence of the corral and stables grew closer, the heads and bodies of many unsaddled horses jam-packing the stockade coming into view. The owner of the corral was getting all the business he could handle from the care and feed of the dozens of horses carrying the spectators who had come from far and wide to witness the first hanging of a woman in the territory, or maybe it was the whole United States, Tuggle wasn't sure. One thing he was certain of was that this corral would be almost twice as full when the rest of the folks came to town that morning. Luckily, it looked like there was room to put their horses, if not much.

The single file line of riders stopped their horses at the gate, and Tuggle dismounted, barely making a sound. He kept his movements to a minimum, patiently crossing to the gate and unhitching it. The men received blank or disinterested stares from rows of sleepy equine faces as one by one the men led their horses into the corral and shut the gate. All of the steeds were in the stable now. Moving with the smooth precision of a well-oiled machine, each of the seven men unbuckled their saddles and removed them with the tack from their horses, then carefully carried their gear into the large, darkened barn and stowed them on the wall pegs by the hay bales. Numerous empty saddles were already hung there, of all sizes and expenses. Tuggle doubted when the owner of the corral checked the barn and corral when the sun rose he would even notice the added horseflesh and saddles because so many were already in his place.

With that the men departed, taking nothing with them from their saddles and saddlebags but their guns—an arsenal of pistols, rifles, and shotguns, and enough ammunition of different calibers to fight an army. Tuggle opened the bag of potatoes and handed each one of his men two spuds, which they pocketed. Loaded down with firearms and cartridges, the seven men slipped out of the barn into the cold clear air of the night, back into the shadows again.

The Victor sheriff's office was quiet and dark, glowing amber shadows jumping in the flicker of the oil

lamp on Sheriff Albert Shurlock's desk. The small
room was fragrant with the smell of fresh brewing
coffee, a toasty scent from the stovetop fire of the
small cast-iron potbellied stove where the coffeepot
bubbled. The lawman was drinking a lot of it because he needed to stay up all night, and he was a
little on edge.

He was going to be plenty angry if Bonny Kate
wasn't delivered as promised. The Jackson U.S. Marshal's office had telegraphed two days ago the prisoner
had set out under armed accompaniment of a deputy
marshal and she was due to arrive this morning. As it
happened, Shurlock knew the man who landed the
assignment—Joe Noose, whom he had done business
with several times and whom Shurlock personally
knew as the toughest and most reliable bounty hunter
he had ever known. So if Noose was in charge of the
escort duties, the female should be here on time and
in one piece because Noose had a reputation for bringing them in alive. The ride across the pass was two
days in the summer—it could take weeks in the winter
but that was six months off. The Victor sheriff was
confident he'd see Joe Noose riding in with Bonny
Kate Valance right around breakfast time, and had
no doubt her hanging would proceed on schedule
at noon.

But it was late, he was jittery from too much coffee,
and the town was so damn quiet—the mind plays
tricks. His stomach was tied in knots, dreading that
something was going to happen. If anything did, he
would be out of a job. The whole damn town of
Victor was full of out-of-towners, over a hundred reporters and visitors from across the country who had

come out to see the hanging. They'd come in by horse, by buggy, mostly by train. Victor's railway line connection had been one of the reasons the town had been selected as the site of the hanging because the politicians and the state capital had wanted to make a big show. The hotels in Victor were full. The restaurants were sold to capacity. Homes were being rented and the owners were charging exorbitant rates to people who had traveled here. The carnival atmosphere had been in full swing the whole last week and the town was raking in money. The economy of the little outpost was booming, and the township of Victor was officially on the map.

But Sheriff Shurlock couldn't help but worry and fret at his desk during the Hour of the Wolf—the name for the anxiety-prone hours after midnight his Swedish relatives called this time of night. What would happen if anything went wrong and the hanging didn't come off as planned? Let alone if it was because of something he and his deputies did or didn't do that he could or should have done as the local lawman in charge on whose shoulders the responsibility fell.

The sheriff of Victor sipped his coffee and regarded his haggard reflection in the window to the empty street outside, the glow of the gas lamp creasing his craggy face with shadow as beyond the glass the street was a void, black as pitch. Shurlock was alone in the office. His young deputy Bob Fisk he could hear sweeping up the empty cell in the jail next door, getting it cleaned up and ready for the brief stay of its new occupant in just a few hours. The sheriff's other older and more seasoned three deputies, Bill Sturgis, Lewis Chance, and Martin Fullerton, were armed and out on patrol, walking the streets and keeping an eye on things. All three were due to return shortly. They'd check in, have a cup of coffee, and go out again—mostly because there wasn't much else to do but wait until sunrise. Maybe he'd switch off with Sturgis or Chance and take the next patrol so he could stretch his legs and get some fresh air, because sitting around the tiny office thinking too much was making him nutty.

It sure was quiet.

Rolling a cigarette in his tired fingers, Deputy Lewis Chance was a little distracted as he turned the corner onto 4th Street. The rangy Idaho lawman was bored, this having been the fifth time in the last hour he had patrolled the darkened block. There wasn't a soul in sight, not even a dog. The wooden one- and two-story buildings stood dark and still against the dim moonlight. The sounds of his own footfalls were all he heard. Licking the paper and tapping in the last of his tobacco, he rolled up the cigarette and put it to his lips, striking a match. Puffing smoke, he resumed his rounds, looking up at the darkened windows on the Rose Hotel. Through the closed doorway, he saw the front desk was empty, all the staff gone home or asleep. The night was cool, but the town was so empty it felt like he was out in the country, which he practically was. Normally he enjoyed solitude, but the long hours he had been working for Sheriff Shurlock with the hanging come to town, and all the people who had poured into the small five-block community had frayed his nerves the last week.

Chance hadn't gotten much sleep what with all the celebratory atmosphere and was half-awake on his feet. His two Navy pistols hung heavy and untouched in his holsters, weighing him down. Just to be thorough, he peered down the alleys but they were just as empty now as they had been the last five times he had checked. A few minutes ago, Deputy Chance had strolled past the corral, and it looked quiet if filled with more horses than he had ever seen in town—and nothing looked out of the ordinary. One more patrol of the streets the sheriff assigned him and Chance would head back to the office and get a much-needed cup of coffee. His dusty boots were the only sound he heard as he walked wearily around the corner into the town square, and there it was.

The gallows.

The platform and crossbeam with the dangling noose reared black and foreboding against the night sky, an instrument of death lying in repose.

The sight of it chilled him.

It was a woman they were killing today.

Chance wasn't comfortable with that. Sure, he'd heard all the stories about the notorious Bonny Kate Valance and about the many men she had supposedly shot in cold blood—the talk was she would as soon murder you as bed you—but she was a woman, nonetheless. The way he was raised, society didn't raise a hand to a lady, let alone execute one. It wasn't right. The twentieth century was almost upon him as the 1800s came to a close and this was a new world, and killing women seemed to be part of it. Certainly that was the example all the politicians were trying to set. As far as Lewis Chance of Victor, Idaho, was concerned, if they had to do it, he damn sure wished they hadn't chosen to spill a woman's blood in his town, where he made his home.

A long, ominous shadow of the gallows in the moonlight passed across him as the lawman walked by, and he shivered, feeling like he was whistling past the graveyard. He hurried out of the square, feeling the air grow suddenly colder.

Chance knew the hangman. His neighbor and friend Jethro Askew had been tasked with the job, having served as an executioner during the Civil War. He was a good man, although a quiet and introspective one, who worked as the town grocer with his wife, Mary. If today's duty putting the rope around the neck of a woman bothered Askew, he didn't let on, but as Deputy Chance walked past the hangman's house just past the town square, he was guessing Askew wasn't getting a lot of sleep tonight, either. The lawman picked up his pace as he approached the house, figuring if he saw a light on, he'd stop by and offer a few words of fellowship to his friend.

A few steps farther and the deputy saw that past the picket fence the hangman's house was dark, and he felt relieved that Askew was at least getting a good night's sleep before the big day.

And that's when he saw the back door hanging open.

Jethro Askew always closed and locked the doors and windows of his house at night for protection—one of the few in town who did. The war had made him cautious and circumspect—no way he would leave it open, especially with all the strangers in town.

Something was wrong.

Drawing his revolver, Chance grew alert and looked over the exterior of the small frame home as he stepped through the gate and approached the back porch. Not a sound did he hear. No movement. He looked left and right, moving the pistol back and forth in a slow sweep where the barrel went where his nose went. His boots creaked on the loose boards of the porch when he reached it. Chance touched the open door and swung it open all the way. Inside, the one-room living area and kitchen was very dark except for a will-o'-the-wisp shaft of moonlight treacling through the lace curtains.

"Jethro? Mary? It's Chance."

Silence.

That's when he saw the blood glinting blackly on the walls above the shot-away head of the familiar body of the man lying dead on the floor.

But he hadn't heard any gunshots.

A creak of a floorboard sounded to his rear.

Deputy Lewis Chance felt the men behind him before he saw their faces as he turned too late, raising the barrel of his pistol. He felt the bullet smash through his chest. He felt himself hit the floor. In his remaining few seconds of consciousness before he died, Deputy Lewis Chance wondered why he never heard the gunshot and why the hell he was covered with wet chunks of potato fragments.

His men were late.

Sheriff Shurlock was up and pacing, his nerves raw.

Chance, Sturgis, and Fullerton should have been back by now. It wasn't like his deputies to be tardy, and all they had to do was a quiet walk-around through the town. The lawman looked at the clock on the wall. Twenty minutes ago they should have returned. The front door to the sheriff's office was cracked open to let in the cool night air, there hadn't been any noises outside, and Shurlock had ears like a bat. The town had been silent, the streets deserted. He was going to have a word with these boys. If one or more of them had fallen asleep . . .

His coffee cup was empty. The fresh pot was percolating on the cast-iron stove. Time for a refill. Tossing a glance to Bob Fisk, who had returned from cleaning the cell, the sheriff saw his deputy was now lazing in a chair, wearily whittling a stick with his knife, trying to stay awake.

"Coffee, Bob?"

"No thanks, Sheriff."

"Looks like you could use a cup. Don't be nodding off on me." Shurlock scowled at the young man.

The deputy sat bolt upright. "I'm awake, sir. I'll take the next patrol. Aren't the boys supposed to be back by now?"

"Yes, they are," the sheriff said, carrying his empty coffee cup to the front door and sticking his head out, looking both ways.

"Here they come. About damn time," Shurlock grumbled to Fisk as he watched the street.

Up the block, he saw the silhouettes of three men in the familiar baggy clothes and deputy-issued lawman vests. Shurlock couldn't make out their faces halfway down the block in the dim, but didn't need to. Badges gleamed on their chests. Sturgis, Chance, and Fullerton were on their way back, finishing their rounds, carrying their guns at ease and coming toward the office in a casual stroll. The cold, stark moonlight behind them extended and exaggerated their elongated shadows on the dirt street in front of them.

The sheriff waved, relieved.

The figures waved back.

Stepping back inside the office, Shurlock turned his back on the door and poured himself a fresh cup of coffee. It would be daylight soon and in a few hours it would all be over, he was thinking.

Behind him he heard the door creak open and the sound of jingling spurs.

He didn't remember his deputies had their spurs on.

Then he saw the stricken look of surprise on Bob Fisk's face and the color drain from his cheeks like milk from a pail.

The sheriff rounded, the coffee cup in his gun hand preventing him from reaching for his holstered Colt Dragoon.

Three strangers wearing his deputies' clothes were standing inside the doorway. All three had big pistols leveled and cocked. They had unshaven, hard faces and cold, dead eyes.

The one in the front, the leader, took a step forward. Putting his finger to his lips in a hushing gesture, he made an upward motion with the barrel of his pistol and Shurlock and Fisk put their hands up and didn't say a word.

The sheriff of Victor wasn't unduly concerned. Didn't think he would get shot. He didn't know who these men were or what they wanted but he was fairly certain they would not dare fire off their guns and make all that noise in a town so full of people. He could see in the leader's cunning eyes he wasn't stupid.

What he saw next was very peculiar.

The leader holding the Remington .40-44 revolver with the eight-inch muzzle reached into his own pocket and pulled something out . . .

A spud potato.

He brought it to his narrow mouth and bit off the end with a *crunch*.

Then he screwed the potato slowly over the barrel of his pistol with a *squeak squeak squeak*.

He pulled the trigger.

There was no gunshot only a muffled *pffft* as the potato exploded into moist fragments as it smothered the discharge of the weapon.

Sheriff Albert Shurlock was shot right between the eyes. He collapsed on the fire of the open stove, knocking over the coffeepot, which doused the flames as the fresh coffee spilled, sparing the shocked face of the corpse burn disfigurement.

Across the room, Deputy Bob Fisk did a lot of praying, getting on his knees and shaking all over as the leader of the gunmen produced another potato, bit off the end, spat it out, and slowly and deliberately screwed it on the wet, steaming barrel of his revolver.

When he pulled the trigger again and blew Fisk's brains out, the floor was covered with chunks of spud but there had been no noise.

The triggerman Tuggle grinned: "Idaho is known for its potatoes."

CHAPTER 22

Joe Noose's eyes blinked open.

It was later but still night. The pain in his chest ached bad, real bad, but he did not have a bullet in him, Noose knew that right away.

Why not? He had been shot point-blank.

He took inventory. Not moving a muscle, he sensed the feeling in all his extremities, knowing he was intact. He played dead, because that tricky shootist thought he was dead and Noose didn't want to dissuade him of the notion.

Eyes slitted, Noose looked down at his chest. That slug sure had put a big enough hole in his coat, but through that hole, he saw metal glint.

Bent metal.

The deputy marshal badge had taken the bullet, blocking the slug from penetrating his flesh. The six-star steel plating absorbed the impact. With a slight tilt of his head, Noose could see the flatted slug crammed into the crumpled badge that caught it like a baseball in a glove.

Noose figured he had Bess Sugarland to thank for making him wear the badge.

He had her to thank for a lot of things.

His chest still hurt like hell, but his head was clearing and his mind assessing his current situation, the first step to formulating a survival plan.

To start with, Noose was slumped against the tree in a sitting position. From the sledgehammering numbness in the back of his skull, he rightly assumed that his head hitting the trunk had knocked him out, not the bullet that blew him off his feet against the tree itself.

His eyes slid sideways, then down.

His holsters were empty. Guns and knife gone. Not good.

Where was his prisoner?

He saw no sign of Bonny Kate Valance in the darkness, and it was too dark to see anything anyway on the pass.

So he listened instead. Hard.

A man's and a woman's soft voices spoke somewhere nearby. Difficult to make out.

Still playing dead until he had a handle on the situation, Noose risked a slight turn of his head to the left. The voices came from that direction. It had to be Bonny Kate and Cisco. The voices were raised in argument, so both were probably not looking his way. Whatever the verbal sparring was about sounded like some urgent business between the two of them. Despite what Bonny Kate Valance had said about her lovers' relationship with Johnny Cisco, it sure didn't sound like a lovers' spat.

This was business.

The ringing in Noose's ears evaporated. His ears were regaining their hearing after the deafening close-range blast of the Colt Dragoon that felled him. The voices were coming from his left side, beyond his field of vision. Noose could make out some words . . .

"—*Money?*—"

"—*Kiss my ass!*—"

"—*Hid it! . . . Gonna tell me or*—*!*"

That's when the female voice started screaming in raw agony.

Cisco was putting the hurt on her. The brutal tone of his savage voice was that of a man with murder in his heart.

Noose had no choice but to look. Couldn't risk playing dead much longer. He had a job to do: save Bonny Kate Valance's life and stop this man from killing her so he could get her to the hangman and they could kill her. Didn't make much sense but that was his job. Sometimes you don't make the rules, you just try to play by them.

Snapping his head left, Joe Noose witnessed a terrible, shocking sight.

In the clearing less than a hundred yards away, Bonny Kate Valance was suspended horizontally three feet above the ground. Her ankles and feet were roped together and tied off to the trunk of a big tree. Her extended arms and roped wrists and hands were tied by lasso to the saddle of a huge, mean mustang. The horse was taking another small step forward, adding tensile tension to the tight ropes already pulled taut, straining the female outlaw's arms and legs in her shoulder and hip sockets, stretching her spine to the breaking point. The ghastly crackling sounds of tortured cartilage and tendons were audible. Bonny

Kate's face was contorted in anguish, tears of pain streaming from her clenched-shut eyelids, teeth gritted against the awful keening mewl forced up from her throat. She was being drawn and quartered!

Sitting backward on the saddle of his horse, legs spread, smoking a cigarette, was Johnny Cisco. He puffed and tickled his horse's flanks with his spurs in sadistic amusement as his merciless cold lizard eyes stared down at the lady outlaw roped to his horse. Noose could see one thing plain from the fearsome, pitiless expression on Cisco's narrow face: this was a very angry man who had been wronged by this woman and he wanted his pound of flesh—and wanted something else. The shootist's eyes were dead. "You're gonna tell me what I want to know, bitch, or I'm gonna spur my stud here and rip you apart."

Whipping her head in fury, Bonny Kate found the gumption to spit at him, but she missed.

"Spitfire hellion. Still got that sauce. Can't say I haven't missed that spirit. But I want my money you stole, Bonny Kate Valance, and you're going to tell me where you hid that hundred thousand dollars."

Joe Noose's brow furrowed as he listened closely. From this distance he could see Bonny Kate was biting her lip so she didn't talk.

"Still not talking? Okay." Cisco scowled. He whistled through his teeth and drove his left spur like a blade into the flank of his mustang. The horse took a step forward and the ropes squeaked with torque as they jerked Bonny Kate's arms in the shoulder sockets. She screamed in pure agony, writhing in pain. Noose winced as he heard something in her crackle and crack, cartilage or bone, he couldn't tell.

The feral outlaw, still facing backward in the saddle, fiercely pulled the reins and halted the stallion.

"Stop it, stop it. I'll talk, I'll tell you everything." Bonny Kate wept. "Please don't kill me. Please don't hurt me anymore."

Cisco snorted smoke. "You're a coldhearted bitch, Bonny Kate Valance, and that's a fact. I rode with you six long years. I was your best gun. Got in the way of bullets for you. And I thought you loved me. Ain't that what you said to me? But you can look a man in the eye and lie like it was a truth. You left me and the boys back there in that crap Arizona town and took all the money without looking back, leaving your gang to get shot to pieces by that sheriff after it was you who shot his boy in the back and then blamed me. You broke my heart, Bonny Kate, busted it to pieces and that was bad. But you stole my money, everybody's money, from that train robbery and that was worse. I want that money. I know you got it hid. You're a piece of work, lady. It's bad enough there's one of you in this world, but if you don't tell me where you stashed my loot, give me the exact location, I'm gonna spur this here horse and there's going to be *two* of you but *both* will be *dead*."

Seeing the icy outlaw's attention was on his female accomplice tied between his horse and the tree and guessing the two of them still had plenty to talk about, Noose made his move. Sparse moonlight trickled through the tree canopy and he sat in a pool of shadow. Noose knew it would hurt when he stood up and was already braced for the pain, locking his jaw shut so he wouldn't grunt or otherwise make a sound and attract attention. It hurt, all right. Hurt plenty. As his muscular legs lifted him upright a shooting agony tore through his chest and his teeth ground as he swallowed a scream—he could hear his molars grind. Then he was done. Joe Noose was on his feet, leaning against the tree for support, feeling the blood rush back into his legs. Then he put one foot in front of the other and advanced.

"What do you want me to say?" Bonny Kate choked, spitting blood.

"I want you to come clean. For once in your life, Bonny Kate, I want to hear the truth come out of your mouth. While you still draw a breath."

A shaft of lunar light through the leaves carved a harsh pattern of illumination on Bonny Kate's pallid face and she looked like a waxwork. The luminescence glinted off the spur on Cisco's boot poised by his waiting horse's flank, ready to kick the steed into motion and spectacularly end the lady outlaw's life with grisly and horrific sadism. Noose moved like a cat, slowly creeping toward the scene in the adjacent clearing, careful to stay in the shadows and watching where he stepped. His gaze swung left and right across the ground, looking for a weapon of any kind, his gaping holsters light on his hips, mocking him. Nothing but leaves and twigs on the forest floor, not even a branch big enough to use as a club. Noose clenched and unclenched his cement-block fists—he was going to have to go bare-handed against the armed shootist and that meant he was going to have to get in close, real close, right next to Cisco to grab him, or if he had a chance, snatch a pistol from the man's holster if he was quick and tricky enough. Just fifty yards to go now, but soon he would be in Johnny Cisco's line of sight.

Noose could hear them clearly now and Bonny Kate

was doing a lot of talking. "Okay, okay, yes. I did steal
the money, all of it. It was your money and the gangs'.
The sheriff and his lawmen had you boxed and the
money was just sitting there and I saw my opportunity
and I took it. There, I said it. You happy now? I took
it. Grabbed the money. Got on my horse and rode."

"You never even looked back. Not once."

"What was there to see?"

The shadowed figure of the lean, leathery cowboy
slowly shook his head, hissing in disgust. "Just us getting cut to pieces."

"I was looking ahead."

"Well, it's like they say, Bonny Kate, don't look
behind you because something might be gaining.
Looks like I caught up. You're getting what's coming
to you."

"We all get what's coming to us."

"You stashed the money someplace before they
caught you. Where's it hid?"

"Idaho."

"Where in Idaho? It's a big state." Cisco's yellowed
teeth flashed in a cynical grin.

Something glittered on the ground. Noose saw
moonlight glint off glass.

A whiskey bottle. Half-full and corked. Amber liquid
gleamed in the dark glass. It gave Noose an idea. He
picked up the bottle and ducked silently behind a tree.

Just around the other side of the trunk not twenty
yards away Johnny Cisco tortured his horribly strung-
up cohort for information. "By a river. Under a pile
of rocks. I can take you there," she croaked. Rope
creaked. Bonny Kate mewled in pain.

Pulling out the cork, Joe Noose yanked the ker-
chief from his neck and plugged up the opening of

the whiskey bottle with the cloth, turning the bottle quickly upside down so the alcohol soaked the rag. Then he reached into his pocket and pulled out a match, striking it with his thumb in a flash of flame under the booze-soaked handkerchief, and the cloth burst into flame.

At the sound of the struck match and flare of fire-light, Johnny Cisco swung his surprised gaze to the tree, already drawing his Colt Dragoon revolver from his holster but by then the burning whiskey bottle was already in flight as Joe Noose leapt out from behind the tree and heaved the weapon at the shootist's head. Before Cisco could raise his gun the blazing whiskey bottle hit him between the eyes with stunning force, exploding to smithereens of shattering glass and splattering burning alcohol that doused his head and torso with liquid fire as he went up in shrieking, screaming flames. The wet blaze of booze splashed all over the leather saddle and cloth saddle blanket and both those ignited in a fiery roar.

Johnny Cisco dropped his pistol and it fell on the ground as he swatted at the whooshing flames on his hair and face and arms as he turned into a human torch.

The mustang suddenly began to rear, pawing the air with its front hooves in terror as the horse began to be burned by the flaming saddle and blanket strapped to its midriff. The panicking stallion's withers were already licked with orange flames and smoke as it tossed its rider from his backward perch on the saddle. Cisco's boot got tangled in the stirrup as the outlaw plunged in a smoking fireball off the horse, his billowing arms and legs thrashing in agony as he emitted hideous high-pitched shrieks. The burning man landed on the ground hard, his leg stuck in the stirrup snapping with a loud *pop*. He was done for. Noose could already smell the ugly stench of burning human flesh.

Bonny Kate Valance threw a desperate anxious glance to Joe Noose as the violent lunging of the rearing horse jerked the ropes on her hands and feet brutally taut, pulling her arms and legs out of their bone sockets. She screamed her lungs out, feeling herself pulled apart.

A pair of big hands grabbed the rope.

Leaping to her rescue, Joe Noose got between Bonny Kate and the horse and caught the rope in both huge fists, holding fast, digging both spurred boot heels into the dirt and throwing his full weight and might into stopping the mustang from advancing. Whinnying in pain and fear as the blazing empty saddle strapped to its back spat flames into its scorched and blackened hide, the horse tried to bolt but Noose struggled to hold it in place. The roasted figure of Johnny Cisco, covered head to foot in leaping fire, half on, half off the mustang with his boot still trapped in the stirrup, was tossed like a fiery rag doll as he pawed the ground with his charred crisped hands.

"Help! Help me!" Bonny Kate screamed.

Noose's boots were dragged in the dirt, his buried heels dredging up soil with each lunging movement of the horse but he hung tight to the rope and pulled back on the mustang with every ounce of strength he had, his face contorted and teeth gritted with the effort, the veins bulging in his neck.

The knot of the rope on the saddle pommel was on fire, blackened and burning in the licking tongues of flames jumping from the steaming blanket beneath the alcohol-soaked leather. With a few ferocious jerks of his heavily muscled arms, Noose snapped the flaming rope apart at the blaze point, showering cinders. The tension went slack and Bonny Kate dropped heavily onto the ground in a cry of pain, with Noose falling on top of her.

He covered her body protectively and they both locked their glances on the untethered horse as it broke away and galloped into the forest, dragging Johnny Cisco by the boot of his shattered foot lodged in the burning saddle. His eyes were roasting in his skull looking right at them as he shrank away, scarecrow face contorted in a ghastly rictus within the ball of fire that consumed his head and body. His body, still alive and thrashing, was a second smaller fireball alongside the larger ball of flame that was the horse, now fully ablaze as it took off through the raw fuel of flammable tinder of the drought-dry forest.

As the burning, bellowing stallion brushed against the packed trunks and branches of the rows of pines it passed during its escape, the flames pouring off the saddle instantly set the woods alight like kindling, igniting a raging inferno as combustions of fire exploded in the trees that lit other trees, the ground behind the mustang erupting in a devil trail of flames in the horse's wake as the dragged, fiery corpse of the shootist set the dry pine needles ablaze.

Sweeping Bonny Kate Valance up into his arms, Joe Noose quickly began to untie the knots of rope on her ankles, freeing her from her bonds. Both watched the fiery runaway horse as if hypnotized by the nightmarish surreal sight of the burning, lunging stallion running in a crazy wide circle of blazing agony through the forest around them, torching the trees in a ring of fire in its flight. The fireball dead body of the outlaw was swung left and right behind the horse like a medieval cavalry weapon, his shattered body colliding with trunks and bushes, and everything the burning corpse hit went up in flames.

Smoke was thickening in the air as Noose staggered away back toward their horses with Bonny Kate swooned in his arms. It was bright enough to see now: the entire surrounding area of woods pulsed with evil orange light that glimmered and danced through the branches, a hellish glare glowing brighter and hotter by every passing second.

The forest was a deadly inferno, growing in size and danger as the runaway horse with fire and smoke pouring off it touched off one tree after another like lit kerosene had been splashed on the trunks and branches. The engulfed stallion galloped in a doomed looping zigzag generating a labyrinth of wildfire, a searing conflagration spreading with every beat of its scorched hooves. Hell came to earth with lightning speed.

Noose set down Bonny Kate onto her own two feet and hauled her by the hand through the unburned section of woods, making good their escape, both of them looking overhead at the canopy of trees above becoming a crackling nest of fire. "We gotta get to the horses!" Noose shouted. "That fire's spreading fast!"

"I don't want to burn, Joe!" Bonny Kate wailed, raw terror etched across her features. "Don't let me burn!"

"Don't plan to!"

They pushed through the woods, feeling the wall of heat on their backs. Swinging his gaze to the left,

Noose saw the twin fireballs of the mustang and the
man it dragged appearing and disappearing behind
the trees, a good distance off. That wasn't a good
thing, he knew, because the farther the burning horse
got, the more of the woods it was going to ignite—it
had already cut a blazing swath of fiery devastation
through the forestation.

Shouldering through the branches, the two people
saw the way was clearly lit by the fulgurations of flames
on all sides, and the congested view ahead began to
look like a landscape hung with fog. Orange patches
of fire bloomed in the haze. The searing air was getting soupy thick with smoke—both the man and
woman were starting to cough and gag, their lungs
hurting from the heat. The snapping sound of flames
was growing louder.

Ahead, the outline of a bronze horse materialized
in the smoke. A second horse was beside it. Both were
tethered to the tree, where they'd been left. Copper's
brown eyes were wide with alarm and it jerked its head
urgently in its bridle when it spotted its owner staggering through the smoke. The brown-and-white-spotted
Appaloosa was less poised, pounding its front hooves
and rearing on its hind legs in a growing panic from
the nearby fire. Whipping its head desperately side to
side, the reins were shearing the bark on the tree and
the bit of the bridle was tearing its mouth. Whinnying
and snorting, the Appaloosa's eyes bulged out of its
head in raw terror. Patting Copper quickly to reassure
it, Noose saw he needed to calm the other horse, the
one Bonny Kate needed to ride, if he could. Letting
go of the woman, he took the mustang's face in his
strong hands and hushed and stroked it.

The effort accomplished little, so Noose rounded on the woman. "You need to saddle up before this horse can't be ridden. C'mon now, move!" Grabbing the woman's arm, he tugged her to the horse but she hardly needed added incentive getting her boot in the stirrup and swinging a leg over the saddle.

"I got it!" Bonny Kate yelled, settling in her seat and unlashing the reins from the tree. "Get on your horse and let's get the hell out of here while the getting's good!"

Sprinting a few yards to Copper, Noose saw the stallion turn to him helpfully as he undid its reins from the tree and vaulted into the saddle. "*Yee-ahh!*" he shouted, and tugged the bridle, rotating the horse around in a half circle and giving it some spur, charging it through the smoke-wreathed trees where the fires hadn't reached yet. Swinging his head to look over his shoulder, he saw Bonny Kate riding like the devil right behind him, controlling her horse by sheer ferocity. The two of them galloped over the uneven ground, logs and ruts appearing in the billowing smoke seconds before the twin horses cleared them. Noose prayed one horse or both wouldn't break their legs. The conifer trees were fully on fire to their rear— gargantuan pillars of roaring, crackling, snapping flames reaching fifty to a hundred feet or more as the dry pines incinerated—the woods had become a raging firestorm.

Noose and Bonny Kate bore down in their saddles and rode hard ahead into the darkness and smoke when suddenly there was a *whoosh* of fireball and heat and Cisco's blazing horse ran directly across their path in front, flames shooting off the saddle and dragging the burning corpse on the ground, tangled in the stirrup in its wake. The banshee screaming mustang was half-burnt alive, flesh and coat charred, and as it passed, torched the pine trees ahead that exploded suddenly into an impassable wall of fire.

Yanking tight on his reins, Noose charged Copper to his left into a section of forest that was still not ablaze. He looked quickly over his shoulder and saw Bonny Kate drive her horse directly after him, although the Appaloosa seemed to be staying right on Copper's sure heels.

A huge loud *crack* above them made Noose duck his head. Just then a giant flaming branch fell from the heavens and crashed on the ground a few feet from his horse's hooves in a fireworks shower of smoldering, flying sparks from the glowing cindered log. Behind him, Bonny Kate veered her horse around it at the last second and narrowly avoided being tripped up by the fiery fallen tree limb.

A gruesome obstruction lay on the trail ahead and Noose saw exactly what it was as his bronze horse came up on it and his nostrils filled with the sweet sickly smell of roasted human and horse flesh: the crisped horse and rider lay in a steaming, blackened pile of bone and burnt meat in the dirt, human and horse skeletons knotted and fused, the blackened saddle twisted with the metal of the stirrups, bridle, and rifles into a melted mass of steel and leather.

Cisco and his mustang were gone but not before setting a catastrophic forest fire, the outlaw ending his life as he had lived it—in mayhem and destruction. Gesturing his arm to Bonny Kate behind him, Noose alerted her to the trail blockage and signaled for her

CHAPTER 23

Three miles south back down the pass, a long way away from everything, the Jackson cabin was a one-room structure at the edge of town, a few hundred yards from the U.S. Marshal's office. Bess Sugarland had purchased it for its proximity to where she worked for the foreseeable future and her need to hobble a three-minute distance on her bum leg was the best feature of the cabin. It was a humble, simple place. A sink. A bed. A log fireplace. A cupboard and dresser. Gun rack. She had moved a lot of personal effects of her lawman father and hers that she'd inherited after he was killed. She had grown up with him in a small house attached to the U.S. Marshal's office in Hoback and this place reminded her of home. She lived alone.

Bess had left her office just after sundown. Much of her afternoon had been dedicated to giving her new deputy, Nate Sweet, a brisk but thorough orientation of the local marshal's duties; showing him where everything was in the office from guns to maps to files,

then riding around the town of Jackson with him in a
horse-drawn wagon giving him a tour of their jurisdiction. Introductions had been made to several local
passersby and the men seemed happy to see a man
wearing a lawman badge in Jackson even if their
wives were less happy about it, being inclined toward
the woman who was the first female marshal. Sweet
seemed a quick study during Bess's peace officer orientation and after she had dressed him down during
their abrasive first meeting his rough edges had softened a bit; Nate Sweet basically kept his eyes and ears
open and his mouth shut. But this was only day one
and the marshal knew the kid had a long way to go to
earn her genuine confidence.

Bess, by nature reserved and brusque around
people, had become cantankerous now she wore a
marshal badge and didn't like shotgun weddings like
the U.S. Marshals Service headquarters in Cody had
given her with this deputy who likely was here to stay.
After his first day of work today, she had assigned him
the night shift, and Sweet was presently on post next
door until she relieved him at daybreak.

Through her window, Bess could see the oil lamp
burning in the office. It actually gave her a sense of
security knowing somebody was minding the fort
while she was off duty and everything did not rest on
her capable if weary shoulders.

Tonight, as she sat in her chair reading a book and
drinking a single glass of whiskey as was her nightly
custom, Marshal Bess was gripped by a peculiar and
uncharacteristic loneliness. The isolation felt tangible
as a cold emptiness permeated the room. It was a case
of nerves. Her skin felt too tight. She was unable to

shake a sudden irrational sense of free-floating dread. Bess was still wearing her work jeans and shirt and couldn't bring herself to put on her nightgown.

It did not take long for her to realize why: There had always been a man in her life every day of her life. Not a romantic figure but a familiar, protective one. First her father, Nate Sugarland, filled that role and then the big, tough, and friendly bounty hunter Joe Noose, who she fatefully had met the first time the day her U.S. Marshal father was murdered; it was as if one had replaced the other.

Her father was no longer with her. His pictures— photographs of him that had been taken and paintings she had done of both of them together as a little girl—were placed all around her house, reminding Bess of his absence while keeping him close in her heart. But he was gone.

Now, for the first time, so was Joe Noose.

Bess realized that for the last three months since the day they had met, difficult and trying though those times had been, Noose was always there, always near her, always in close physical proximity. After the battle with the evil Butler Gang, he had gotten her to Jackson and safety, been there every day while she healed, been around every day when she was assigned the new U.S. Marshal's job she now held.

Noose wasn't always in the same room or on the same street, yet he always felt near. She always felt safe, like he could get to her if she needed him. Like a big and powerful but gentle and protective guard dog you always knew was around. She was cranky to him half the time, and there was nothing romantic between them—they were friends, true friends, was what it was. The marshal hadn't realized until tonight—

She thought to throw another log on the fire but then noticed the huge glow of fire on the wall and smelled the burning pine, thinking even though the logs looked burned out the fireplace must need no stoking.

Taking another sip of whiskey, Marshal Bess faced the fireplace and felt the good numbing, warming burn of the liquor going down her throat.

Noose was gone now, too. She had sent him away.

On that fool's errand riding that crazy outlaw wench over the pass. Bess blamed herself—it was all her fault. Why did she send him? She could have deputized any one of— *But she didn't send him; he offered to do it. Made the offer because he knew it would help her out and she couldn't do it herself because of her damn bum leg. Helped her out because he was a friend. Did the same thing for her she would have done for him had their roles been reversed. She would not have had to be asked.*

But Marshal Bess had a bad, bad feeling about that female outlaw Bonny Kate Valance and knew the minute she saw Joe Noose ride off out of sight with her there was going to be trouble. But by then it was too late.

Those shots Bess thought she had been hearing all day had been rattling her, too, but she couldn't place them as far as direction, and the lady outlaw didn't have a gun, so the marshal kept telling herself it was hunters in the mountains.

Still . . .

Too much whiskey. She needed sleep.

The pulsing fire glow seemed oddly to be growing—

it bloomed hungrily around the fireplace, andirons, and wall. The ominous effect of the baroque luminescence was grandiose and infernal.

Her senses numbed by alcohol, things took too long to register for Bess.

Her toes were freezing. The logs on the fire were blackened char. Her fire was completely out.

Yet the reflected firelight reared diabolically up the cabin walls and ceiling in flaming shapes like hellish demons. And her nostrils were filled with the stench of burning logs.

No!

Marshal Bess Sugarland whirled around and saw the windows behind her brightly ablaze with the enormous glare of a gigantic fire, the view of the Teton Pass her shutters faced obscured in a titanic fiery glow outside, fogging the glass with heat.

Leaping out of her chair, Marshal Bess staggered to her door and threw it open. The heat and overwhelming stench of the forest fire in the fresh Wyoming air hit her like a kicking horse and knocked her back. She clung to the door and threw herself forward into a hurricane of light, smoke, ash, and cinders, hobbling out onto the grass to behold hell itself.

It was as if night had turned to day and a biblical apocalypse had come. The Teton Pass was on fire.

The sky was bright with flames consuming the forest in a raging conflagration, a towering firestorm reaching a hundred feet high. The whole mountain was burning.

Covering her nose and mouth, staring in speechless shock and awe up at the vast blazing tableau of the whole mountain range engulfed in flames, Marshal

Bess stood small and alone outside her cabin, dwarfed by the staggering forest fire only a few miles off.

That bitch Bonny Kate Valance was responsible somehow, Bess just knew. But that didn't matter right now.

Joe Noose was up there. And there was nothing Bess could do.

But she had to try.

Wild with panic, Bess Sugarland screamed her lungs raw until her chest hurt and she had no voice or spit left. She was screaming, "*Sweet!*"

It didn't matter that her leg hurt like a railway spike had been driven through it, didn't matter that she could barely walk, she did anyway. Her mare was a hundred yards off in the corral behind the office, the buck-and-rail fence incandescent in the hellish bloom of the distant forest fire. Glad she had decided to stay in her clothes, Marshal Bess staggered to her doorway and jammed her bare feet into her cowboy boots she left on the porch, grabbing her coat and hat from inside the doorway and throwing them on as she force-marched herself limping across the grassy field. The wooden brace on her leg began to splinter and crack from the pressure but Bess didn't care, shoving aside the gate of the stockade with both big hands and gimping her way to her new horse, a powerful paint. Her saddle was set on one of the wooden rails of the corral. Bess snatched a saddle blanket and tossed it over the back of her mare then half stumbled to the heavy saddle and hauled it into her arms, an effort that caused her leg to collapse under her—she tripped and fell on her face in the mud with a cry of agony. The wooden leg brace shattered but she ignored it as she pulled herself up the stockade fence and climbed to her feet, heaving the saddle over the blanket on the back of the frightened horse, whose eyes were riveted on the fires in the mountains rearing over the town of Jackson.

"*Sweet*!" she roared, buckling the saddle under her mare's chest. "*Sweet, get your damn ass out here! Where the hell are you?*"

Finally, the U.S. Marshal's office door was flung open and Deputy Sweet staggered out, clenching his rifle, looking like he'd just woken up, and immediately he stopped dead in his tracks, transfixed by the great forest fire to the north.

Cinching the saddle, Bess stuck her good leg in the stirrup and heaved herself onto her horse with a gritted-teeth grimace. "Sweet! What the hell do you think you're doing? Grab me a rifle and get us some ammo then get your ass on your horse!" Hauling hard on her reins, Marshal Bess wheeled her horse around and rode over to Sweet to glare commandingly down at him.

The deputy, realizing how tough his boss had to be, getting on her horse like that with a badly wounded leg, and cognizant of the fearsome fury in her face, gave her no argument and scrambled into action. Ducking into the office, he snatched the rifles and bandoliers of cartridges and had his hat on and was back out the door in less than a minute. Tossing her up a Winchester and an ammo belt, Sweet vaulted onto his own horse he had left saddled, then rode up beside her, his gaze still drifting over to the roaring fires on the pass. Sweet indicated it with a nod and looked Bess a question.

"Yes. That's where we're going."

He looked her another question.

"My friend is up there. We're gonna go save him."

And it was in that moment as Marshal Bess Sugar-land saw fearlessness in Deputy Nate Sweet's strong eyes as he nodded dutifully and his horse fell in right behind hers as she galloped straight for the pass, that she liked him right down to the ground as they rode into the breach.

CHAPTER 24

Somebody was shooting live ammo at Noose and Bonny Kate.

A fusillade of gunfire immediately followed in a thundering series of staccato reports that boomed over the crackling roar of the forest fire. With a quick look back Noose saw that Sheriff Waylon Bojack and his posse of Arizona deputies were hard-charging their lathered horses through the leaping flames like a pack of demons unleashed from hell, guns drawn and muzzles flashing in hot pursuit. Bullets zipped and zinged, ricocheting off the fire-wreathed trees ahead of Noose and Bonny Kate as the two of them drove their spurs into the horses and galloped on ahead.

Out of the frying pan and literally into the fire.

"Ride!" Joe Noose yelled.

"Damn straight!" Bonny Kate shouted back.

They dug in their spurs but the horses hardly needed incentive, dashing like their asses were on fire. Noose rode ahead in the lead, hugging his horse, bent close to the saddle as Copper skillfully navigated its speedy, sure-footed escape through the forest fire, dodging trees and low-hanging branches, placing its galloping hooves well, somehow finding a clear trail through the confusing maze of forestland. Bonny Kate's horse followed Copper step for step, trusting the bronze stallion's alpha leadership. Trees came rushing at the people's faces, more and more now on fire.

Hell was in front and hell was behind. Getting burned or shot or both seemed an absolute certainty. The smoke was getting so thick in the woods it was hard to see more than fifteen yards ahead.

The air was cacophonic with deafening sounds of raging fire and gunshots but suddenly there was a gigantic *boom* that sounded like a stick of dynamite going off. It came from behind Noose and Bonny Kate, who turned their heads in alarm just in time to see the blazing hundred-foot pine tree burn through and collapse, falling like a giant flaming pillar onto the trail behind them, showering fire and sparks and shaking the ground in its colossal impact. The sheriff and his deputies had abruptly stopped shooting and were looking in raw terror upward toward the ten-ton tree's fiery descent toward their very heads.

Bojack and his men picked up their pace on their horses, riding for their lives. He and one of his men got through, the other didn't. The tree landed right on top of Jed Ransom. Bonny Kate averted her eyes and Noose winced as the titanic, fiery beam crashed down on horse and rider, squishing the lawman into his saddle as the impact broke all four of the stallion's legs like toothpicks and both horse and rider were crushed flat and consumed in a billowing combustion of exploding fire from the crash of the blazing, fallen tree. Sparks and smoke plumed.

Catching a quick glimpse of a mask of bitter grief on Sheriff Waylon Bojack's fire-emblazoned bearded features, Joe Noose ducked as he saw the lawman's head quickly snap his way as the old man raised his Winchester one-handed and fired, spinning the rifle around his hand and levering another round into the chamber and firing again. Copper was running in a zigzag pattern to avoid the pine tree trunks that lay like an obstacle course in their way, throwing Bojack's aim, and the Arizona sheriff's shots went wild.

Fifty feet directly ahead, Noose saw a huge galaxy of orange and yellow evanescence in the dense smoke screen before him then an immense glowing, brightening shadow and saw another burning tree was falling right in his path. A wave of heat washed over him. "*Look out!*" Noose yelled to the lady outlaw riding close behind. Yanking on the reins, Noose heaved Copper sideways out of the deadly way of the toppling tree, but he jerked too hard and the ground was too soft and his horse lost his footing and fell sideways as both went down in the dirt just as the fire-engulfed conifer came to earth in a ground-shaking smash. Noose stayed in the saddle, throwing his weight left as Copper scrambled upright to his four legs, the man working the reins, and in one smooth movement, they were at a full gallop again.

A minute later, once his horse had its feet under it, Joe Noose looked over his shoulder to check Bonny Kate Valance was still behind him.

The woman was gone.

So was the posse.

When he heard the fierce barrages of rifle and pistol shots back down the trail Noose knew the lawmen were shooting at someone and he had a good idea who.

Unarmed and defenseless, Bonny Kate Valance was easy prey for the Arizona constabulary if the lawmen had caught up with her . . . and it sounded like they had.

Pulling his horse to a sudden, abrupt halt, Joe Noose wheeled Copper around to face the way they came. Copper didn't like that at all and looked back at Noose with its wide, moist, brown eyes communicating an unmistakable look that its rider was crazy. Noose patted the stallion on the withers, his eyes fixed on the wall of fire that blocked his return the way he had just come—a dangerous woven tapestry inferno of burning branches crisscrossed on blazing trees . . . it looked like the gate to hell.

Bullets still sounded in steady ear-shattering volleys ringing through the forest.

They hadn't got her, not yet.

"C'mon, old horse." Noose stroked Copper's shivering, muscular neck as they both stood stationary, their eyes locked in fear and awe on the fiery curtain before them that rose a hundred feet into the sky. It was a furnace in there. "It's up to us. We got to go back. We got to save her."

As Joe Noose gave Copper a decisive spur to the flank and the horse lunged into motion, charging straight into a solid wall of flame that would probably burn them to crisped ash, Noose figured he had at least one thing going for him:

No way that sheriff and those Arizona boys would be expecting him nor any man of sound mind to ride back *into* the fire . . .

CHAPTER 25

They came upon the first body not fifteen minutes out of Jackson.

Deputy Sweet saw it first—a sprawled body flat on the grass at the beginning of the trail up the Teton Pass. Marshal Bess Sugarland first felt a stab of fear that it was Joe Noose but the closer she rode quickly saw the man was too small, a kid, and the clothes he wore were not those of her friend but instead that of the Arizona posse that she had encountered earlier that day.

Trotting up to the corpse, she made visual confirmation it was one of that old sheriff's deputies. Bess did not bother to dismount because she was in a hurry; neither did she need to: the corpse was well lit enough for identification, bathed in the glimmering light of the forest fire miles on, and it looked like he had been shot square in the belly with a single kill shot, judging by that big messy exit wound out his back.

"Not your friend?" Sweet asked, reading her face.

"Not him." She nodded. "But my friend shot this one."

"What's going on, Marshal?"

Bess looked at Sweet and quickly explained—he needed to be brought up to speed. "This afternoon a posse of lawmen well out of their jurisdiction rode in from Arizona and showed up in my office. This dead kid was one of the deputies, I'm certain of that. The sheriff wanted to know about a female outlaw I deputized my friend this morning to escort over the pass to Victor, where she's going to be hanged tomorrow. I just now figured out these boys from out of state want to kill her themselves, so they went after my friend. If they tried to stop him from doing his job getting her to Idaho he would have shot those lawmen dead to rights without hesitation. That's exactly what happened here."

"Just so I got this straight," Sweet answered. "These lawmen are after this friend of yours and that female prisoner somewhere up the trail."

"Right."

"How many bad guys are there?"

"Five."

"Five against one is bad odds," Sweet said.

"For them it is. They need more men."

"One against five?" Sweet scratched his head. "I don't know, Marshal."

"You don't know Joe Noose."

Spurring her horse, Marshal Bess quit the idle chatter and galloped onto the trail leading into Teton Pass. Deputy Sweet's horse was right on her hooves as they charged toward the fires up the road to hell.

CHAPTER 26

Waylon Bojack saw the bitch clearly down the notches of his Winchester repeater as his finger tightened on the trigger. She was hiding, cowering behind her bullet-riddled dead horse sprawled on the ground, so far the bulky stallion corpse taking all of his and his deputy's shots as Bonny Kate Valance crouched behind the saddle and tried to squeeze under the heavy weight of the equine carcass. A few flowers of blood punched out chunks of fur and flesh on the fallen Appaloosa—Bojack's green deputy couldn't shoot straight and was wasting bullets, distracted by all the fire around them and wondering how the hell they were going to get out of here alive—but the sheriff paid no attention to the fire and didn't care whether he got out of here alive because right now, he had one of that female outlaw's big tits in his crosshairs, the left one, where the heart, if she had one, would be, so he took careful aim because he was going to kill her right now and nothing else would ever matter again.

Bonny Kate saw Bojack, locked eyes with him, raw fear in her gaze seeing her own death.

Good.

Waylon Bojack's finger tightened on the trigger.

Then suddenly his gun exploded in his hands in a sparking shrapnel of mangled steel and wood that tore through his hand and the right side of his face and his blood was everywhere—the sheriff thought first it was a misfire then he thought better of it when he saw the gigantic silhouette of the huge cowboy on his leaping horse with pistols in both hands blazing as he came flying through the ring of fire.

It was that son of a bitch marshal!

Bleeding like a steer, clutching his damaged face with one hand, Bojack staggered back on his boots, screaming in fury that the marshal had shot his rifle out of his hand and ruined his kill shot on that evil outlaw Bonny Kate Valance. The bitch was still alive and kicking, crawling her way across the dirt out from under her horse in a flash of blue cloth and flaming red hair—right toward Joe Noose, who landed on his horse beside her, the stallion coming to a dead halt, the marshal's clothes partially ablaze as he fired both pistols into the surprised deputy, shooting Fulton Dodge twice in the chest.

Dodge fell back, spurting bright red blood from his mortal body wounds, the gun flying from his hand, face frozen in shock, reflexively reaching for his other revolver. Noose dealt pure death in the brace of pistols in his hands he fired again and again, his gaze switching in lethal accuracy, blowing pieces off the man as he shot down the deputy in a space of seconds.

The sheriff stood over the sprawled, bullet-riddled

corpse of the last of his fallen deputies. A choked cry
of anguish was strangled in his throat. Overcome with
grief and remorse for having gotten all his men killed,
Sheriff Waylon Bojack's ragged ruin of a face a punctured bloody red agony of metal and wood shrapnel,
he was suddenly a very old man who sagged, knowing
the very worst had happened.

Fumbling agedly for his pistol, knowing he would
never get it out of his holster much less a shot off
before Noose shot him, he looked up in dread to face
the most terrible thing he possibly could have: Bonny
Kate Valance escaping his grasp, having taken everything from him and leaving him only failure—he
failed to avenge his son, he'd gotten his men killed,
he'd left his wife a widow. Every ounce of his man-
hood was now stolen and he would take that to the
grave. Right now, he jerked on his pistol with a fumbling hand, watching the unthinkable . . . Bonny
Kate Valance being swept off the ground by Joe
Noose's massive arm and slung safely onto the back
of his horse.

Bojack's eyes met Noose's, the marshal looking
straight down the barrel of a Colt Peacemaker. The
meaning of the look in Noose's mean, hard eyes
was clear.

The look said: *I warned you.*

Hammered back from the shot punching him in
his chest before he even saw the muzzle flash, Bojack's
legs crumpled and he sank to his knees—as his vision
went blurry he saw Bonny Kate Valance and Joe Noose
mounted on the bronze horse whose golden coat reflected the fires all around like glorious armor as they

CHAPTER 27

Finding Joe Noose wasn't going to be easy, not in the impassable blaze of that immense forest fire up ahead.

The only hope was he was this side of it.

Marshal Bess tightened the handkerchief over her face below her Stetson after splashing and wetting the old cloth with water from her canteen. Looking over at the other horse she saw her deputy doing the same. Both pressed wet cloths over their mouths and noses so they could breathe clean air amidst the choking haze of dense, foul-smelling smoke hanging over the Teton Pass trail they rode their horses up.

The farther the lawmen rode the smokier it got. At the top of the mountain, huge, turbulent mushroom clouds of orange fire and oily black smoke billowed high into an incendiary sky diabolically lit from below by colossal mouths of flames chewing a path of fiery destruction through the forest. Far ahead before them, row after row of dead pine trees engulfed by walls of fire exploded and collapsed in showers of sparks and flaming, falling timber. Bess didn't know how close they were going to be able to get before they had to turn the horses back. Not much farther, she reckoned.

Already the two skittish horses Bess and Sweet rode pulled against their bridles and jerked their necks on the reins, both recalcitrant steeds requiring plenty of spurring to advance farther up the trail into danger. The humans riding them weren't happy about it, either.

A sudden flurry of flapping wings came at their faces and they ducked just in time as the sky was filled with great flocks of crows flying past them like hundreds of black teeth silhouetted against the flaming sky, some of the birds already on fire and dropping like tiny blazing cinders into the yawning canyon darkness far below.

In the last few minutes, a stampede of wildlife had rushed past the lawmen down the trail, escaping the spreading firestorm in the mountains above. Bobcats, deer, antelope, wolves, coyotes, and smaller raccoons and squirrels had fled past their horses, the fleeing animals whether predator or prey ignoring each other in a singular desperate flight for survival—the forest animals simply ran away from the fire. Swiveling her gaze upward then downward, Bess saw the shadowy flow of shapes of dashing wildlife in the hills above and plunging precipice below.

The whole gorge was illuminated with the evil, pulsing incandescence of the forest fire a mile ahead that was coming their way fast, furious roiling flames devouring the dead trees in their path like an incendiary demonic maw. The night canyon was brilliantly and dangerously lit up. Monolithic shadows and glowing pools of infernal radiance bloomed below over the rocks and boulders in the hundred-foot ravine on the edge of the trail . . . and it was within those hellish pools of light that Marshal Bess Sugarland spotted the body.

The shattered corpse of the man lay twisted at the base of the gorge plunging off the edge of the trail they rode. It looked like a tiny broken toy from this height. The marshal's sharp eyes spotted the body and instantly her heart leapt into her throat. Pulling up her horse, she signaled with a raised hand for Deputy Sweet to halt. He did. Then she pointed down the cliff toward the mangled figure on the bottom. The body was too far away and cloaked in darkness to identify from where they sat in their saddles but her first fear was that it was Joe Noose. Bess could not tell from the clothes because they were only one color— the dye of the brackish red blood that soaked the garments completely. This man had died badly.

"Is that him?" Sweet quietly vocalized her worst fear.

"I don't know." Bess choked. "We need to go down and see."

"The horses won't make it down that gorge," he replied sensibly. "It's too steep. We'll have to try on foot." The marshal appreciated that her deputy voiced no complaint—not that she would have broached any argument—and he simply followed orders and offered his opinion on a solution. She was liking him better every minute.

Bess's guts were tied in knots as her gaze kept traveling to the corkscrewed body on the rocks below that had died a very hard death. She was still too high to identify it in the darkness but she had to know, so she dismounted in dread and led her horse to a tall nearby pine tree and tied off the reins. The animal did not like it, being this close to the fire, and snorted and

whipped its head against the bridle but she got it tied.
Sweet wasn't having any easier time with his own stallion, she saw—the deputy had already dismounted and
was practically dragging the big horse across the trail
to where hers was. Both of the horses felt the danger,
even though the fires were not yet close enough to be
life threatening. Bess patted and tried to calm her
steed to little effect, then walked several paces to help
Sweet lead his horse beside her own. Her deputy
swiftly lashed the reins to the tree and both horses
were sorted.

Having spied a series of descending rock ledges
down the edge of the canyon a few minutes earlier
from her saddle, the marshal figured she had found
a possible passage to the base of the ravine twenty
yards back down the pass. She went straight to it with
her watchful deputy just behind her. At the brow of
the precipice, Bess crouched down and peered
over the edge, once again spotting the rugged declination of cliff outcrops, a series of shelves jaggedly
dropping a hundred feet down to the rock-strewn
base upon which lay the corpse. Her sharp eyes had
not deceived her.

Swinging her glance to Sweet, Bess pointed down at
what looked to her like a path. "We can get down
that way."

He didn't look too sure.

"Go back to the horses and get us two coils of
rope," she said. "Together it's about a hundred and
fifty feet of lead and we can use the rope to get down
and back up. Tie the first rope to that tree by the
horses, then the second rope to the first in a big 'ol
triple knot so it's tight and secure." He just looked at
her. "What are you waiting for?"

Still crouched, Bess Sugarland watched the new kid snap to it like his legs had springs. Sprinting back to the horses in a few long strides, Nate Sweet hauled the two coils of rope from the saddles, lassoed one around the heavy tree trunk, knotted the two leads together with a swift yank, then rushed back to her side in less than two minutes. The deputy hadn't even broken a sweat.

"Give it here," Bess said, clapping her hands, so Sweet tossed the coils of rope into her waiting open palms.

"You want me to go first, Marshal?"

"No, I'll take point."

"You sure about this?"

Her answer to him was to rise to her feet and chuck the coil of rope over the cliff. They both watched as it unfurled as it fell, landing ten feet from the broken corpse with length to spare. Bess had kept one hand on the line and now wrapped it loosely around her waist and once between her legs. Feeding the rest of the loose lead between her hands over the edge of the canyon, she tugged on it with all her strength, and it went taut against the tree—it would hold her and him, too.

"Okay, let's go."

The marshal nodded, and he held her hand at the lip of the gorge as she swung a leg over the edge and found purchase on the ridge. She dropped her other leg over and both boots met solid stone. Then she released the deputy's hand and grabbed hold of the rocks, clinging to the edge of the gorge, thinking if she was wrong about this, it was a long way down. The rope tightened at her waist and crotch under her weight.

A few steps later she was able to slide safely onto the next table of firelit rock below. The brow of the cliff was now fifteen feet above her, a massif of shadow looming dark against the night sky. She saw Sweet's lanky silhouette now appear climbing over the edge, the tight length of rope extended from his waist where he had it wrapped around securely. In the light of the flames a mile off, his face looked like forged steel, and his eyes shined metallically as they remained fixed on her from above. Dislodged pebbles spat from his boots and struck her on the arms. Marshal Bess knew they had to keep up the pace, so without wanting to, she looked down.

The canyon yawned below, a drop into the shadowy abyss, bathed in ominous firelight. More confident in her step and the security of the towline, Bess rappelled down the face of the cliff, her boots finding footing on the crags of rock, letting line out between her gloves with each drop. Shifting her gaze upward, she saw the deputy right above her making steady progress down, then looking below again, she saw the crushed body of the dead man getting closer and closer. Far above, the top of the ridge and the trailhead where their out-of-sight horses were tied seemed now a world away—getting back up would be harder than getting down, for sure. But they were almost there. Jumping from one outcrop down to another rock shelf, Bess could feel the heat closing in from the natural basin of the bottom of the gorge—it was like a furnace down here and her clothes were soaked with sweat and sopping wet.

About fifteen feet to go.

Her boots hit the floor of the canyon.

Like a shot, she ran straight for the crushed body splattered on the rocks, its shattered limbs jutting akimbo at unnatural angles and hanging loose in their sockets like a doll stomped to pieces by an unruly child. It had landed face-first and lay on its stomach. In the florid bloom of the firelight, she could see the corpse was bathed head to foot in blood as a result of the fall, but the messy bullet hole exit wounds in its back were visible.

No, please, no was all Bess Sugarland was thinking as she reached the body and took it in.

She turned the body over.

CHAPTER 28

It wasn't Noose.

The corpse's face was crushed in, a red pulp of bone and cartilage, but she instantly knew from the clothes and size of the body it was another one of the Arizona deputies.

Bess exhaled in relief.

Joe Noose was alive. That was all that mattered. That the second deputy died by Noose's gun was a certainty, as was the fact that the posse was running out of men. Less and less Bess worried for her friend.

What happened next happened so fast she barely had time to react . . .

One moment the body was there, the next instant it wasn't as the sweep of the huge claws raking across the dead man's back tore the body in half in two clean pieces that flew in both directions, dousing her face and chest with cold, sticky blood. Suddenly everything was cacophonic noise and her eardrums almost burst from the assault of deafening sounds that followed: the savage, ferocious animal roar answered by booming gunshots from above that made the gigantic grizzly

bear bellow even louder in raging agony as Sweet's
pistol shots slammed into the beast's hairy shoulder
and hammered it back.

For a dangerous few seconds Marshal Bess stood
paralyzed frozen in terror, eyes widened in shock as
the colossal grizzly rose on its hind paws, towering
over her, its gaping fanged jaws bared, ready to sink
into her flesh. The world went black around her in
the darkness of the predator's rearing shadow, a mon-
strous silhouette blotting out the roaring forest fires
on the mountain above.

The bear stood fifteen feet high on its back legs.
Its yellow saucer eyes rolled around in their orbits in
feral whorls of bloodthirsty panic—its whole world
was on fire and the wounded beast's brain was an un-
stable confusion of fight-or-flight impulses. Trapped
in the gorge, the disoriented grizzly didn't know
whether to run or kill. The marshal just stood there,
knowing what everyone did, that no human being
had a chance of outrunning a full-grown grizzly and
all you could do was lie down and play dead and hope
it wouldn't tear you limb from limb. The stench of the
grizzly's filthy matted coat and roasting flesh and fur
stung her nostrils and Bess could see smoke wafting
off the burned-bare blackened patch on its chest
where the bear had been scorched by the fires.

Unable to make her limbs move, her body not re-
sponding to her mental commands, Bess was thinking
she was about to die very badly.

"Get out of there! Use the rope! Now! Move, Marshal!" Deputy Nate Sweet's loud, urgent shouts from
above snapped Bess out of her fog. She grabbed the
rope with both hands, used her arms to pull herself
upward, and jumping with all her strength was off the

ground, boots and spurs finding purchase on the face
of the cliff. Looking up desperately, Bess saw her
deputy ten feet above her on a ledge, holding the
rope with one hand, his other fist pointing his smoking revolver down past her toward the bear. "Climb!
Don't look down! And duck!"

His Colt Peacemaker boomed again.

The slug clipped the grizzly as it launched itself up
at the scrambling woman, both paws striking the granite wall where her legs had been an instant before,
dragging its claws down the rock, sending up showers
of sparks like struck flint. The bellowing creature
sounded to her terrified ears like the beast was on top
of her and it nearly was. The dead-meat stink of its
breath was all Bess smelled as she imagined its teeth
sinking into the flesh of her back with each desperate
hand-over-hand pull of her fists up the rope and every
clank of her spurs as her boots scaled the cliff face.
Until, suddenly, she felt Sweet's strong arms close
around her and heave her safely onto the outcrop
where he stood.

Marshal Bess gasped for breath, her heart racing,
seeing spots in front of her eyes. Catching her breath,
she swung her gaze over the edge of the ledge and
bore witness to the biggest grizzly bear she had ever
laid eyes on pacing below, snarling up at them with
baleful eyes, a string of red drool spilling from its
snout. The grizzly wanted to eat them in the worst way
but both were now safely out of its reach.

The gargantuan blaze burning its way through the
dry tinder of the pass way above kept getting closer,
towering steeples and spires of fire climbing hundreds
of feet into the sky—the dreadful orange radiance

emblazoning the grizzly made it look like it came from hell.

As far as Bess was concerned, it did. She had a coughing fit. It was hard to breathe with the soot and char in the air and every breath made Bess's lungs burn, a searing pain that got worse with every physical exertion. She huddled on the ledge as Deputy Sweet drew his second revolver and took careful, deadly aim on the bear below them, aiming straight between its beady eyes—but before the lawman could pull his trigger, the grizzly suddenly bounded off with a purpose, charging on all fours around the bend in the gorge where it ascended to the pass. The bear vanished as quickly as it had appeared.

Sweet slowly released the hammer of his unfired pistol and slid the gun back into his holster. "I think it had enough. It ran."

"Bears don't run toward fire. Bet that grizzly has something else in mind."

They exchanged urgent glances.

"We better get back to the horses. Right now."

Both using the rope, the two lawmen began to climb back up the side of the gorge with all possible haste, clambering up the ascending ledges of granite outcrops, keeping tight grips on the line. Sweet stayed in the lead this time, Bess close behind. The base of the gorge fell away behind into a deep chasm the higher they climbed, each officer gasping and grimacing with exertion. Ever upward, the two scaled the face of the cliff.

Marshal Bess's eyes were fixed on the brow of the ridge fifty feet above them past Sweet's shoulders. The rope was pulled taut against the jagged edge of the lip of the crevice, the line vibrating under the strain of their combined weight. Here the outcrop ended—it was a straight climb up a sheer perpendicular rock face the remaining distance to the top. As if reading her mind, Sweet shot a glance down at her and nodded *Ready?* Bess nodded tightly and both lawmen kicked off the ledge, each now dangling off the side of the cliff in midair above a hundred-foot gorge with nothing but boulders far below.

It didn't take much to imagine what they would look like if they fell, for she had lately seen the condition of a body that did. She used every ounce of strength she could muster to climb upward, foot over foot up the granite wall, hand over hand up the rope, gaining a few feet each time. The heat was incapacitating but her deputy was managing the climb better than she.

Thirty feet from the top now. Almost there.

Sweet chose that moment to look over his shoulder to check on her progress.

So Sweet did not see the falling, burning tree branch toppling onto the edge of the cliff and suddenly setting the dried scrub brush on fire along the lip of the chasm.

The climbing line lay in the center of the burning bushes, stretched to the breaking point with torque.

The rope was now on fire. Flame sizzled on the coiled twine that was starting to blacken and unravel.

And it was burning through quick.

"Climb!" Bess shouted. "The rope is burning!"

Turning his gaze upward, Deputy Sweet put his back into clambering hand over hand, hauling himself up the rock, cowboy boots dug in against the face of the gorge. Aching with pain, Marshal Bess dragged herself up after him, her lungs seared by the heat and clogged with ash, choking for breath. She felt for sure she wasn't going to make it.

Her fellow lawman was ten feet from the top now, the lip of the cliff nearly in reach, when the rope lurched sickeningly and the line jarred and slipped a few feet—the jagged edge of the rock slicing through more of the smoldering rope with every strain on it from the weight of the officers. Sweet almost lost his grip and plummeted to his doom, but some reservoir of strength inside the stubborn young man fueled a burst of sudden movement and looking up Bess saw Sweet had one hand on the top of the gorge dangling by it when he released the rope and grabbed onto the brink of the cliff with both hands. Then with a struggle the deputy hauled himself back up onto the solid ground of the trail and was leaning over the edge, reaching down, extending his open hand to the marshal.

"Grab my hand!"

Bess was almost there—a few more feet to climb. The energy had drained from her limbs and her body was going numb. She slackened, certain she could go no farther, and was about to fall when she locked eyes with Sweet and saw the steel determination in the young deputy's glance, so in the force of his gaze the marshal absorbed his strength and made it the last two feet. Reaching up her hand, Bess felt both Sweet's hands clamp her wrist as he heaved her up over the edge of the cliff and onto the dirt of the Teton Pass beside him. Both lawmen rolled onto their backs and caught their breath.

"Much obliged," she said.

"Just doin' my job, Marshal." He nodded.

"I think you're going to work out just fine, Deputy."

"Happy you feel that way, ma'am."

They both got up and stood and stared off at the apocalyptic fires reducing the trees to burning matchsticks on top of the mountain less than a mile before them. Blasts of heat hit them from the inferno that lay ahead. At the tree, the frightened horses reared and whinnied in raw terror, front legs pawing the air with their hooves.

Bess looked to Sweet. "We've gone as far as we can go. No way those horses gonna go further. We gotta turn back. That posse or what's left of 'em is the least of Joe Noose's worries now. He's either got to safety past the flames, and if there's a way to do it for sure he has, or his fate is out of our hands now. Let's get mounted and get on back to Jackson."

"Good plan, Marshal." The deputy nodded. Both of them sprinted across the trail to their tethered horses and swung into the saddles. The steeds were relieved to be getting the hell out of there and cooperated as from the saddles the riders, leaning forward in their stirrups, untied the reins from the tree.

As she swung her horse around facing down the trail, Marshal Bess tossed a last dread-filled glance up at the fire on the mountain and had a bad feeling she was never going to see Joe Noose again.

The bear's paw came out of nowhere—its claws struck the side of her mare's skull with savage force and the surprised horse's head was ripped clean off its shoulders in a gruesome mess of jetting blood and tearing meat with a sound like tearing canvas drowned out by the ferocious roar of the giant grizzly. Bess Sugarland's horse went down instantly, lifeless legs collapsing beneath its heavy torso as the decapitated mare fell sideways onto the trail, smashing the woman hard on the ground and pinning her leg beneath the saddle.

Bess's sudden view of the towering grizzly bear she had met at the bottom of the gorge was flipped sideways as her horse flung her to earth and stunned her—terrifying jumbled glimpses of yellow eyes, gaping maw, slashing claws, scorched flesh still steaming and matted, punctured fur wet with blood from Sweet's bullets. The bear was rearing up on its hind legs—it wanted a piece of her, or more accurately, her in pieces.

Marshal Bess ducked and covered her head as the grizzly dropped on top of the horse, swiping both front paws, raking its claws through the headless mare's chest and belly, splintering apart bone and digging through intestine, disemboweling the horse while trying to get at the woman. An oceanic wave of blood showered Bess, who didn't know if the blood was the mutilated horse's or her own.

The weight of the saddle pinning her wounded leg, made much heavier with the bulk of the bear combined with the crushing mass of the horse, became agonizing—Bess imagined she could feel the bones of her left leg splintering as the pain from bullet wound she had already sustained became unbearable and caused her to almost pass out as unconsciousness overtook her.

Then she heard the thunder of the Winchester rifle shots close at hand—five sharp blasts in swift staccato rapid-fire succession and just like that the bear was off her.

Looking up blearily from the ground, her sideways vision blurred with blood, Marshal Bess saw Deputy Nate Sweet in the saddle of his horse with his repeater rifle socked to his shoulder, quickly levering and firing round after round into the grizzly in a precise string of head and chest shots that hammered the beast back toward the edge of the gorge. Again and again Sweet fired, empty casings ejecting from the breech of his trusty Winchester, gleaming spent shells glittering in the glow from the forest fires and the muzzle flash discharges, the grizzly staggering upright on its haunches, balance unsteady as more bullet holes punched through its face and barrel chest as the beast tottered by the edge of the precipice. Dead while it stood up on hind legs, the giant grizzly bear disappeared from view as it fell off the cliff and dropped into the deep gorge with sounds of hard impact that grew distant until they stopped altogether—it was the last thing Marshal Bess Sugarland heard as she blacked out.

The next thing she knew, it was some time later and she was having a dream she was riding a horse down some darkened trail but strangely she wasn't holding reins yet somehow staying in the saddle anyway. It didn't feel real but somehow it was. A man was behind her holding her up as she leaned against him, and it was his competent hands reaching around her hips, clenching the reins, and driving the horse, his arms holding her in the saddle, and it was real.

When she spied the faraway lights of Jackson Hole she knew her deputy Nate Sweet had ridden her to safety and her last thought before she passed out again was she had misjudged the young man and would have to make it up to him.

CHAPTER 29

The heat lessened on their backs.

The spreading fire had not as yet reached the woods ahead and before them lay an unburned phalanx of trees as Joe Noose and Bonny Kate Valance galloped through the forest on the sure-footed horse whose path was clearly lit by the baleful glow of the inferno to their rear. The air was wreathed in smoke, but the haze thinned the farther they got. Out of harm's way for now, they had ridden beyond the reach of the flames and were leaving the fires behind.

She sat behind him in the saddle with her arms wrapped around his massive torso in a vise clench, her exhausted head resting against his big shoulders. Every tense muscle in Noose's body screamed *We're not out of this yet*. He was still in a state of high alert until they were truly clear of the encroaching blaze. His control of his horse, Copper, was absolute—rider and stallion were like one animal as they rode with precision and sped through the clearly lit gaps between the trees, out of danger for now.

A half an hour had probably passed before the air

began to cool and the cover of darkness descended again. Noose slowed his tired horse to a trot. Disengaging his canteen from his saddle, he uncapped it with his teeth and leant forward to give Copper water to drink. The horse tilted its big head sideways to receive the spout and gulped down half the water in the container thirstily through slobbering lips into its parched gullet. When the stallion had been refreshed Copper politely stopped drinking, seeming to know it had to leave some refreshment for its passengers.

Noose then passed the canteen back to Bonny Kate. She shook her head. "You first."

"Ladies first."

"I ain't no lady."

"All evidence to the contrary."

"Stubborn—" She took the canteen and sipped, passed it back. He took just a swig. "You hurt?" he asked.

"Nothing a hanging won't fix."

"I have medical supplies. You ain't hanged yet."

"I'm okay. Thank you."

Noose nodded and gave Copper a tap with his spurs and the horse set off at a brisk trot. Noose was staring straight ahead. His voice was low. "You been lying to me, Bonny Kate. About everything. You're gonna tell me the truth now."

"What difference does it make?"

"That man Cisco wasn't after you because he was in love with you and he wasn't trying to rescue you. He was trying to steal you away because he was part of your gang and you ran off with their robbery money and he wanted it back. Wanted to know where you had the loot stashed. Ain't that the truth?"

"I'm too tired to argue," Bonny answered. "Yes,

that's the truth. I took the money. I left them to get captured. Had my reasons."

"A whole money bag of 'em, I reckon."

"It warn't just about the money."

He said nothing. She sighed, then said, "Okay, it *was* all about the money. I saw my opportunity and I took it."

"It took you to the gallows."

"I still have the money, Joe."

"Figured you did, Cisco trying to find out where it was from you 'n all."

"You listening to me, mister?" she demanded. "I still have the money. I'll split it with you, you let me go."

Noose shook his head. "Not interested."

"Ain't interested in fifty thousand dollars?"

"Nope."

"All right, I'll give you all of it, then. A hundred thousand dollars. You promise you let me go, I'll take you right to it. Three, maybe four days' ride from here."

"I don't want your money, Bonny Kate. I already got me a job and I'm doing it. I didn't shoot them lawmen back there so I could profit from stolen loot, I did it because they were breaking the law to stop me from delivering you to the gallows, and that wasn't right. I don't expect you to understand. Maybe I don't understand, myself."

Bonny Kate was silent for long minutes then Noose heard her softly crying, and this was no act this time.

"What's wrong?" he asked.

"Why did you do it? Why did you come back and save me back there? You coulda died. Died hard. Died painful. You could have burned up or been shot and for what? For what? For nothin'! I'd've been dead by that fire or that posse's bullets same as I'll be dead at the end of that rope in a few hours! You don't make no damn sense to me, Joe Noose."

"I told you. Told you before, last time you asked. Same thing each time."

"Tell me again! Make me understand."

"I swore an oath to get you where I'm taking you. I have my word."

"People's word don't mean shit. What makes you so different? Nobody's word means nothing in this crazy world."

"Mine does. Least it does to me."

"Why?"

"It's the right thing to do."

"People don't do the right thing!" she suddenly screamed.

"I guess I ain't most people, then."

"No, I reckon you surely ain't. I can't figure you. Just can't."

Copper's hoof slipped in a ditch and Joe Noose was distracted for no more than a split second righting his balance and that of his horse but that was all the time Bonny Kate Valance needed to snatch the Colt Peacemaker out of his holster—she was fast, very fast—and get it cocked with the muzzle pressed against the back of his neck before he could lift his hand to prevent her. He froze. Exhaled.

"Get off the horse," she said with a vacant coldness in her voice. "Real slow. If you make any sudden moves I'll blow your head clean off. You know I'll do it. Nice 'n easy. Dismount."

Noose dismounted, hands raised. She didn't have to ask him to do the second part. His spurs *clinked* as his boots met the earth. He stood on the ground, hands up, back to her.

"Now turn and face me. I know you and your horse are married or something but don't try to whistle or signal him to throw me or I'll shoot it before I shoot you, but I *will* shoot you both."

Noose turned and faced Bonny Kate with his hands up by his ears. She sat calmly in the saddle, her expression dead, her gaze blank—the face of a killer. The big pistol, held in a steady, small hand with a firm grip on the stock, finger on the trigger, was leveled at his head, five feet away. "Now you're gonna unbuckle your gun belt, real slow, and let it drop. Then kick it away. Gentle."

Very carefully lowering one big mitt to his buckle, Noose undid his belt and let it drop with the remaining pistol, stepping out of it, sliding the gun belt away with the tip of his boot. He didn't take his eyes off hers and he didn't blink.

Neither did she.

"I done everything they said I did, Joe Noose. I stole that money. I left my gang to get shot. I even shot that sheriff's son in the back like he said I did. I done all that and more. And I'd do it again. People don't know half of the stuff what I done. I'm telling you this because I want you to know what you went back and saved. Want you to know just exactly who and what I am. Because I ain't sorry for none of it. Ain't sorry for nothing I done in this dirty world. This is what I'm going to do now. I'm taking your horse. I'm riding out of here. Not telling you which way I'm going. By the time you walk to Victor I'll be a day's ride away. I know you love this horse and as soon as I can find another I'm gonna leave him for you to find. I may be bad to the bone but I ain't that cruel. And I'm not going to shoot you." Her gaze flickered. "I should, though. Shouldn't take no chances with a man like you." Her eyes became black holes. "Yeah, I best believe I better shoot you."

Bonny Kate raised the gun to fire.

Her thumb cocked back the hammer, forefinger tightening on the trigger. Joe Noose knew he was dead, braced to hear the blasting discharge of the pistol, but was surprised to hear the synchronous sound of a second cocking hammer instead.

So was she.

"Lower the gun, bitch," a familiar Arizona drawl intoned. The recognizable figure of Waylon Bojack stood unsteadily in the shadows behind Bonny Kate. His arm was outstretched and the muzzle of his Colt Dragoon pressed hard against the base of her spine above her rump in the saddle. Sweat and blood gleamed on the sheriff's ravaged face.

"You don't kill so good, mister," Bonny Kate hissed, but lowered the pistol into her lap with a flinch.

Noose flicked his gaze past the looming figure of the lawman behind Copper and saw another horse standing fifty yards back in the darkened trees. The fires rising high into the blackened sky over the forest cast it in glimmering silhouette. Bojack had obviously escaped the flames, but he hadn't escaped Noose's bullet—he saw the rip in the right side of Bojack's shirt, drenched with glistening blood. His badge, crooked and bent, had partially deflected the shot and gleamed in a deformity of its original shape. The Arizona lawman looked like a bronze statue, framed with the epic firelight behind him that glimmered on his beard, but he was almost dead and his body was powered and animated by the last dregs of his will. Waylon Bojack was a dead man walking. Noose didn't move, knowing he would never get to his gun before the sheriff gunned him down, so he stood and watched, waiting to see what would happen next.

Bonny Kate, jaw grindingly set, stared straight ahead as Bojack spoke quietly to her from behind, his voice hard as lead. "This bullet will blow you in half, bitch. Bust out your spine and gut-shot ya. You'll die screaming and you'll die for a long time and it's just what you got coming. You shot my boy in the back. Heard it just come out of your own lips. I promised his mother I'd kill you and now I got you under my gun. You're gonna die, bitch. So say your prayers."

"Ain't nothing to pray to or for, old man. Do it."

"Loosen the hammer of that pistol in your hand."

The female outlaw did as she was ordered and there was a slow, low *snick* of a hammer being replaced.

"Toss your pistol to the marshal."

Noose cocked his head, surprised.

Bonny Kate chucked him the gun and Noose caught it. Flipping it around in his hand, Joe Noose had it pointed at Sheriff Bojack so quick he might have stood a chance of shooting the old lawman before he shot him if that was what Bojack had in mind, except he didn't, so Noose didn't shoot.

Staggering to his knees, the sheriff holstered his pistol as he dropped into a kneeling position and looked up at Noose with failing, dying eyes. "Take her to the gallows, Marshal. I'm truly sorry I got in your way and tried to interfere with you doing your duty. Vengeance got the better of me and my sworn oath but you're a good man and you got a job to do like I would have done once, like I used to do."

Noose shifted the aim of his Colt up at Bonny Kate as he walked up to the kneeling Bojack, and he wasn't looking at Bonny Kate but could feel her paralyzed figure on the horse, knowing he didn't need to look at her to shoot her in the head. Noose stood and looked down at the broken man. "We all make mistakes, Sheriff. It's easy to go astray. You did the right thing, right here, right now, and that's what counts."

The lawman coughed blood. "My mistakes killed my men. That can't be forgiven. But I want to go out clean like I did my job most of my career, do that for them. Means I can't kill this woman as much as I want to and I got to let you take her in. I'm dying, Marshal, and I know you got no reason to but want to ask you one favor."

"Name it."

"My wife, Margaret, is ailing at our home in Phoenix, Arizona. When they hang Bonny Kate Valance, when her neck is good and broke, will you send word to her that justice has come to the woman who shot our boy?"

Noose nodded. The life was draining from the fading, pale-eyed gaze of the dying sheriff looking up at him. "I will do that, sir," Noose said. "You have my word."

"Thank you, son," Bojack said in a final grateful whisper as Noose realized he was looking down at the old man's open eyes that had no life left in them.

Sheriff Waylon Bojack lay on his knees, dead, head raised, eyes open to the sky.

Joe Noose reached out and closed the lids gently with two big, respectful fingers.

A wad of saliva splattered the old man's bullet-mangled sheriff's badge, spat from the saddle.

Noose's eyes narrowed dangerously.

"You men make me so sick with all your manly hero talk about right or wrong, it just makes me wanna puke—" Bonny Kate Valance didn't finish her sentence because Joe Noose's closed fist punched her right in the face, very hard, knocking her out cold. When the female outlaw regained consciousness two hours later Sheriff Bojack was already buried, miles behind, and she was roped hand and foot and tied to the saddle of Joe Noose's horse as he rode into the outskirts of Victor, Idaho.

He could already see her gallows rising up like a steeple against the dawn sky from here.

CHAPTER 30

"Do you smell smoke?"

Bill Tuggle looked up from the sheriff's office desk in Victor, where now he wore the sheriff's badge. He had been leaning back in his chair with his feet on the desk, pretending to catch a little shut-eye, Stetson tilted over his face. Comstock stood by the door, sniffing, a funny look on his face. It was he who had spoken. The impostor sheriff smelled the air. He shrugged.

"I've been smelling it all morning," Comstock complained. "You can't smell that?" he asked again, fingering his nose. "There's a fire somewheres."

Tuggle sniffed. "Now that you mention it."

The gang had occupied the sheriff's office for exactly four hours and twenty-three minutes since they had dispatched Al Shurlock and his three deputies with the guns, using the potato silencers. Nobody in town had heard a thing. The first hour after the murders, after assuming the purloined badges and identities of local law enforcement, the gunmen had been busy as they worked hastily to clean up the blood before dumping the bodies in the back room and locking the door. The gang was quiet and efficient and three hours ago had finished their work while the town slept without a soul on the street and none of the citizens the wiser.

Now the phony lawmen were killing time waiting for daybreak and the approaching morning hours when the package would be delivered. It had been a long train ride before the Victor gunwork and Tuggle knew he and his crew had to be sharp for the job that lay ahead today—he had told his boys to catch some sleep and said he would wake them at sunrise.

But now it appeared a problem had arisen. One they had not expected and could not have anticipated.

The impostor sheriff looked back at Comstock. "Looks like you were right. There is a fire. Let me see." He got up from the desk and walked to the window.

Bill Tuggle acted like he could scarce believe his own eyes. The mountains to the south were on fire.

But he already knew that. In fact, he had been up before dawn, awakened in the safety of the sheriff's office by the ominous red glow blossoming through the window curtains and filling the inside of the room with a pulsating evil glare—the light of the forest fires on the top of the Teton Pass was turning the night into the day before the sun rose. The smell of burning timber was acrid in his nostrils. Tuggle had looked over at his sleeping gang, whose slumber seemed undisturbed, then soundlessly trod to the window of the office.

The view past the curtains looked out south, and the fires and smoke billowed against the sky ten miles away. Bill Tuggle knew this posed no imminent threat to his person or to the safety of the town of Victor, but his stomach churned with dread nonetheless. It wasn't from fear of being caught in the fire—there was scant chance of that because there would be plenty of time to evacuate by railway by the time the conflagration grew close enough to worry about—he guessed that time was a day away at least.

What caused Bill Tuggle such severe apprehension instead this morning was the possibility that there would be no hanging for the woman who was scheduled to swing today. She could not have made it through the forest fire and was undoubtedly reduced to ash by now.

Bonny Kate not arriving in Victor was bad for Bill Tuggle and his gang of thugs for a lot of reasons.

Dawn would soon be upon them. Varney, Gannon, Flannery, Mesa, and Hondo were waking up, checking their pistol loads, ready for action. One by one, they noticed their leader standing with Comstock by the windows framed with fire and they got up to take a look.

Restless and queasy with tension, Tuggle paced the office, gesturing his gang away from the window and with a series of hand signals directing them to appointed tasks in the interests of readiness.

There came a knock on the door of the office.

"Excuse me," the impostor sheriff said. Going to the door, he opened it.

Standing in the doorway on the boardwalk was a well-dressed man.

"Can I help you, sir?" Tuggle inquired.

"Where is Shurlock?" the man replied, taken aback.

"Who's asking?" retorted Tuggle.

"I'm Ralph Wiggins, the mayor of this town," the

official huffed. "And I'm here to see our sheriff, Al Shurlock. This is a momentous day, you understand."

Tuggle was glad he had scrubbed and shaved himself before posing as the lawman. He doffed his Stetson and assumed the appropriate deferential attitude and demeanor. Clearing his throat, the impostor sheriff kept his watchful eyes fastened on the mayor's. "Sheriff Shurlock was unavoidably called away on urgent business last night, Mr. Mayor. My name is William Tuggle. Call me Bill. Al's my friend and colleague in the Teton County Sheriff's Association and I'm his temporary replacement, acting in his stead until he returns. Shurlock's orders, sir. My regular duty is acting sheriff of Swan Valley and Al called me in last night to keep an eye on things so everything goes smoothly with the hanging today."

"I see." If Wiggins was surprised or taken aback by Tuggle's rehearsed patter, it didn't show on his well-fed, none-too-bright face. The mayor simply said, "Fine. Is everything in order?"

The impostor sheriff smiled a little too confidently. "It is indeed, sir. The hanging will go off without a hitch. I've added three additional deputies so we have things well in hand."

Scratching his head, Mayor Wiggins looked confused as he saw six new faces wearing deputy badges and carrying firearms. "So our deputies Chance, Fisk, Sturgis, and Fullerton, they will be here today?"

"Unfortunately they had to ride with Shurlock, sir. I brought six new men today on temporary assignment."

The mayor peered in at the six new faces standing inside the sheriff's office, looking back at him with competent and respectful expressions, awaiting orders.

The politician nodded to them and awkwardly smiled at Tuggle. "You all look like good men, capable and competent indeed."

"The best that money can buy," Tuggle retorted with a smile.

The mayor shook the new sheriff's hand and took his leave. "Very good. Glad to hear everything is under control."

"Everything but the fire on the pass, sir. That's a bit of a concern."

"Indeed so."

Exiting the building into the street, the cold fresh Idaho air filled Tuggle's lungs refreshingly even though it was tinged by the acrid stench of burning lumber. The whole sky was aglow with sapphire color, brighter in the direction of the mountains to the south, where the fires rose hundreds of feet in the air in the distance.

Tuggle's heart sank into his bowels as he gazed blankly at the distant inferno. Nobody could get through that.

There would be no hanging today. Not for her. Not ever.

If Bonny Kate Valance was dead, that changed every damn thing, it surely did.

Then Tuggle squinted. Rubbed his eyes. He thought he detected movement in the smoke, about a half mile off up the trail toward the pass. Couldn't be. He rubbed his eyes again against the stinging tears from the smoke and he saw it again: someone was out there. Surely his eyes were playing tricks on him, causing him to imagine things in the wreaths of smoke weaving ghostly wraiths in the swirling gray smog from the forest fire. It had to be his wishful projections,

this phantom in the vapor coming slowly toward him
and gradually growing corporeal until the ghost suddenly became flesh as a big man on a burnished gold
horse riding out of the smoke onto the outskirts of
Victor . . . and on the back of his saddle was a hog-tied
woman whose flaming red hair was recognizable even
from this distance and identified her indubitably as
the lady the waiting gallows had been erected for.

CHAPTER 31

Joe Noose was tired and his eyes were slow to focus. Even so, he didn't recognize the three lawmen standing on the street at the edge of town, looking in his direction. Noose saw their badges clearly enough, tiny dots of gleaming metal reflecting off the blaze behind him, but the figures that wore them were unfamiliar. They weren't the faces of the Victor sheriff and his deputies Noose was used to seeing in his regular bounty hunting business. The closer Noose rode to the lawmen, the more he realized there was nothing wrong with his eyes—these were definitely not the same men. In fact, their clothes didn't even seem to fit.

The welcoming committee was sure glad to see Noose, though. The three lawmen damn near broke into a run and got to his horse just as a weary Copper trod onto the main street, dominated by the austere spire of the gallows. Hands patted Noose's arms and back and grins flashed in his face and Noose was so exhausted he barely heard the words, which were all congratulatory.

"By God you made it, Marshal!" the sheriff crowed. "You brought this outlaw to face her comeuppance. You have done a man's job, sir!"

Hog-tied to the saddle behind him, Bonny Kate Valance was stirring, and behind him Noose could feel the surly energy radiating off her. The two deputies had stepped in her direction and she was being roughly handled from the sounds of things, not that Joe Noose cared. He could give a spit.

Pulling up his reins, Noose stopped Copper and leaned forward to give his stallion a guzzle from his canteen before drinking some water himself and splashing some on his face. It poured off him black with soot onto his shirt. Noose got a glimpse of his reflection in his canteen and two white eyes stared out of a mask of char. Noose noticed that Copper's usually bronze coat was dulled with ash. The horse turned its head to look back at him in relief that they had arrived safely to their destination, and he threw some canteen water on its snout to cool it. He patted the animal: *Good job, old pal.*

"How the hell did you get through that forest fire?" The sheriff gasped in admiration.

"With difficulty," Noose replied gravelly, his voice hoarse. "Some others weren't so lucky. The undertaker here has new business. He best ready seven fresh graves. You'll find the burned skeletons of five of 'em when the fires die. The other two bodies are back down the trail a ways." Noose tossed a somber glance back toward the pass, then lowered his gaze.

"Sounds like it was a long, hard ride," Tuggle said with an appreciative whistle.

"It was."

"Well, you're here now, with her, and that's what matters."

The sheriff saw the once-over Noose was giving him. It made the impostor lawman edgy. "Where's Shurlock?" Noose asked. "What happened to the regular sheriff? I don't know you boys."

"Replacements," Tuggle replied, scratching his eyebrow, noticing Noose's hand rested on his thigh right by his holstered, loaded Colt Peacemaker.

"Replacements?"

"The sheriff got called away on business."

"What kind of business?" Noose asked.

"The urgent type."

From his saddle, Noose saw the grin starting to look plastered on this sheriff's face whose eyes weren't smiling as they looked up less welcomingly at him on his weary horse. He was too tired to think straight, having been shot twice, lost a lot of blood, and hurt all over. *Maybe they were replacement lawmen like the man said*, Noose told himself. He'd been tasked to bring Bonny Kate Valance to the gallows and his job was done, the hanging platform a stone's throw away from the wench on the back of his saddle. *Leave it alone. Let these boys handle the rest.*

Noose jerked a thumb back at Bonny Kate tied up on the saddle. "She's all yours," he said in a gravelly voice, sounding plenty glad to be rid of her.

"We'll take her from here," Sheriff Tuggle said, roughly hauling the woman off the saddle and getting her onto her unsteady feet. The female outlaw just glared at the lawman with a surly blue-eyed stare and refused to look at Noose.

Noose didn't give her a second glance as the sheriff roughly held her and nudged his jaw to his two deputies, who produced handcuffs from their belts and unceremoniously shackled Bonny Kate Valance's hands in front of her at her waist. "Welcome to Victor, Miss Valance. Your hanging's at noon. Hope you brought some clean undies. Let's lock this bitch up, boys."

Sitting in his saddle, Joe Noose watched as the three lawmen force-marched Bonny Kate Valance across the square in the morning sun beneath the shadow of the gallows platform toward the sheriff's office and jail at the end of the street. Her shapely, worse-for-wear figure shrank smaller in his field of view, flowing mane of red hair blowing behind her.

She didn't look back, not once.

Then, a moment later, the lawmen pushed her through the door into the jail and she disappeared from Noose's sight.

With a sigh, Noose found himself wishing that would be the last he'd see of her.

But he knew he would have to stay and see her one last time.

When she took the drop.

"You're a mess, Marshal."

Joe Noose had been shot twice and needed to see a doctor. His wounds had to be tended to. He hardly needed to be reminded of this fact when a few minutes later Tuggle returned from the sheriff's office after locking up his prisoner, ambling over to where Noose sat on Copper, letting the horse drink from a nearby water trough. "Looks like you've been shot," observed the lawman, looking him over. Noose thought that fact was fairly obvious the moment he rode into town, given the two bloody, ragged bullet holes in his shirt, but figured maybe this peace officer was simple.

Joe Noose nodded and held up two fingers, too

tired to bandy words. He felt like he was on his last
legs even though he was seated in his saddle. It was
all he could do not to fall out of it. Copper was holding up better than he was, but Copper hadn't been
shot twice.

Tuggle wore an exaggerated expression of grave
concern. "Marshal, you gotta get to the doctor directly."

"Just tell me where," Noose growled, more out of
exhaustion than aggravation.

"Okay, Marshal, you ride right down this street here
half a block and you'll find the doc on your left there."
Tuggle pointed directions helpfully. "Got a big sign
on the door. Can't miss it. Doc will get you fixed up."
The sheriff looked genuinely worried at the sight of the
bloody cowboy on the horse. "I'll lead your horse and
help you over there."

"I got this," Noose snarled as he gave some boot to
his stallion and rode past the sheriff crowding him.
The man stepped aside and watched him go. It was
taking all Noose had to sit straight in the saddle but he
wasn't about to show weakness in front of a stranger
he didn't trust. And he was still wondering what happened to Sheriff Shurlock. These new lawmen didn't
pass the smell test.

"Let me buy you a drink when you get fixed up,
Marshal," Tuggle's voice called out behind him affa-
bly but there was a mocking in his tone. "You sure as
hell earned it." Noose looked back and didn't answer
as he rode off.

With a flip of the reins in his wrist, Noose steered
Copper in a brisk trot past the gallows through the
square onto the main street he figured was the street
that sheriff mentioned the doctor was on.

The sun was coming up hard and hot—it was already

hotter than normal. Hanging smoke and reeking stench of char in the air from fires on the pass burning out of control imparted an uneasy sense of danger and foreboding to the atmosphere . . . that and the blood in the air—because everybody in the town today who didn't live here was here to see a woman get killed; the folks wanted blood and you could almost taste it in the air.

The hovering sooty haze stung Noose's eyes and was keeping people off the street but he could see the town was packed for the hanging. As he rode past the corral, he saw the stockade was full of horses. Sold out.

A large, colorful banner hung across the street announced the hanging of Bonny Kate Valance. It was decorated in the ornate way of a Buffalo Bill Wild West show.

Rounding the corner, Joe Noose rode up a wide dirt main drag walled on both sides by boardwalk, storefronts, saloons, and hotels. NO VACANCY signage was hung out on the doors of the lodging establishments. As Noose trotted past the larger of the bars, he saw through the windows that the place was packed with a wide assortment of people crowding the counter, beginning their imbibing early; a few shots of whiskey improved the enjoyment of a hanging for some, Noose figured. It turned his stomach. So did the posters and carnival circus celebration portraying the hanging of Bonny Kate Valance. It wasn't that Noose felt Bonny Kate didn't deserve killing for her misdeeds, he just didn't like making a big show of it for people's entertainment.

And probably some politician's election campaign. It made Noose sick.

He knew Bonny Kate and had ridden with her by his side for two days and had risked his life for her and she was a person to him, even if she was a bad one who had it coming. Suddenly he wished he'd have let that Arizona sheriff kill her clean and quick with a bullet as he would sure have done given half the chance; that angry old man just wanted to be the one to pull the trigger. That way, the woman would have been spared this public spectacle.

As if a fateful reminder of why everybody was here today, the town clock tolled the hour with eight loud *bong*s. Swiveling his gaze to the left, Noose saw the clock tower with the hands snapping into place with a click of unseen clockwork machinery on the eight and the twelve.

In four hours, Bonny Kate would die.

Joe Noose wondered if that was what she was thinking, aware that in the jail she surely heard that clock strike the hour.

Two hundred and forty minutes.

In two and a half hours they would come into her cell and get her ready, he reckoned. The crowd would be assembling in the square around the gallows platform, rubbernecking for the best viewing position for the execution. Reporters would be setting cameras, scribbling in their notebooks. Ten minutes later a priest would show up at the cell and ask her if she wanted to make her confession. Noose smiled to himself, thinking Bonny Kate could give herself a few extra days of breathing life if she confessed all she'd done, but he figured she'd just laugh at the padre.

Fifty minutes to go, she'd be led into the sheriff's office under armed guard.

Ten minutes to go, the posse would be walking her to the gallows, down that long street on her last mile, past the parting crowd, up the wooden steps, and a rope placed around her neck by the executioner.

A minute later, Bonny Kate Valance would be no more. Despite it all, Joe Noose would miss her.

When she was gone, the world would be a little less interesting.

Inside the small, empty jail Bonny Kate was pushed through the barred iron gate into the single open cell.

Sheriff Tuggle stood in the open doorway, his deputies fanned out behind him.

The female outlaw turned slowly to face him. Raised and held out her handcuffed wrists.

The sheriff took his key and unlocked them. The cuffs fell from her hands and hit the ground with a *clank*.

She smiled.

They all smiled.

CHAPTER 32

It took him no time to find the doctor's office. It was just where that dodgy sheriff said it was.

The small wooden single-story building was right across the street from the feed store on the board-walk. Weathered plank siding and a brick roof and a few small windows and a well-used door. A metal sign hung on the front that read, J. STONEBRIDGE. DOCTOR. The place looked open for business.

Urging his tired horse across the street, Joe Noose pulled Copper up to the hitching post. The getting off the horse part he had been dreading. Gathering his strength and putting a rolled-up cloth in his teeth, the big cowboy put his weight on the boot in the stir-rup on his uninjured side. Slowly, painfully, he eased off his saddle, the cloth of his pants sticking to the leather seat with dried, bad-smelling blood. His. Using his muscular arms to cling to the pommel, he bit down on the rag and very slowly got first one boot down on the ground and then the other and then he was off his horse but barely on his feet. Copper's big fluid brown eyes worried into his own.

"I'll be all fixed up in a few minutes, friend," Noose said, patting his amicable and loyal horse's snout. Copper snorted hot breath onto his hand. "Then we'll get ya over to the corral and watered and rubbed down and fed. How's that sound?"

Copper gave him the side-eye.

Turning away from the stallion tied to the hitching post, Noose staggered stiffly to the door of the doctor's office and rapped sharply with his knuckles.

It opened presently.

Standing in the doorway was a woman of about thirty, wearing spectacles and a clean shirt and white smock. Her hair was pulled back over a strong rural high-boned face and her intelligent gaze was direct and observant of his.

"I need to see the doctor," Noose mumbled through gritted teeth.

"You're looking at her."

"'J. Stonebridge,' the sign says."

"The *J* stands for Jane. Most people around here just call me Doc. Anyway, you've come to the right place." The doctor's hazel eyes behind her spectacles narrowed in abrupt concern as they looked Noose up and down and took in the extent of his injuries. "Mister, you been shot to pieces."

Hovering in the doorway, Noose returned a weary amicable cracked grin. "Still in one piece that's got a few holes in it."

Dr. Stonebridge swept open the door and helped him limp inside with surprising country farm strength in her arm. "Lordy. Get the heck in here and let me

have a look at you." She led him through a small but
functional hospital room to a table and helped him sit
on it. He managed with a grunt. She saw the bullet-
crunched chunk of metal on his chest that had saved
his life last night. "I see you got a badge. Or it used to
be one. Who the hell did this to you?" Dr. Stonebridge
had already turned to the medicine cabinet and was
quickly snatching up handfuls of bandages and bottles.

"It's a long story."

"What's the short one?"

"My job was to bring Bonny Kate Valance to Victor
from Jackson over the pass. Some people didn't want
her to get here. I disagreed. You could say I won the
argument."

That got him a scrutinizing, disapproving glance
from the physician. "So those people won't be having
need of my services, I take it."

"Services, just not yours."

"The woman you brought here." The doctor com-
pressed her lips tightly. "She would be the one all the
fuss is about?"

"The same."

Noose watched Jane Stonebridge, noticing the
clenched expression that had suddenly come over her
features. "Is something wrong?"

"Looks like one bullet went clean through. The
other got blocked by the badge. These wounds need
to be stitched up and it is going to hurt. And you got
some broken bones ought to be set."

"Please stitch up the bullet holes for now. I'll come
back later for the splints."

"When?"

"Few hours at the latest."

"Where you planning on going?"

Noose's eyes stared straight ahead, his mind working. "Not sure yet. I'll know in a few minutes."

"Stay still." She was dabbing his wounds with a sharp-smelling solvent that stung like a hive of hornets but he didn't move. "I have painkillers if you need them. Laudanum."

He shook his head. "I need to keep my head clear. Stay sharp."

"You got that woman here. They're hanging her at noon. Your job is done. Keep your head clear for what?"

"In case this ain't over yet."

"Why wouldn't it be?"

He swiveled his powerful gaze to hers and she didn't blink. "You tell me."

Dr. Stonebridge took out her needle and thread, focused her gaze on the bullet hole in his side, and began stitching it closed. "I'm sure I don't know what you mean."

"Anything strange going on in town?"

"Like hanging an outlaw woman and having people come from across the country to watch it?"

"Other than that. Is there going to be trouble?"

She stopped stitching to look straight at him. "Mister, I best believe you're a better judge than me if there's going to be trouble or not."

"That's not an answer."

Dr. Stonebridge sighed, tight jawed. If she knew something she wasn't saying, Noose reckoned—then, in her way, she did: "Let me just say this. If there is going to be trouble, the sooner I get these holes stitched up, the sooner you can get back on your feet and deal with it, because, mister, any fool can tell that's what you do."

In no time at all, his bullet wounds were stitched and bandaged.

There was a knock on the door. Noose looked up to see Sheriff Tuggle, a big grin on his face, walk in like he owned the place.

"Mr. Noose, I'd be obliged if you'd let me buy you a drink."

Noose nodded.

A few minutes later, the two men walked across the street into the saloon.

CHAPTER 33

The noise of the whiskey pouring into the shot glass was music to Joe Noose's ears and the woody smell of the aged sour malt in his nostrils told him it was the good, expensive stuff as the bartender poured two stiff glasses from a fine bottle behind the bar and handed one to him and one to Tuggle.

The men clicked glasses with a melodious collision of glassware. "To a job well done. Damn well done, Marshal," Tuggle said with an admiring grin.

Noose drank a deep draft as did his counterpart. The fine whiskey went down his throat in a smooth, syrupy burn that warmed his insides with a pleasing, numbing fire. Noose took another sip, watching the sheriff the whole time.

A minute ago he had followed Tuggle into the luxurious comfort of the plushly outfitted saloon. Before he did, Noose tied up Copper by a water trough, patted him down, massaged the stallion's sore muscles, and brought him some fresh hay. The sheriff had politely stood on the boardwalk in front of the bar without complaint, watching patiently as Noose tended to his horse first. Then, when good and ready, the big cowboy followed the sheriff watchfully into the saloon and now they were having a drink.

"Hits the spot," said Noose.

"I figured it would," replied Tuggle, signaling the bartender, who lifted the lid of a desk humidor exposing a full stock of fine-smelling fresh cigars. "Buy you a cigar?"

Noose slowly shook his head, "Bad habit." He took another sip of whiskey, carefully scrutinizing the bar. It was just the two of them in the main area, with two curtained compartments leading off it. Leather couches. A full brass-railed bar. A wall-sized mirror. Oil lamps. Oriental carpeting. The row of Remington shotguns and Winchester rifles mounted on the wall caught his attention. The town had gone all out in refurbishments for the history-making hanging and business should be booming, but nobody was in the bar but him and this dodgy lawman. Like the townsfolk had been told to stay away, or just knew to. This saloon was too quiet, and Noose got the distinct impression that this sheriff was stalling for time. But why?

There was something else that raised his suspicions.

He knew this man Tuggle. Couldn't put a face to a name, but they'd met before. A long time ago. He got the sense from the occasional odd glance that Tuggle recognized him, too. Something about the man was wrong.

"One of many vices I subscribe to," said the sheriff, selecting a cigar, snipping the end off with guillotine cutter, putting the stogie in his lips, striking a match, and lighting up. Through the cloud of rich-smelling smoke, he looked past the glowing coal of cigar at Noose looking at him.

"We've met," Noose said.

Tuggle watched him through the smoke. "Don't think so. I'd have remembered."

"You sure?"

"Yeah. You make an impression on a man. But I sure am glad to have made your acquaintance. You must be plenty tuckered after that trip. Please relax." Sheriff Tuggle leaned against the bar, drink and cigar in hand. Noose sipped his whiskey and watched his counterpart very carefully with his steady pale blue–eyed gaze, a gaze that unnerved many, given the size of the man behind it, but if the other man was rattled he didn't show it. He remained cordial and affable. "She give you trouble, did she, bringing her over the pass?" Tuggle said.

Noose shook his head. "Her, not much. An Arizona sheriff and his posse, plenty. Seems the sheriff wanted to kill her himself because she shot his son and I had to convince them otherwise in harsh terms."

Behind a cloud of smoke, Tuggle's eyes widened and he sat forward. "Sir, are you saying that you engaged with armed lawmen? Do I understand you correctly that you gunned those men down escorting the outlaw here?"

Noose sipped his drink and nodded tightly. "They weren't Wyoming or Idaho lawmen and they were out of their jurisdiction, breaking the law trying to kill a prisoner under U.S. Marshals Service escort to her lawful hanging. I warned them."

"Then those were righteous kills, sir! You were doing your duty."

"It was the other one that was the bigger problem, the old gang member of Bonny Kate's come after her to get back the money she stole and hid."

Tuggle listened closely. He scratched his ear like he had a nagging itch. "Someone was after her for . . . money? This is the first I've heard of this." He scratched again.

Leaning his boot against the brass rail, Noose took a slow sip of his whiskey and clinked the ice. He regarded the sheriff over the glass. "A hundred thousand dollars it seems she has socked away. Only the lady knows where it's hid. Reckon the location of that money is going to die with her in a few hours."

Tuggle watched him steadily. "Reckon."

"All that money." Noose whistled. "Never to be spent."

The sheriff scratched his ear again. He sniffed, sat upright, straightened his vest, stuck out his bearded jaw, and struck a pose of determined integrity. "And so it should be. It is blood money if her hands touched it. Ill-gotten gains no doubt robbed and stolen. Let the secret die with her, I say, as it should."

Noose smiled. And finished his drink. But he didn't blink. "Sure."

Inside the empty saloon, Joe Noose propped up one side of the bar facing Sheriff Tuggle propping up the other side but the atmosphere had changed almost imperceptibly. Noose definitely surmised the lawman was keeping him occupied and stalling for time.

"Let's sit. I'm sure you'd like to get off your feet." Tuggle gestured to a table and chairs. Noose shrugged and took a seat after the sheriff sat down first. "Another drink?" Tuggle asked.

"You a poker man, Sheriff?" Noose asked in response.

"Yes, I am."

"Not a good one, my guess is."

"Care to play a few hands and find out?"

"I'd beat you."

"How can you be sure?"

"I already know your tells."

"Not sure I take your meaning, sir."

"A man has tells when he bluffs. His face, his movements, might be just a twitch, but no matter how good his poker face, his tells give him away."

Tuggle scratched his ear again. Noose pointed at his hand. "You scratch your left ear when you're lying. That's your tell, friend." Noose put down his glass on the tabletop with a solid *thunk*, his hand dropping to his gun belt. "Bonny Kate Valance, she has her tells, too. She was scared of getting killed, sure enough. That's a fact. When that sheriff showed up and started shooting in her direction, then when her old outlaw buddy showed up and loosed some bullets her way, Bonny Kate, she got a high color to her face and those red freckles of hers got bright as smallpox. Also, Bonny Kate got this quiver in the lip on the right side of her mouth. I saw this happen every time she faced death. That was her tell." Noose's face turned rock hard. "You know what never brought those tells from her, friend? *This hanging.* She was never the slightest bit scared of being brought to this gallows and she always acted not the least bit concerned. I just put it together right this very second. It was because Bonny Kate knew she wasn't going to be hanged in Victor, not today, not any day." Noose smiled coldly, his unblinking eyes hard as metal bits as they drilled into Tuggle, who was starting to sweat. "She'd never face death at the end of the rope."

"I don't know what you're talking about," Tuggle retorted. He made a big show of checking his pocket watch on the gold fob on his vest. "She hangs at.noon. Three hours, twenty-four minutes, and . . . ten seconds from now."

With a slow shake of his head, Noose kept his eyes on the impostor lawman. "Now, you and I both know that's a lie, friend. She ain't gonna hang. She made sure of it."

"I don't take your meaning, Marshal."

"Did she pay you half up front, the other half when she got away? Bonny Kate tell you she would take you where her stash of money is hid? And like a fool you trusted her. Sure, you know what I'm talking about. Your lips may lie but your eyes don't. Your tells give you away. The money she stole from that train, the money she got away with and hid in a bunch of different places. The money Johnny Cisco was chasing her to get back. The hundred thousand dollars Waylon Bojack had chased her down for before she shot his boy in the back and then the money didn't matter to him anymore nor his badge because he was chasing her for revenge. It was her insurance policy to bribe her life back when they caught up with her like she had to know they would. She paid you off to arrange some men to break her out of jail and escape her from the gallows today, didn't she?"

Tuggle said nothing. Just glared. All pretense of friendliness was gone from his beady eyes.

Noose continued, "You don't need to say nothing, friend, not even nod or shake your head, because I didn't need to play cards with you to notice your tells and I see all of 'em in your face."

Tuggle leaned back and crossed his arms. "You have no proof of any of this."

"My question is how Bonny Kate got to you. Must have been somebody came to visit her when she was jailed in Jackson. She gave them a message to give to you. I can't imagine she got many visitors, so I wonder who it was."

"A priest." Tuggle smiled like a snake. "Least I was pretending to be. Nobody would suspect a man of the cloth. My pappy was a reverend, you see, and I learned everything I needed to know about acting the part, once I heard Bonny Kate was locked up in Jackson. Information travels fast when it has to. How long have you known?"

Joe Noose's hand rested on his Colt Peacemaker he had slid out of his holster and had pointed under the table at the sheriff. "I know the lawmen in Victor. You see, outlaw, marshal ain't my real job, just a favor I'm doing for my friend the marshal in Jackson who deputized me for the purpose. My regular occupation is bounty hunter, and I knew the sheriff and his men in Victor real well. I say *knew* because I'm guessing they're all dead by now. I did a lot of business with Shurlock and Sturgis and Chance and I sure as hell know what they look like. The minute I rode in here an hour ago I didn't recognize the sheriff or his deputies. They were all new men and that didn't make sense to me because Sheriff Shurlock has been lawdog in Victor forever. The men taking their place I reckoned killed them, starting with you, all of you hired guns enlisted to replace them. The rest of it was easy to figure. In a few minutes, you boys are gonna change clothes and put kerchiefs on your faces and start riding around and shooting and break Bonny Kate Valance out of jail, making like her gang come to bust her free."

"You got it all figured out."

Noose nodded. "'Cept what I'm gonna do with you since you're gonna be charged with multiple homicides of Idaho lawmen and consorting with a known convicted outlaw. There's good news and better news, friend, or maybe I best just call you Bill Tuggle, because I remember your damn face now. The good news is you ain't sheriff no more. The better news is you're gonna hang for your crimes, right after Bonny Kate does today. The folks came here to see a hanging and they'll get two for the price of one."

Surprisingly, Tuggle laughed. It actually brought tears to his eyes. "Fact is, you is just a bounty hunter in it for the money. I don't suppose you'd be open to being paid handsomely to keep your mouth shut, Noose? Say, fifteen thousand dollars to get on your horse and ride away. Your job was to bring Bonny Kate Valance to Victor to the gallows and you've done it. What happens to her after she is handed over ain't your problem. Your record stays clean, and you ride away rich."

"Not my style."

"What does that mean?"

"I don't always know what's right, but I know what's wrong."

"What do you want?"

"I want to do the right thing." When Noose cocked back the hammer of his gun, he heard another gun cock behind him and froze, feeling the presence of the man behind him as he heard another ratcheting hammer. In the mirror behind Tuggle across the bar, Noose saw one impostor deputy step out of the darkness of the closet, aiming a double-barreled 8-gauge shotgun at the back of his head at point-blank range.

Swinging out of his chair, Joe Noose dived for the floor then turned and rolled and took two-handed aim just as both barrels of the shotgun exploded and filled the room with light and noise.

Exposed now to the gunmen as Noose dived from view, Bill Tuggle took both barrels of the outlaw deputy's shotgun blasts directly in the chest, his back disintegrating in messy showers of blood, flesh, bone, and cloth that sprayed across the walls and ceiling as his body was lifted from the chair and flung across the bar, a dead expression of shock and surprise on his face matched the impostor deputy's own as from the floor Noose shot him once, cleanly between the eyes, and blew the top of his head off. The corpses of both outlaws hit the floor at exactly the same time, equally deceased.

Jumping up on his feet, Joe Noose snatched the smoking cannon of a shotgun from the outlaw deputy's lifeless grip and scooped handfuls of shells from the dead man's blood-splattered pockets, jamming the rounds in his own pockets as he cracked open and reloaded the scattergun, then jacked it closed. Already, outside, there were the sounds of commotion.

Bonny Kate Valance huddled against the side of the door of the sheriff's office, stuffing .45 rounds in her SA Army revolver. She had a second loaded SA Army in the holster of the gun belt that she had just put on and buckled to her hips and a Winchester repeater slung on a strap on her shoulder. The firearms had been acquired from the rack in the office. Her face was twisted in raw fury as she took cover, listening to the sporadic loud gunfire outside coming from the direction of the saloon. People were running up and down the street, getting the hell out of the line of fire.

The lady outlaw met the questioning gazes of her armed gang crouching on both sides of the open door and answered in an animal growl, "It's *him*! Noose!"

"What the hell?" Varney was rattled.

"Tuggle's dead. So is Flannery. Joe Noose just plugged 'em. Told those fools to watch out for him."

"Who is this guy?" Varney spat, unnerved.

"A pain in my ass," Bonny Kate retorted, and spat. "Kill him. And when you're sure he's dead shoot him again. Noose, he don't kill good. But he's one against the six of us. And don't take any chances. He's dangerous. You're professionals so act like it."

Poking her head around the corner of the door to sneak a peek, she saw the big shape of the man in the color of shirt she had come to recognize dart out of the bar. She ducked back into the sheriff's office and cursed a string of profanity, cocking her pistol. "I just saw Noose. He's alive. That means Tuggle and Flannery definitely ain't. It's us now, boys."

"The horses are all saddled, Bonny Kate. Waiting for us."

She nodded with a toss of her red mane of hair, face flushed with color, blue eyes glittering. "Get to the corral. Shoot anybody gets in our way. Man, woman, or child. Knowing Noose he's got our whole setup all figured out, figuring we's a-headed to the getaway horses, so expect trouble. *Do not* underestimate this man. He's the best hand with a gun I ever seen or heard of."

Bonny Kate respected no man and her accomplices knew that about her—the phony deputies looked at the tense combination of fear and admiration in their leader's face and took her at her word. So they cowboyed up quick.

The woman was through the door first, shooting with both guns, one in each hand, at anything that moved.

CHAPTER 34

The shot came from above—one direction Joe Noose wasn't expecting—so he dropped and rolled, hitting the ground on his back, fanning and firing up at the top of the feed store.

The gunfighter wearing lawman's clothes staggered back as his chest exploded, revolver spilling from his dead fingers, as he clutched his wound and fell forward somersaulting head over heels off the roof of the building and landed limp and sprawled on the boardwalk.

Sweeping his gaze to the left, Joe Noose looked up the street and two blocks away saw the corral.

Behind the fenced pen, over a dozen horses were stomping around in agitation, alarmed by the noise of the gunshots.

Townspeople were running to and fro on the sidewalks, mostly taking cover. A few well-dressed businessmen fled into the hotel. Several cowboys hid behind some barrels. A mother wearing a shawl and clutching her little daughter's hand pulled her into an alley. The folks had come to town for a show but this had not been the one they were expecting.

Taking position behind a post beside the doorway of the saloon, Noose squinted to his right and saw Bonny Kate duck out of the sheriff's office with four of her gang in tow, all of them heavily armed. The gang were still wearing their stolen deputy clothes and badges but they were clearly outlaws and the badmen looked ready to shoot anything that moved.

They would be heading for the corral to get their horses and make their getaway, Noose was certain. It was what he would do in their position. The small town was in the middle of nowhere and with a huge, growing forest fire in one direction and low range-lands in the other, and making a break for it they weren't going to get far on foot.

The only other way out was the train. The parked and shut-down locomotive lay six wagons down the rails in the direction of the corral. He was closer to it than Bonny Kate and her crew were, but they were on the move. The cowboy knew he had to remove both escape options from the female outlaw. Keeping low, carting the loaded 8-gauge scattergun with his two loaded Colt Peacemakers in his holsters, Noose sprinted down the side of the train, staying trackside to the railroad. No shots came his way, yet, but he was ready to engage in gunfire any second as soon as the outlaws spotted him.

Looking ahead up the street, Noose saw that most of the horses in the corral were unsaddled. This was good, because if Bonny Kate Valance and her gunmen got there first, they'd be delayed a minute or two saddling up their mounts, which would give Noose all the time he needed to do what he needed to do in the drive cab of the locomotive to disable the engine. He

made a break down the train and reached the steam
engine in no time flat.

Clambering up the ladder onto the footplates of
the drive cab, he found the tool he needed right
beside the boiler. Behind the grate the coals were
cold. He set down the 8-gauge shotgun, picked up the
crowbar beside the boiler, then swung it hard against
the steam gauge and the throttle inside the engineer's
booth, smashing both controls into useless bent metal
with a few well-placed blows in a shower of sparks. The
locomotive was now disabled and nobody was driving
it anywhere without many hours of repair. Grabbing
his shotgun, Noose took cover behind the tender and
peered over the lip of the coal bin, which provided a
clear view of the corral and stable across the street.

Bonny Kate and her gang were coming. He saw their
figures two blocks away, running with their weapons
drawn like their lives depended on it. Their constant
defensive looks in all directions with their loaded guns
slowed their approach somewhat, giving Joe Noose all
the time he needed. Leaping from the tender, he hit the
trackside in a crouch, leveling the shotgun at the five
outlaws up the street and firing both barrels. The discharge of the scattergun was deafening and though the
lady outlaw and her cohorts were out of range and
the pellets fell short, the nasty sound of the blasts gave
them incentive to take cover before returning fire. In
that space of time, Noose made it across the street,
cracking his shotgun, ejecting the smoking empties,
and sticking in two fresh shells.

Noose got to the corral first. Up the street came
crackling reports of rifle and pistol fire. Bullets whistled
past his ears. Yanking open the gate and leaving it wide
open to the street, he dived in and hit the dirt. Looking

up as he rolled over onto his back, Noose braced as he saw the stamping hooves of a dozen agitated horses stomping the ground inches from where he lay—it was all he could do not to get trampled. Hearing the shouting male voices of the fast-approaching outlaws and the one female voice of their leader louder than the rest, Noose knew he had to act fast and scatter the horses before the gang could get to them. Aiming his scattergun straight into the air, he triggered two loud double-barreled blasts into the sky and that was all it took.

The horses bolted. Spooked at the close-range gunfire, they took off at a panicked gallop in the only direction they could—through the open gate of the corral. Noose was up on his feet, tossing the empty shotgun and drawing one of his Colt Peacemakers, which he fanned and fired several times through the fence posts at the shapes of the outlaws running after the horses to try to grab them before they got away, but the added shots gave the fleeing stallions even more incentive: they escaped in a furious gallop up the street in one charging herd out into the open countryside before any of Bonny Kate's gang got even fifty yards near them.

Joe Noose grinned savagely, knowing the outlaws were unhorsed. They were trapped in town in his killing range and none of them was getting out of here alive.

Hearing the barrage of gunfire coming in a steady fusillade from the gunfighters who had taken cover behind a row of barrels and crates on the sidewalk, Noose ducked into the open barn where one horse remained.

Copper looked happy to see him.

* * *

It was Comstock who first saw the last horse bolt out of the corral. The ragged outlaw saw the bronze stallion come galloping through the gate, fully saddled, and knew it was his damn lucky day. The horse looked magnificently golden as if it were armored in metal, and the steed was fifty yards off, coming his way, hooves kicking up dirt, so the hired gun broke cover and ran to intercept it. It was the last horse in town, his one chance. Comstock was hurt bad, his side bleeding all over the place from the marshal's bullet that had just broken his ribs, but this horse was his ticket out—the coward pushed past the pain as he ran flat-footed in his bloody cowboy boots, holstering his near-empty pistol and reaching out both desperate hands ahead of him for that big saddle and pommel so he wouldn't miss his chance. Behind him, Comstock heard the angry yells and curses of Bonny Kate and the rest of the gang and with every step toward that hard-charging horse he expected a bullet in the back but it never came. This gunfighter Noose was too damn dangerous and it was every man for himself if any of them were going to get out of here alive. The stallion was coming straight for him and Comstock's eyes were singularly focused on that saddle nearly within reach of his big mitts and then he felt leather in his hands and had good hold of the saddle as the horse galloped past. Using the steed's charging velocity to heave himself off the ground, the outlaw dug a spurred boot into the stirrup and swung a leg over the other side of the saddle, the physical stress of this activity and sitting upright sending a stab of agony through the bullet wound in his side as his busted ribs ground together. But then Comstock was on the horse, galloping the hell out of the meat grinder the town had become, and for a blessed second or two he felt relief.

Until he looked over the left side of the horse and saw Noose clinging to that side of the saddle where he had been hiding, looking Comstock straight up in the eye right up the barrel of a Winchester lever-action repeater he one-handed aimed right between his eyes.

The last thing Comstock saw and heard was the explosive muzzle flash that loosed the .45 caliber round that blew a hole through the front of his face and took the back of his skull off, ejecting him from the saddle, but his boot caught in the saddle so instead of flying off the horse he hit the ground like a bag of meat and was dragged by the one shattered leg at full gallop down the gravel-and-dirt street, smearing a snail trail of bright red blood and brains in his wake like a stripe of red paint.

Bonny Kate saw the whole thing from her hiding place with her three surviving gang behind the barrels and started cussing in frustrated rage, watching from her place of concealment the fast horse dragging her second-best man like a tattered rag doll—

—until she realized the horse was now in full view as it passed the barrels and crates on the street, which meant she and her men were now exposed on the boardwalk, which was Joe Noose's plan all along.

Right as Noose swung upside down beneath the horse from his perch on the other side of the saddle, Comanche-style, opening fire with his Winchester rifle, blasting and levering off round after round at Bonny Kate and her three gunfighters, who were hit by a storm of lead slugs fired between the stallion's legs by Noose as he rode past.

Varney took three in the chest and was flung backward through the window of the grocery store, his chest blossoming like rose bushes as he collapsed inside in a shower of shattering glass fragments, dead as it gets.

A little quicker than the rest because she saw it coming a fraction of a second earlier than her men did, Bonny Kate flattened herself against the boardwalk footboards.

Hanging upside down under Copper, his legs gripping the side of the saddle, Joe Noose aimed under his bronze horse's belly at the figures blurring past on the sidewalk, making a split-second decision. His shot at the woman wasn't clean so he levered and jacked another round into the chamber and shot dead-eyed into the biggest target—the fat outlaw's big belly.

Spewing a mouthful of blood, the obese Mad Cow Hondo looked down at his blown-out stomach spilling all over his boots and it was a mess as his shotgun barrel dropped in his hand as his finger tightened on the trigger by reflex, blowing both his own feet off as the scattergun emptied into the ground.

Cocking his pump shotgun Jim Gannon showed some guts at least as he broke cover and ran out into the street, diving onto the ground to get a clean shot at the man under the horse running past. As he drew a bead, catching a glimpse of Noose before Gannon could pull the trigger, there was a flash of lightning from the upside-down marshal's weapon. The single .45 round drilled through the top of the outlaw's skull into his brain like an oil derrick gushing blood instead of crude, and Gannon's face sank in a puddle of it.

Bonny Kate watched her last man die in the dust.

Her eyes were ice-cold.

Her gun was loaded.

Down the notches of her pistol, Noose was dead to rights. It was an easy shot.

She aimed at the horse.

As the bullet slammed into Copper, the horse let out a bellow of pain and fell violently sideways. Noose was tossed from his precarious perch on the saddle and hit the ground hard at the speed of a full gallop. The world spun around and around as he saw his beloved horse toppling onto the ground and lying on its side in the middle of the street in the settling dust.

"Noooooooooo!" Noose screamed.

The sound of his own scream strange to his ears, Noose staggered upright on his boots only to stumble down to one knee beside his wounded stallion. Without realizing it, Noose had automatically drawn his gun, prepared to put his horse down if a mercy killing was required. Noose wasn't a praying man but he prayed the gunshot wound was not fatal—fingers feeling, touching, tracing the blood, finding where the bullet hole was.

Not a head wound. Good, the horse wasn't dead.

Not a leg wound. Good, not lamed.

It had been just the one shot.

Noose felt around Copper's huge, panting, shivering, prone mass until finally he located the bullet wound under the pad of his fingertip. It was a shoulder wound: big, messy, and seeping—but not life threatening. Copper wasn't going to die. It would take a good veterinarian but his horse would eventually recover. Noose willed it to be so.

Shooting a fearsome glance over his fallen steed, Noose caught a quick flash of a flapping shirt as Bonny Kate Valance ducked out of there around the corner of the building toward the town square.

Perfect, thought Joe Noose savagely, *run toward the gallows,* and the thought curled his mouth as a cruel smile came to his lips. *Because that's where this ends, lady.*

"Good boy," Noose said softly, reassuringly patting Copper, who looked miserably up at him. The horse's breath came in panting gasps. "You're gonna be fine. Gonna get you fixed up. Right as rain. Just got to leave you for a few minutes then I'm coming right back. You got my word on it, old friend."

Noose cocked his Colt Peacemaker.

"Got me a piece of business I got to put paid to."

Noose stood and strode like a force of nature in the direction the female outlaw fled.

Entering the town square alone, Noose reloaded his revolver, standing in plain view.

The street was empty.

Nearby, the gallows stood tall and grim, austere in the blowing dust around the creaking wood platform. The rope noose swung in the wind.

Hefting his gun, Noose switched his keen gaze in both directions, looking left and right.

A shot rang out and a bullet clipped his arm, tearing a rip in his shirt. Noose quickly ducked behind a wood pile by the boardwalk. Gripping his pistol with the long barrel up by his face, he snuck a peek through the piled wood and saw movement in the empty square.

Bonny Kate Valance stepped out from behind some barrels, holding a little pigtailed girl across her chest as a body shield. One of her hands clutched the sobbing kid by the throat, the other clenched a Winchester rifle with the muzzle pressed against the girl's head. The lady outlaw walked boldly out in the open in the middle of the square near the gallows.

Bonny Kate's eyes were wide with vicious, savage fury. "Come on, Joe! Shoot me! Go ahead! You'll hit the girl, though! 'Cause even you ain't that good a shot!"

Joe Noose stepped out, his empty hands raised, his holsters empty. "Let her go, Bonny Kate. Even a woman as low as you don't want to kill no child."

Jamming the barrel of the rifle harder against the little girl's skull, the feral female gunslinger used the muzzle to describe circles in her hair. Bonny Kate grinned sadistically, her lips sickeningly moist. "Oh, Joe, you ain't got a brain in your head. I killed lotsa kids. Age don't matter to me none. Hell, I shot my big sister when I was no bigger than this young 'un is. Let me see those hands. Up."

Raising them higher, Noose fixed his gaze on the piece of the side of Bonny Kate's head that showed behind the bawling, hysterical child's face.

That was when Bonny Kate Valance made her move. She was quick, almost too quick, as she swung the barrel down from the kid's head in a straight, lowering, swift arc, aiming it across the space at Noose's chest—and as she did her head moved an inch out from behind the little girl's and when that happened Noose dropped to a crouch, his hand whipping behind his back to his belt where he had his Colt Peacemaker stowed and hidden—he had his gun out, fanned, and fired so fast Bonny Kate never had time to get a shot off before his .45 caliber lead slug drilled a bloody red

trench along the left side of the lady outlaw's head
and blew her left ear off in a gory shower of flesh.

With a horrific high-pitched screech of horror,
Bonny Kate Valance was blown off her feet and hit the
ground hard. She dropped the little girl, who landed
in a screaming heap. The child had not been hit. By
then Noose was on the move, running as fast as his
boots could carry him for the helpless child, his revolver aimed straight-trained on Bonny Kate, careful
not to fire and hit the kid. Wailing like a banshee,
Bonny Kate clutched the side of her head, holding on
to the ragged stump of skin that was all that remained
of her shot-off ear, her tousled red hair glistening with
redder wet blood, trying to hold the ear that wasn't
there on, and she had already grabbed the Winchester
rifle off the dusty ground, had her finger around the
trigger, and loosed an enraged shot at the oncoming
Joe Noose. "You took my ear! You took my ear, you
dirty, miserable son of a bitch!"

He was at least twenty paces from the little girl in
the cloth dress up on the ground, covering her head
and screaming—the dress was splattered with blood
but Noose saw it was from Bonny Kate and the child
had not been hit.

Not yet.

The first rifle shot buzzed past his face as he ran, so
close he felt the wind of the passing slug.

Noose dodged left to right in a zigzag movement to
throw Bonny Kate's aim as she levered the repeater
rifle with the bloody hand she pulled away from her
head, loaded, and fired again just as Noose veered in
the other direction, coming on relentlessly. Taking aim
with his Colt Peacemaker, Noose saw he had a clean
shot as the lady outlaw on the ground wormed her way

across the dirt, bending at the waist, inching herself toward the safety of the alley while she levered the Winchester again—he fired, but missed, the bullet exploding an inch from her head, showering her bloodied, twisted face with pebbles, and when he aimed again it was at her boots scrambling behind the alley wall.

It was a clean shot—Noose could have blown both of Bonny Kate's feet clean off at the ankles and that would have slowed her progress some and she'd have bled out and died in minutes—but he had a split-second decision to make: he had reached the little girl and all he could think of was getting her to safety—the child was out of the line of fire for a few seconds while the lady outlaw pulled herself into the alley, and if Noose was going to get the kid out of there it had to be now.

Scooping the little girl up off the ground in his arm, he holstered his pistol and covered her with his other big, muscled arm and upper body, turning his broad back on Bonny Kate in the alley and, with the rescued kid, running for all he was worth for the safety of an open barn a hundred yards away.

He might get shot, but his body would shield the little girl from any bullets the lady outlaw fired, though just the same Noose hoped he wouldn't be on the receiving end of any—that depended on how fast he ran and he ran fast indeed, reaching the barn in fifteen seconds and tossing the little body through the door onto a bale of hay shielded from gunfire as Bonny Kate's first bullet rang out right as he dived chest first to the ground and slid and rolled twenty feet behind the wood pile where he had left his other guns a few minutes before.

Leaning against the cords of lumber, Noose quickly knocked out his empty shells and slammed fresh loads into his Colt Peacemaker. He had two rounds. Then he was out of bullets.

Bonny Kate had a lot more weapons. And on the other side of the square, an easy walk or crawl to her dead gang and their weapons that she could take from them. The lady outlaw's voice shouted from across the square: *"You took my ear, you no-good bastard!"*

"You shot my horse, bitch!" Noose hollered back.

"I was aiming at you!"

"The hell you was!"

"That's no way to treat a lady, shooting her ear off!"

"You're a lot of things but you ain't no lady!"

"You shot my ear off and messed my looks up permanent and I'm gonna settle up proper with you for that, bet your ass on it, you son of a bitch!"

"You got a date with the noose today, Bonny Kate. I mean to see you keep it."

"Want to repeat that? Can't hear so good outta my left ear."

"You heard me just fine!"

"That noose ain't around my neck yet! It's down to just us now, Noose! Just me and you! Been a busy two days! You killed that Arizona sheriff and his boys! You killed Cisco. You killed Tuggle and all my boys here. You killed everybody but me! You hear me, Joe Noose? I said you ain't killed me! The butcher's bill ain't been settled!"

"The bitch's bill is about to get settled and I'm putting paid on it!"

"I'll see you in hell, Joe Noose!"

Noose clenched his revolver and listened, taking cover behind the chunks of lumber. No bullets came his way. He didn't hear her voice anymore. It was too quiet. As the seconds ticked by, Noose no longer sensed her presence in close proximity and sensed she had changed her position to a more advantageous one. Bonny Kate Valance was smart and only a fool would underestimate her. Joe Noose was no fool, but that would not make him any less dead if he didn't stay one step ahead of his deadlier-than-male quarry.

He checked the loads in his pistol. Two bullets left. His belts were empty.

He knew that Bonny Kate would be counting his bullets—know he was down to a couple rounds. The only way to rearm was grab the guns and ammo off the dead gang members, but the lady outlaw had positioned herself between Noose and those weapons and already rearmed herself.

Where was she?

Two shots. Make 'em count.

Peering through the space in the pile of lumber, Noose saw the town square was quiet and still. No sign of anybody. His eyes narrowed as he surveyed the surrounding buildings. Nobody on any of the rooftops.

Nothing moved but the empty noose on the hanging rope dangling from the yardarm of the gallows platform, slowly swinging back and forth like a pendulum in the breeze.

Noose needed an overview of his surroundings. He needed to get the high ground.

There was only one place.

Noose ascended the gallows.

The shadow of the rope fell across his face.

CHAPTER 35

Crawling up the ten wooden steps on all fours in a quick crab walk, Joe Noose flattened himself on the wooden planks of the gallows near the trap door and lever. He was twelve feet off the ground—the height the contraption was built to allow for the drop so the tallest man's feet would not touch the ground, allowing their broken, stretched neck sometimes added a foot to their height. Noose knew he could not be seen from the town square and intersecting streets, just from the hotel across the street but nobody was up there. He could see, though. Lying on his belly, he had a 360-degree vantage point on the surrounding town.

Cocking the hammer of the Colt Peacemaker in his fist, he watched the cylinder rotate the first of the last of the two rounds into the chamber with a solid *click*. Keeping the barrel pointed ahead, his fist clenching the stock on the planks, his other fist clutching his gun hand's wrist to steady his arm, Joe Noose kept his eyes peeled on the lookout for Bonny Kate Valance to show herself. She was out there somewhere.

The deafening pistol shot was so close and loud it

caught Noose completely unawares as the fist-sized hole exploded through the planks of the gallows . . . *from below*! Sawdust sprayed him but the slug just missed.

Rolling desperately out of the way, Noose caught a flash of movement of colored cloth in the gap between the planks and fired his gun at it. It was answered by a second shot up through the planks from Bonny Kate Valance, who had ambushed him from below, and this one clipped Joe Noose on the elbow and he leapt to his feet and fired his last round down at the hidden, unseen lady outlaw positioned beneath the gallows. The slug punched a big hole in the floor planks on the platform and showered splintered wood.

When he heard her merry laugh, he knew he had missed.

Noose crouched on the gallows platform and pulled the trigger of his Colt Peacemaker, knowing it was wasted effort.

The hammer of the revolver snapped on an empty chamber. He was out of bullets.

And when Joe Noose heard the *click* of a gun being cocked behind and below him he froze, because he was unarmed.

The female voice was one he knew well: "You're empty," Bonny Kate Valance said, cold as ice.

Wincing, Noose raised his hands away from his holsters and stood straight, slowly turning and expecting the impact of the bullet at any second—he knew it would come before he heard the shot.

There she stood at the foot of the hanging platform by the wooden steps. Bonny Kate held the Smith & Wesson SAA pistol straight-armed up at him about twenty feet away. Her eyes were dead. "Why didn'tcha?" she said.

Noose looked left and right on the wooden gallows platform. There was nowhere to run—he was right out in the open, an easy target. The trapdoor was a foot from his boot. The rope noose swung lazily in the breeze right above it. A foreboding sign if there ever was one.

Bonny Kate's foot took the first stair of the platform steps, slowly advancing on him, her gun deadly steady, her finger tight on the trigger, her blue eyes locked with his. There was death in her pitiless gaze, but something else, too—something that bothered her like a stone in her boot, an itch she couldn't scratch. "Why didn'tcha?" she repeated as her boots took the second stair, then the third. The wood creaked below her weight but there was no other sound in the oppressive silence on the gallows.

Noose just stood there, facing her, his face showing nothing. He let her do the talking as she came up the steps toward the top of the hanging platform, holding the gun rock steady on him.

"Why didn'tcha just go when you had the chance? What did it matter to you whether I got hanged or not? What's it to ya?" Raw emotion tinctured her coarse, whiskey voice. "Why did you come back for me in that fire when as far as you knew I was gonna die anyway? Why did you risk your hide to save me from that sheriff and Cisco?"

Noose didn't blink, just held her gaze in his own.

She was halfway up the platform now and the words tumbled from her lips. "Why didn't you go for yourself? What makes you so different from anyone else?"

She was now ten feet from him, her head and

shoulders rising above the edge of the platform, the
revolver level with his knees and aimed right at his
nose. Her wild, untamed beauty was a sight to behold
with her face flushed and her blood up, her expression fierce and conflicted behind her flowing red
locks. "What makes you want to be a hero? You think
it's because you're good or something? You ain't
good. You and me, we both know that. You're just as
bad as everybody else in this shithole world."

The creak of her boots echoed on the wood planks
as Bonny Kate Valance climbed to the top of the steps
and stepped out onto the gallows platform. Her left
ear was shot away and that side of her face and clothes
were soaked with blood. The two of them stood eight
feet apart from each other, the dangling noose between them on the hanging structure, like they were
the only two people in the world. Her revolver was
held steady, the hammer cocked back on a hair trigger. She was just out of reach and if he made a move
to grab the gun he was a dead man.

A dry, hot wind fragrant with the smell of the forest
fire whisked up and blew her flaming red hair and
clothes, flapping them around her face in the swirling
dust and soot.

For a moment he just stood, locking eyes with her.

Moisture welled in her eyes.

"*Why?*" she whispered.

The gun wavered. She couldn't do it. Couldn't
shoot him.

Her boots stood on the trapdoor.

Noose's countenance softened as he reached out
his hand and touched the barrel of her SAA revolver.
His big hand closed around the gun and tugged it
from her grasp.

EPILOGUE

The forest fires raged through the month of August.

In the months that followed Bonny Kate Valance's death, the flames bellowed against the sky but never came nearer than a mile from Victor, so the town was safe. In early fall, the great Teton fires of 1888 roared their last when mud season came early in October, bringing the rains as the skies opened and a torrential flood doused the inferno in two days, leaving the Grand Teton mountain range a vast blackened no-man's-land of scorched earth, charred trunks, and fallen, cindered trees lying spread across twenty muddy miles of deforested land like millions of burnt toothpicks. The trees would grow again, and in a few years the Tetons would again be lush and green with conifers. Such was the cycle of nature in Wyoming.

Joe Noose remained in Victor through the first snowfall in early November, for he had matters to attend to that would keep him there until the temperatures grew very cold and winter descended and the land grew icy and dark.

By popular vote Noose had been appointed interim

sheriff of Victor, given his fitness for duty, a job he agreed to do until a replacement could be found for Al Shurlock. The fact he had single-handedly gunned down all the bad guys gave the locals confidence the bounty hunter turned marshal should wear the sheriff's badge for a while. Joe Noose didn't ask for the job—the mayor asked him the day Bonny Kate and her gang were laid to rest in the local cemetery—but Noose didn't say no. He could use the money.

The fact was, he had no choice but to remain in Victor for several months during his horse, Copper's hospice. Noose had no intention of leaving town until he could ride out of town in his friend's saddle, but the medical treatment for the wounded horse was going to take many weeks while the animal healed from its bullet-shattered shoulder, and in the early days it would be touch and go. The veterinary treatment was expensive, and Noose needed the money from the sheriff's job to pay for the medicine and equipment, so that's the way it went.

Everybody told him to put the horse down. There was no way to save a lamed steed. It was just a horse. But Joe Noose never made a habit of listening to people and it wasn't just a horse—it was his best friend. Copper had saved his life more than once, and a debt was owed.

He rented out part of the stable in the town corral and had a chain and leather harness built that he chained around a winch on the beam in the rafters. Strapping his fallen horse into the harness, Noose winched the horse upright off the ground, where its hooves were off the floor. He changed Copper's bandages and cleaned its wound and applied fresh

ointments and solvents several times a day and
night—Noose rarely slept much; he warmed the re-
covering, weakened horse with blankets on its back,
fed it the best hay as its appetite slowly returned, and
kept it hydrated with water. He scrubbed his stallion
down with soap and water and manually massaged it.
For two months Joe Noose rarely left Copper's side,
and his equine friend knew it, and felt the comfort,
the glow slowly returning to its warm brown eyes.

Folks were still telling him to put the horse down,
that it would never walk again. Noose didn't listen, like
he never did.

The long days and nights in the passing weeks,
when Joe Noose wasn't on patrol in the town or in the
sheriff's office, he was at Copper's side in the stable.
Noose never smiled, rarely said a word to anyone that
wasn't sheriff-related business.

After the burial service, Joe Noose never once vis-
ited Bonny Kate Valance's grave, and nobody ever left
flowers. The lady outlaw had signed her death warrant
the moment she shot Noose's horse. The gallows had
been dismantled after her hanging and, at Joe Noose's
directive, the wood of the yardarm and platform and
trapdoor were used to build an equipment shack
behind the sheriff's office. There would be no more
hangings in Victor, the town decided, and the mayor
put it into law—one execution had been enough.

Noose largely ignored the everyday goings-on in
the town that didn't directly concern the sheriff's
office and kept to his duties of disarming and locking
up rowdy cowboys and wranglers who caused a fuss.
One time he broke the nose of a john who beat a whore.
While sheriff, he shot only one man—a booze-crazed

young gunfighter who drew his gun in the street and waved it aggressively at passersby, and after fair warning Sheriff Noose drew his Peacemaker and shot the kid's gun hand off at the wrist. The youngster would survive, but had better learn to shoot with the other hand. Noose advised him if he ever returned to Victor, he'd shoot the other one off, too. The kid never returned, and Joe Noose's tour of duty as sheriff of the town of Victor was otherwise uneventful.

He slept beside his horse, wrapped in a blanket, his arm around his stallion. One day, there was a change.

In late October, as the sky steamed from the doused trees as the heat from the blackened forest rose in the relentless assault of the rain, Joe Noose disengaged the harness, and Copper stood on its own four powerful legs for the first time in two months. Noose just smiled and patted his horse's head, as if to say *We did it.* Then he opened the gate of the stall and led Copper slowly, tentative step by slow step, out of the stable and into the corral and the heavy rain that was falling. Man and horse stood getting drenched in the rain, up to their ankles and fetlocks in heavy mud, standing together. Copper threw its head back and opened its mouth, refreshed by the downpour and lapping the fresh water and nostrils flaring, breathing in the cold, wet air. Noose's face broke into a big, cracked grin, the first time he had smiled in two months since coming to town. Copper was back. Horse and rider just stood in the rain getting wet, and the man was laughing, and to the few wet cowhands who witnessed the scene, it seemed like the damn horse was laughing, too.

Nobody ever told Noose to put his horse down again.

* * *

It was the first time Joe Noose had seen Bess Sugarland in five months.

In early November Idaho saw its first snowfall of the
winter. The air was chill and a carpet of soft flakes
gently fell on the landscape, coating the buildings and
streets of Victor. The white of the snow was peppered
with black smudges of ash from the burned mountains
that lay to the south; flakes of ash flitted through the
air with the fluffy flakes in dots of black with the white.

Noose had been on patrol, wearing a heavy coat he
had recently purchased with his sheriff's salary, since
the end of mud season had brought a plunge in tem-
perature to where his breath condensed in the air as
he sat in Copper's saddle. His trusty horse was now
fully back on its feet, and Noose had taken to using his
daily patrols of the town as an excuse to walk the horse
and exercise its legs and wounded shoulder, which
had completely healed. They were presently trotting
down the snow-dappled main street that faced the entrance to the Teton Pass a few miles off. The winter and
muddy fall before it had turned the landscape brackish brown, black, and white, a subdued palette of color.
There were few people on the streets, and Noose kept
his hands loose on the reins, away from the twin re-
volvers hung in his holsters, for he did not sense any
trouble. Breathing deep of the frigid air, he exhaled
a lungful of chill mist that clouded below his low-
tipped Stetson.

As he gazed again south out at the distant pass,
Noose thought of Jackson, several miles across, and of

Bess Sugarland. There had been no word from her, not
that he had expected any. The summer's fires had cut
off any communication between Victor and its sister
city in the Jackson Hole valley just across the border in
Wyoming. She had no way to contact Noose, nor he,
her. The pass had been utterly impassable during the
great fires and the rains that finally extinguished
them—for the last couple months, what remained of
the Teton Pass trail was a mess of mud and fallen,
charred trees that made passage equally impossible.
Noose knew Marshal Bess probably thought he died
during the fires and over the last months had wished
he could get word to her. There was every likelihood she
had received a telegram from Cody or one of the other
U.S. Marshals Service offices saying that Bonny Kate
Valance's execution had taken place, which would have
made her realize Joe Noose had made it through the
conflagration and had survived to successfully complete the job she had tasked him. At least he hoped that
information had reached her one way or the other.

Noose felt bad that his female peace officer friend
would be worried he was dead, because she would be
blaming herself.

He missed her.

Besides his horse, Bess Sugarland was his best friend.

That was the truth.

Now this morning on Main Street in Victor, sitting
astride his healthy and vigorous horse, Noose saw
something he didn't expect to see in the distance. It
was a foggy view through the cloud of condensed
breath he was exhaling.

Movement on the pass. Coming in his direction.

Two riders on horses a mile off.

No, three. One was small.

"Ho." Joe Noose reined Copper and sat in the saddle, shielding his eyes from the snow and squinting into the distance.

The three riders were getting slowly closer, but they were too far off to recognize. They had come over the Teton Pass, so must have come from Jackson.

Joe Noose had a damn good idea who at least one of them was.

The snow fell in a vast flurry, bringing with it a gigantic winter hush over the world, where all Noose could hear was his own breathing and the *flit* and *tap* of the snowflakes on his coat and gloves. There he sat, watching the approaching stick figures; dark, indiscernible shapes on the white canvas of the pass until a glint of metal on the woman's coat caught his eye and then he was sure.

His smile grew incrementally broader the whole ten minutes it took Marshal Bess Sugarland to ride up in front of him and Copper with the two mounted strangers at her side. The woman looked healthy, her ruddy outdoor face red from the cold but her eyes warm and cozy as two campfires as they locked on his. She was tearing up, and not just from the cold.

"I knew it was you." She grinned, her voice cracking.

"What took ya so long?" He grinned right back.

They hugged right there in the saddles of their horses.

Shutting the door to the sheriff's office behind them, Joe Noose showed Bess and her two companions to three chairs set in front of the wood-burning stove. The office was cold and their breath condensed on the air.

She had still not introduced her fellow travelers to Noose. He guessed she would in her own good time, and that they were here for a reason. One was a young, rugged, brooding U.S. Marshal, the other a quiet, reserved little boy of maybe nine or ten, Noose guessed. The kid seemed nervous and fearful and stayed close to Bess as she showed him a seat then took one herself.

"I'm the interim sheriff while they find a replacement. Bonny Kate's gang killed the last sheriff and his deputies before I did for them and the town needed someone to wear the badge. Seemed like the right thing to do when they asked me. You maybe heard about all that." A nod from Bess. "I don't have any deputies. Think I got the situation in hand. But I'll be moving on soon, I reckon."

"Bounty hunter, then marshal, now sheriff. A body has a hard time keeping track of your movements, Joe," Bess cracked. Noose was glad to see she hadn't lost her ornery sense of humor, but was worried about the huge wooden leg brace she wore on the wounded leg—it was bigger than the one he last saw her wear, and he hoped that the bullet Frank Butler had given her to remember him by wasn't going to mean she would lose that leg. Bess saw him looking at her brace and looked crossly at him. "It ain't gangrene. I'm not losing the damn leg. Just got it jacked up again when my horse fell on me while I was riding up the pass with my deputy, looking for you during the fires. Thanks to you."

With a sigh of relief, Noose looked over at the lawman who had just sat beside her by the stove. The young man had a hard, angular face and an intense, dark gaze and was watching Noose closely. "That him, your new deputy?" Noose asked.

Bess shook her head. "No, my deputy is a greenhorn

named Nate Sweet I left back in Jackson to man the
U.S. Marshal's office while I came here. Somebody had
to mind the store while I was away. Good man, Sweet
is, lots of promise." She looked over to the lawman
with her. This here is Marshal Emmett Ford."

Joe Noose gave Marshal Ford a long, hard stare—
something was familiar about his face, but he couldn't
quite place it. "We met before, Marshal?" Noose asked.
"I seem to remember your face."

Ford held his gaze respectfully and shook his head,
demurring. "No, sir. I don't rightly recollect so."

Noose shrugged. Maybe he was mistaken. He
looked a question at Bess. Drew her gaze with him to
the silent little boy bundled in coats, sitting staring
into the fire. She spoke up. "The boy, we don't know
his name because he won't talk. Marshal Ford brought
the boy to me a few weeks ago. So I brought him to
you. He's why I come, Joe."

His brows furrowing, not following her conversation, Noose went to the stove, where the pot of coffee
brewed, filling the room with a warm, toasty aroma.
Without asking if they wanted any, Noose poured
two cups and handed them to Bess and Ford, both of
whom accepted the hot beverages gratefully and
sipped. The boy just watched the fire.

"Sit down, Joe," Bess asked politely. He did. He was
about to hear the story and the reason for her visit.
"I'll let Marshal Ford tell it. Go on, Emmett."

The young lawman cleared his throat and spoke
plainly. "This boy was the only survivor of the massacre
of his entire family near Alpine. Father, mother, two
sisters all cut to pieces and strewn about."

"Indians?" Noose asked.

"No."

"Go on."

"They weren't the first victims of this killer. We think it is one man. Twenty-five people, families, men, women, children, have been butchered by this fiend. The ones we know about, anyhow. He has been leaving a trail of bodies from the southern border of Idaho, and I've been hunting him ever since." The marshal spoke gravely and the intense, personal dedication to catching this killer was plain in his eyes. This was a mission for him.

"Good hunting," Noose said.

Bess interrupted. "I came to you for a reason, Joe. So did Marshal Ford."

"What reason?"

Ford answered, "You're the best bounty hunter in the western states, Noose. Everybody knows that. There ain't a man in the world you can't track down and apprehend. I haven't been able to catch this killer on my own. I need your help. And there is a twenty-five-thousand-dollar bounty on this monster."

"That's serious money," Noose replied, warming his hands by rubbing them together by the fire. "Very serious money. But the thing is, Marshals, I took a job as sheriff here in this town and gave my word I would perform those duties until a replacement is found. Nobody's arrived to relieve me yet, don't rightly know when they will. I'd surely like to chase down that bounty, but I have a job."

Rising to her feet, Bess's boots jingled as she walked to the wall and leaned against it by the stove, fixing Noose in her persuasive gaze from an elevated vantage. "Only you can catch this man, Joe." Noose raised an eyebrow in question, letting her continue. "You don't know the rest. This killer, he always leaves one alive, like this boy. And he does something to them . . .

leaves his signature. One you'll understand, Joe."
Gesturing to the boy, Bess made the motions with her
hands of opening her shirt. "Show him," she gently
but firmly bid the child.

Swallowing hard, his eyes vacant, the little boy obe-
diently unbuttoned his coat, then opened his ragged
cloth shirt to expose his chest.

When Noose saw what was there, his eyes widened
in raw emotion, and he rose from his chair to his towering full height, staring unblinkingly at what was on
the kid's naked, chicken-bone chest: *The brutal mark of
a red-hot branding iron was savagely burned into the child's
very flesh—half-healed and raw was seared a single upside-
down letter . . .*

$$\eth$$

It was the same brand that Joe Noose bore forever
on his own chest, a mark burned into him when he
was little older than this boy, by the same man. He felt
his own long-healed scar burn freshly under his shirt
like a phantom pain, feeling again the white-hot agony
of long ago. Noose was speechless as he just stared at
the poor child looking up at him with hangdog eyes,
displaying his disfigurement with shame.

His knuckles whitening, Noose's fists clenched at
his sides in a murderous cold fury that made the cartilage crackle.

When his gaze swung back to Bess Sugarland, she
held it confidently. "This is a job for you, Joe. Only you
can stop this man."

Nodding, Joe Noose pulled the sheriff's badge off
his coat and laid it on the desk.

Did you miss the first book in the
Joe Noose western series?
Keep reading for a special excerpt.

NOOSE
A JOE NOOSE WESTERN
by Eric Red

MEET JOE NOOSE.
A GOOD BOUNTY HUNTER WITH A BAD ATTITUDE.

In the cutthroat world of bounty hunters,
Joe Noose is as honest as they come. Which isn't
saying much. Just look at his less-than-honest
colleagues. They framed Joe for a murder they
committed. They made sure Joe's face wound up on
a wanted poster. Now they're gonna hunt Joe down
and collect the reward money. There's just one
problem: Joe Noose thinks it's his bounty.
It's his reward. And it's their funeral . . .

Look for NOOSE.
On sale now, wherever books are sold.

CHAPTER 1

A lone wolf is an easy target.

Joe Noose considered this as he raised his Winchester rifle to his shoulder, settling the crosshairs of his gunsight on the distant figure standing by a horse near the Hoback River two hundred yards away.

Adjusting his aim an inch up and to the right of the figure's shoulder for trajectory in the northwesterly wind, he calculated for windage, elevation, and bullet drop as he felt the cold metal of the trigger resistance against his forefinger.

No mistaking his target even from this distance—nor the missing nose on his face from the wanted posters for Jim Henry Barrow that offered a thousand dollars reward for his capture, dead or alive.

Noose's gloved finger was tight on the trigger and his quarry in his rifle crosshairs had not spotted him yet.

The bounty hunter would try to take him in peacefully, picking his moment to call out the man's name and order him to put his hands behind his head.

If he resisted, Noose would put one in his shoulder, which usually subdued even the most uncooperative type.

He meant to take his target in alive like he always did.

Noose heard something. His finger loosened infinitesimally on the trigger, senses alert.

There it was again—a near-imperceptible disturbance in the distant woods like horses' hooves stepping on fallen leaves and twigs, but slow and quiet like the horses were being ridden with stealth.

It wasn't the first time the bounty hunter had heard the horses; he had heard them on and off all day throughout the full twelve miles he had ridden chasing down his latest meal ticket.

A twig snapped to the east a few hundred feet out.

Who they were and why they were following him, Noose didn't know, not yet at least, but he was aware of their presence. Being alert and ready was the most important part of avoiding an ambush. He doubted the unseen riders were part of any gang Barrow belonged to because Barrow, as far as he knew, rode alone. The thug was too stupid, drunk, and violent for even the most low-life gangs to claim as a member. Yet anything was possible.

These riders moved like ghosts. They were good. He had to give them that.

It had taken Joe Noose less than a week to catch up with Jim Henry Barrow.

While pulling a stickup, the bank robber had shot a guard in the Victor bank and fled across the Wyoming landscape up into the rugged and treacherous Hoback Canyon. He'd gotten away with a hundred and twenty three dollars and in the escape lost the handkerchief on his face so several customers had been able to identify him by his distinctive bullet scar that had taken his nose years before. Barrow had an hour head start on the local Victor lawmen who had been forced to turn back when one of their horses broke a leg. Noose happened to be dropping off a prisoner to the jail when he heard about the robbery and the killing. The sheriff had wired the U.S. Marshal's office in Jackson Hole and gotten the reward authorized and Noose had gone after it.

It had been a long hard ride across twelve miles of sheer forest and steep mountain range that was as hard going down as up. The trek had nearly killed his horse and he had to walk the animal half the time, but the outlaw's trail had been fresh. Noose expected, rightly so, that once Barrow made Jackson Hole, the big valley on the other side of the pass, he would get a boat and make off down the Snake River. Which was exactly what the man Noose was aiming at was doing this very second.

It was the tracks of the other horses that unnerved Noose. He made them out to number twelve, riding together.

In the last two days, he had crossed the fresh hoof-prints twice while doubling back after a wrong turn. The bounty hunter figured it must be a gang. Who they were Noose didn't know but he wondered why all those men and horses had fetched up in the remote wilderness with him and Barrow. What worried him was whether Barrow had a gang Noose didn't know about and planned to meet up with them. It could be the presence of these others was sheer happenstance: a group of settlers or hunters passing through. But Noose didn't believe in coincidence; his belly tightened because he knew if it was a gang and they were with Barrow, it was going to get bloody, very bloody, very fast.

Another broken twig on a pine tree. A little piece of

torn duster. More tracks. The riders' sign had caught his attention repeatedly during his pursuit of Barrow. Noose hadn't seen them because he had been staying out of sight, keeping downwind, not wanting to get made if whoever this gang was, was with the man with the thousand-dollar reward on his head. As far as Noose could tell, they had not noticed him, either. But who were they? he kept wondering.

Now, here, by the river, his man was alone and Noose had him in his gunsights—it was time to make his move.

"Barrow!" he shouted from his safe cover.

The outlaw suddenly straightened and made a quick break for his saddle and the rifle stock that jutted out. Quickly adjusting aim, Noose squeezed the trigger—the gun bucked, and an explosion of stones flew up at Barrow's feet, stopping him dead in his tracks. He winced, put his hands behind his head, and shouted up onto the ridge where Noose was dug in. "Don't shoot! I'm unarmed, dammit!"

"Throw down!" yelled the bounty hunter, leaping out of his cover and side-skidding his boots down the ridge, scattering pebbles and rocks, keeping his rifle leveled with one arm as he kept balance on the hill with the other. "Kiss the ground!"

The criminal lowered to his knees. "You the law?"

"Close enough," replied Noose, who had crossed the bank of the river in three long strides and produced a set of steel cuffs.

"Bounty hunter?"

"That's right."

"You son of a bitch." The man flattened.

"Shut up." Noose patted him for weapons, confiscated a Colt Peacemaker, and cuffed him. In one swift move, the bounty hunter pulled the rifle from the man's saddle and quickly rummaged through the saddlebags for firearms or knives but found nothing but a ratty bedroll and some week-old jerky. Tossing the other rifle back toward the ridge, Noose grabbed the glum man by the scruff of the neck, heaving him to his feet and shoving him up into his saddle on his horse. The bounty hunter moved with practiced professionalism, like a well-oiled machine. "I'm taking you back to Idaho," he said. "We can do it the easy way or the hard way."

Boom!

A big red flower bloomed in Jim Henry Barrow's chest, blossoming out his back, and he was catapulted clean out of the saddle, landing flat on his back on the ground, stone dead with his torso blown out. Blood pooled in a huge lake beneath the blasted corpse and ran into the river, in a spreading red discoloration.

Noose whirled, clenching his rifle with both hands, looking wildly around him for whoever shot the man.

Then the riders appeared. There were twelve. They rode down the ridge, across the river, and out of the trees.

Twelve rifles. Twelve Stetsons. Twelve dusters. Twelve killers blocking out the sun.

"He's ours," said the leader.

Noose gazed up at a tall, skeletal man with gaunt features and a handlebar mustache. He was looking down the barrel of a smoking Sharps rifle at him. The killer had black bullet eyes. "I would drop the gun," he advised.

So Noose did. Slow.

"You murdered him," Noose said coldly, keeping his empty hands in the open.

"Reward's the same either way." The leader smirked. "We just put paid to it."

"I was taking this man in alive," Noose said, unblinkingly holding the mounted man's mean gaze. "I had him disarmed and restrained. He was mine and that reward is mine."

The gaunt scarecrow of a bounty killer smiled. "We say it's *us* got him and we say the reward belongs to us. It's your word against ours, mister, twelve to one." He indicated his gang, a few of whom chuckled. "You can count, can't ya?"

"What's your name?" Noose snarled.

"I'm Frank Butler."

"I'll remember it."

"You do that. Now shut the hell up, you're sucking my air. You just lost money, you could lose a lot more," Butler said coldly. "Don't be stupid. Walk away. Our business is done here."

Noose just stood and looked on as one of the big feral bounty killers Butler addressed as Sharpless dismounted and heaved the bleeding corpse face-first over the dead man's empty saddle.

"Let's get back to town before this crud starts to stink," said Butler as he and his riders spurred their horses and rode off with the dead man's horse in tow.

Noose stood by the creek. He whistled to call his horse. It trotted out of the trees to him.

Five minutes passed before he swung into his saddle and followed the gang's tracks.

He figured he'd given them enough head start.

CHAPTER 2

Times were tough for killers, Noose reckoned.

A thousand dollars wasn't much divvied up twelve ways.

The corpse was slumped sideways over the saddle, festering in the sun and buzzing with flies. The horse was tethered to the rail outside the bar, alongside the twelve other horses, who kept their distance from the other animal, tails swishing at the swarming insects. Noose could see why. Barrow was already starting to stink.

The men must be inside the bar.

There was nowhere else they could be, because other than the saloon there were few other buildings in Hoback, Wyoming. It was barely a town. Noose trotted slowly on his horse, eyeballing the feed store, the corral, and the U.S. Marshal's office. There were two horses in front of that.

The bounty hunter tethered his horse outside the corral. He swung out of his saddle onto the hard earth, checking to be sure both his Colt pistols were fully loaded before he entered the bar. He could use the drink, if not the company, but it was the company he was here to deal with. Shooting a glance to the hot sun overhead, he tipped his hat brim to shade his face.

Today was going to be a hot one.

So he entered the bar, and sure enough, there they all were.

As Noose pushed through the swinging doors, the twelve hulking figures of the big men assembled around the saloon became visible in the gloom, bent like a row of malignant vultures over the long wooden bar, just big shadows until Noose's eyes adjusted to the dim light and he could make out the faces. It was them, all right. Stink eyes slid buzzardlike to regard him over their hunched shoulders over their shot glasses of whiskey as he entered, spurs jingling, in the quiet room. Nobody moved.

The gang would be here in Hoback to see the local marshal and turn the body over to him for the reward. The lawman needed to sign off for the release of the money and that was whom the killers were waiting for now. It would be the marshal's duty to telegraph Jackson Hole for authorization, and soon the money would be waiting for pickup by these bounty killers. That was their plan.

Noose meant to interfere with it.

He figured his presence was a fly in the ointment for these badmen and seeing him here they must figure he was brave or crazy. Noose figured he risked getting shot but not before the marshal came and the men got their reward money.

His spurs jingled as he entered the bar. Crossing the spare barroom built of unfinished pine boards, Noose saw that besides the gang there was nobody else present other than the bartender, and he wasn't much, just an old coot. The saloon was little more than a hut. A table and two chairs. A clock. The clock was ticking. Sauntering up to the other end of the bar from the bounty killer gang, the lone bounty hunter signaled the bartender.

"Buy him a whiskey. Least we can do," said Butler, smiling quietly.

"It's paid for," replied Noose, flipping a coin onto the counter.

The barman grabbed a bottle from the rack, eyes cautiously taking in his fearsome customers and the cool new arrival, and poured a drink. Noose stood tall at the bar, his ten-gallon hat tipped low over his forehead, boot braced on the wooden rail, taking a slow sip of his drink and staring straight ahead. He didn't need to look at the men to know they were watching him. Each and every last one of them. He'd made an entrance for sure, he figured, because he was the last man any one of these killers had expected to see. But Noose didn't fully know whom he was dealing with, at least not yet, and had to be careful that while he'd entered the bar on his boots, he didn't leave it in a box.

Time passed. Just a bunch of guys drinking.

Smells of dust and wood and sweat and leather filled Noose's nostrils, then the stinging tang of the cheap whiskey as he raised it to his face and sipped. His senses were suddenly more alert, as they always were when facing death. What if this was his last drink? he thought. He swallowed and felt the good burn of the liquid down into his gullet. It numbed him. Facing death made the whiskey taste better.

Noose took inventory of the logistics of a gunfight. He was in a good position at the end of the bar

because all the gang were stacked up down the bar
one past the other and if any one of them drew they
would be distracted for a split second trying to shoot
around the others between them and him—he just
had to turn to have both his irons out and pump lead
into the badmen and send them falling like a row of
dominoes. Noose would most likely die in the shoot-
out, but he'd kill or mortally wound most of the rest.

They were clearly thinking the same thing.

Two of the gunmen stepped away from the bar.
One took a seat at a table to his right, crossed his legs,
and leaned back, spinning a spur with a gloved hand.
The other killer sauntered to the beam against the
wall behind Noose, hands dangling near his holsters,
casually eyeballing the hot dirt street out the window.

These men were professionals.

The clock on the wall ticked. The barman, growing
more nervous, cleaned glasses with a cloth.

"What are you doing here?" Butler finally asked.

Noose just took another sip of his drink. He heard
a few random hollow clicks of hammers pulled back
on pistols under dusters, heard the clink of his shot
glass on the wood counter as he set it down, heard
flies buzzing, and he even heard the faint splat of a
drop of sweat pouring from one of the posse's fore-
heads onto the bar. Still he stared straight forward,
feeling the hard eyes on him.

"I asked why you're here."

"Same reason as you."

"We got business with the marshal."

"So do I."

"That boy slung over that saddle out there is our'n."

"You murdered him."

"Mean to dispute the reward?"

Noose sipped his whiskey, staring straight forward. He didn't answer. He wasn't unduly worried about being shot because the gunmen were not going to shoot him without sufficient provocation: it would be messy to explain when the marshal got there with the bartender as witness and might complicate getting their reward for Barrow. And Noose knew they knew he knew it.

Butler looked into his own glass. "Reckon you want a cut of the reward?"

Noose shook his head. "Nope."

"Want the whole reward?"

Noose finally looked at Butler and the others, and his gaze was sure and steady. "I brung him in alive. You boys murdered him and you're gonna pay."

The leader of the bounty killers reared up from the bar and swept a huge, incredulous look across the amazed eyes of the hardened grizzled gunmen lining the bar. A chuckle passed through the men like the sizzling fuse on a stick of dynamite, burning down to Butler, who laughed cold and mercilessly.

Noose didn't laugh. "You boys must be desperate. I figure the reward for Barrow comes out to less than a hundred dollars each. Maybe you should get real jobs. You know what they say, boys . . . you're worth what they pay you."

"Well, mister, what you got in mind to do about this here situation?"

"I'm gonna tell the marshal you killed Barrow."

"Twelve of us says different."

"We'll see." Noose just smiled to himself, which riled the killers. "Meantime, nothin' to do but wait."

Connect with Us

Visit us online at
KensingtonBooks.com
to read more from your favorite authors, see books
by series, view reading group guides, and more.

Join us on social media

for sneak peeks, chances to win books and prize packs,
and to share your thoughts with other readers.

facebook.com/kensingtonpublishing
twitter.com/kensingtonbooks

Tell us what you think!

To share your thoughts, submit a review,
or sign up for our eNewsletters, please visit:
KensingtonBooks.com/TellUs.